WE'LL

FLY

AWAY

BRYAN
BLISS

GREENWILLOW BOOKS
An Imprint of HarperCollins*Publishers*

We'll Fly Away

Copyright © 2018 by Bryan Bliss

The text of this book is set in 11-point Goudy.
Book design by Paul Zakris

Library of Congress Cataloging-in-Publication Data is available.

ISBN 978-0-06-249427-6 (hardback)

18 19 20 21 22 PC/LSCH 10 9 8 7 6 5 4 3 2 1

First Edition

GREENWILLOW BOOKS

To Martha and Michael,
Thank you.

"It is easy to forgive the innocent.
It is the guilty who test our morality.
People are more than the worst thing they've ever done."

<small>SISTER HELEN PREJEAN</small>

November 5

T—

The Sister said it would be good to write to you, but after everything—I don't know. What am I supposed to say? It's not like
you're going to listen, and I stopped really talking to everyone a
long time ago. So what the hell is writing a letter to you going to
help?

But Sister wants me to speak honestly, to let my feelings out.
And holy hell, writing a letter is definitely better than doing one
of those stupid art projects where Sister has me *paint my feelings*.
Can you imagine that? Last time, I painted a tree with a sun coming up over the top of it, because I knew she would eat that mess
up. Sister told me it meant I was growing.

Growing!

And ha-ha, man, you wouldn't believe how fat I've gotten. Before the Row, I'd been in county for months. I was doing push-ups and sit-ups every day. That was the only way to make it. The dudes in here can still be pretty rough, don't get me wrong, but it's nothing like that place. Every night somebody would start screaming, getting their ass beat for the simplest of things. Ramen packets, cigarettes. So I bulked up. Took on anybody who came in my direction. They looked at me wrong, I threw a fist. Eventually it becomes second nature. Eventually you just turn yourself off.

But now? Damn. I'm round as hell! There isn't much else to do here but sit and eat and think. Some of the dudes—like Eddie— play ball, take classes. But what's the point? Every guy in this place has a ticking clock hanging around his neck. Sister says my depression makes me say those things, but like I told her—I'm not depressed. I've just got my eyes wide open. Whenever I say that she mm-hmms it away and tells me not to waste her time.

When she first came around, I got hard with her. Told her not to bother with me. Thought I'd really told her what's what too. Eddie and everybody lost their minds when that happened, laughing like I'd stood up and told a joke. Because sure enough, the next day, here comes Sister stomping down the Row in those red cowboy boots. Loud as hell. Sat down right in front of me and started talking like I'd never said a sideways word to her. Eddie says once she's got an eye for you, you're through. And I guess that's why I'm writing this bullshit letter, right?

I swear, T. Sometimes it feels like the walls are closing in on me. I can't say I wish you were here, but maybe you know what I mean.

Luke

1

LUKE and Toby didn't know a thing about planes, hadn't even set foot in one before they found that rusted-out crop duster halfway between Highway 10 and a little gas station that marked the end of incorporation and the beginning of what people simply referred to as *county*. But you wouldn't have known it, not with how they went at that fixed-wing plane.

Every can and bottle from there to Charlotte was claimed and redeemed, five cents that neither of them had before. And what they could, they pawned. Old bikes. A forgotten guitar. The collection of centennial quarters Toby's mom had given him before she split.

This was about building bank, cash money. Green.

So forget candy and movies. Forget baseball or swimming at the public pool, which was just an excuse to stare at the college girls who spent their summers guarding from those tall towers. Forget all of it, because that summer was nothing but duct tape and two-by-fours. Hours and hours and hours, ditching chores and trips to the mall. Dropping everything for that plane.

The summer passed, and they never got the wing reattached to the body, the fuselage mended. They grew too tall, too old to spend their time on fantasies—to believe that the plane held any magic. At least, that's what they told themselves. But they kept coming. Kept that plane like a military secret.

If he had to swear to it now, Luke still dreamed he'd come through the stand of trees and see the plane transformed. Feel the engine in his chest. The wind in his hair. And Toby. Standing proudly with his arms spread wide like, I told you. *I told you.* He'd get in that plane with his best friend of years and years and take off—never looking back. Never seen again.

Luke downed the last of the Mountain Dew as Toby watched, fascinated.

"What?" Luke asked, throwing the bottle behind him, where the cockpit should've been.

"You drank an entire two-liter," Toby said. "By yourself."

Luke shrugged, hoping the subject would pass. But of course it didn't, not with Toby. His mouth moments from a grin. From the shit he was constantly talking. Toby, who was always boasting how his friend was the best wrestler the state of North Carolina had ever seen. A straight-up monster.

"I thought you were cutting weight," Toby said.

Luke squinted into the sun. It was close to five. His mom would need to be woken up; she'd just gotten on at the Pepsi factory, working third shift. It was the reason they had the out-of-date, nearly flat soda in the first place—the only thing he'd put in his stomach all day.

"I'm going to make weight," he said, trying to force confidence into his voice.

He was still four pounds over, which seemed impossible, seeing as for weeks he'd been living on cereal and whatever his brothers left on their plates. When he decided to drop to 170 and take on Connor Herrera, Coach O tried to talk him out of it. Dropping twelve pounds wouldn't be easy, even for somebody as committed as Luke. And honestly, there was nothing left to prove.

As a freshman, Luke had been a scrawny but tough 125-pounder. He surprised everybody by winning the state championship. Especially the senior from Chapel Hill he destroyed in the final. From there it was 135, 155—he went three for three, taking state every year. At 182, there was no real competition. He'd add his fourth championship the same way he'd taken the previous three—joining maybe ten other people who'd ever finished with that number.

Connor Herrera was on the same path, just twelve light pounds under Luke. He also had three state titles and—thanks to an expensive club team Luke couldn't afford—a shiny new junior national championship. Luke could go 182 and nobody would fault him. But he wanted Herrera.

He'd lose the pounds. He would make weight.

"But you drank *the whole thing*," Toby said, as if reading his mind.

"I've got a week," he snapped. It was the same way he worked on the mat, quick and decisive. Moving before his opponent even had a chance to think. One two three, done.

Luke knew Toby had more to say. Usually, Luke would just let him talk until he lost interest. Sometimes it took an hour, but eventually Toby would sit back like he'd just finished a big meal and sigh long and steady. Luke didn't want to talk about the scale for another minute, let alone the next hour.

"Mom said you could spend the night again, if you want."

Toby's entire body relaxed. Luke didn't miss how he tried to keep his face from going slack too. From showing even a moment of relief. All Toby said was, "I get the couch."

Home was a one-bedroom apartment half a mile from the plane, shared by Luke's mom and twin brothers, Jack-Jack and Petey, hell-raisers even at five. By now, both of them would be screaming about dinner, how they were starving, and his mother would have another excuse for why she hadn't put anything on the stove yet. For not shopping.

Luke looked up at the sun again. "It's fine. I'll sleep on the floor," he said.

They should leave, but he didn't want to stand up. Out here, he didn't have to think about wrestling, the scholarship offer he'd just accepted, school, any of it. Time stopped in this small grove of trees, and he wanted to believe he could spend the rest of his life sitting here drinking soda, eating whatever he wanted. Talking shit with his best friend until the sun went down.

But Toby slapped the side of the plane and stood up. Even sitting, Luke's head came past his waist. And when the sun was behind him, like now, you could almost see through him. Every drop of blood, every vein twisting under his skin. That meant somebody had to have seen the bruises that sometimes peeked from under Toby's shirt. But other than one do-gooder teacher in sixth grade—who they ignored and was gone a year later anyway—no teacher or principal or any other adult had ever said a thing.

As soon as he walked into the apartment, Luke knew his mother was still asleep—that she'd be late for her shift tonight. The apartment wasn't big, but he still ran across the living room, nearly killing himself when he didn't see one of the boys' scooters lying across the floor. Behind him, Jack-Jack and Petey were taunting Toby. It wouldn't be all that long before they'd be bigger than his friend, too.

He knocked on his mother's door. The only sound was the fan, clicking each time it oscillated across the room.

"Mom?" he said, opening the door.

Inside was hot, the air a mix of cigarettes and stale soda. Across the small room, the twins' mattress was on the floor, a mess of blankets and dirty stuffed animals. He spoke softly into the dark room. A shadow moved, followed by his mother's tired voice.

"Jesus, Petey. I told you to get some cereal."

"Mom," Luke said. "It's nearly six."

At first, Luke thought she'd fallen back asleep—that's how long the pause was. But then she sat up, knocking the fan over as she ran to her closet, naked and cussing.

"Six o'clock? Where the hell have you been?" She flung clothes out of the hamper, finally pulling out a light-blue Pepsi shirt and putting it on.

Their father had left when the twins were barely home from the hospital. Luke had been thirteen, old enough to realize that his parents weren't in love the way people seemed to be in movies and on television shows. And once his dad was gone, Luke just assumed that was something that happened—that people left you without a word.

His mother was still spinning around the room. "You were supposed to be back at five."

"I didn't realize it was so late," Luke said.

"Well, we both fucked up then, didn't we?"

Luke turned and started back to the living room. She wasn't wrong. He should've been home at five, to make sure she was awake and didn't have to deal with the twins as she was getting ready to leave. To make sure she kept this job longer than her stints at the hosiery mill, or as a waitress at the Waffle House. But he couldn't keep the indignation from rising up. His mom knew how to set an alarm. And she didn't need to spend her mornings watching trashy television when she could be sleeping.

Toby had the twins pinned to the carpet, smiling as he ate a banana, the peel spotted black. Luke had no idea where he'd found the thing. The boys called for help as he passed, laughing out every other word.

"Stop bothering Toby," Luke said, pretending to be mad as he went to the kitchen.

They howled and spit and laughed.

He made his mother a sandwich, peeling the last thin pieces of turkey out of the package and pressing them between twin slices of white bread. Chips. A small apple from the back of the refrigerator. There wasn't much else, so he put a handful of cereal into a plastic bag and set it on the table just as his mom hurried into the room.

"Hey, Doreen," Toby said.

She waved without looking. "I need you to figure out dinner, Luke."

Toby let the twins off the floor and they came running to their mother, talking a mile a minute, barely breathing between their words. She nodded distractedly as she searched for her lighter.

"And take them to the park or something," she told Luke. "God knows they need to get out of the apartment."

Luke didn't move. Of course they'd go to the park. He took them to the park nearly every day. He tried to hide his annoyance, but Doreen saw it immediately. She came over and put a hand on his forearm. "Listen, I'm sorry. But I depend on you."

Luke knew that too. He couldn't take more than a few steps—could barely breathe—without a reminder of how much she *depended* on him. He forced himself to look her in the eyes. When he was a kid, he would tell people she was the most beautiful woman in the whole world. They'd laugh and he never knew why. She was still beautiful, even now, her eyes hung with perpetual black circles. Her clothes stained and wrinkled.

She reached for him again, as if she might ruffle his hair the way she had when he was younger, before stopping herself. She sparked her lighter instead, taking a long drag and speaking through the exhale.

"I'll see you in the morning. Okay? And boys—be good. Listen to your brother."

The door slammed behind her, and a few seconds later, the truck rumbled out of the complex parking lot.

It was quiet when Jack-Jack came barreling toward Luke, arms out like a glider. Right before the collision, Luke dropped to a knee and swept the wriggling kid up, squeezing him close to his shoulder. Petey came at him fists balled and face lit with a goofy smile. Luke scooped him up too. They both struggled, kicking the air and yelling to be let down. Luke bounced them once, feeling their ribs against his shoulders.

"All you're going to do is come back at me," Luke said, squeezing them again. They were one voice with their promises, their assurances. And of course when he put them back on the carpet, it was only a second before they attacked. Toby jumped in then, grabbing Petey and crying out when the kid tried to bite his ear—dirty to the end. Luke held

Jack-Jack at arm's length as the boy twisted, contorting his body back and forth like a wild animal. The twins were both laughing, but even then they were liable—and the perfect height—to take a swing at your crotch.

Luke's mother always said her people were hot-blooded, angry like a stick of dynamite. She said it casually, a way to explain behavior at family reunions. But Luke wanted her to keep going. To tell him and the boys that they needed to be more than a wild card—to control the explosion, because that was just as much a badge of strength. Luke needed something he could hold on to, could use to navigate the world.

The first time he had wrestled, he nearly got himself kicked off the team, wrenching a boy's head and throwing him to the ground like he was made of air. The kid was crying when the ref slapped the mat and Luke came up proud, arms raised. That same murder in his blood. But Coach O had laid a look on him that could have withered an oak. All he said was, "Never again. Not on my mat."

Control. Balance. Discipline. How many times had Luke beaten somebody stronger and faster only because he understood these things? The need to pause and breathe and not come out swinging. And when it was time, you attacked fast and hard. But that didn't mean shit if you went off half-cocked at every word said against you.

"We're going to the park," Luke said.

Petey gave Luke a skeptical look. "What park?"

"Wildcat. The one with the wooden castles."

The twins shared a defeated but happy look. And for a second, Luke let his defenses down. Which was exactly when Petey clocked him hard in the nuts, cackling as he ran away. Luke fell on the couch in pain. The twins tore for the front door, and Toby followed, laughing just as hard.

They watched the boys run against the deep sunlight, not talking until Toby yawned loudly and said, "I need to get a job. Maybe bagging groceries at Food Lion. I saw this sweet pickup for sale on Fairgrove Church Road."

"You'd be a terrible bagger," Luke said.

Toby had only recently gotten his license, showing up late to school with it still in his hands. Luke had been a wreck all morning, expecting the nurse or the principal—who would it be?—to pull him out of class. To tell him his friend had finally been put in the hospital, or worse.

"We could take it up to Bakers Mountain," Toby said, ignoring him. "Throw some sleeping bags in the back?"

The excitement and possibility came off him like day-old booze.

Luke watched Jack-Jack push Petey, who immediately

tackled him. They wrestled for a few seconds before Luke stood up and yelled their names. They separated and went back to running. As he sat down, Toby was still talking. He nodded absently. Camping.

"We'd find some girls. Bring some ladies with us? Damn, man. *Damn*."

And then he was off, standing up and humping the air vigorously until Jack-Jack and Petey came over, out of breath and utterly confused, a look on their faces like "Is he having a seizure?"

Luke stood up and pushed Toby, stopping the gyrations, but hard enough that Toby hit the ground. For a moment there was a flash—like a knife coming out—across Toby's face. Luke had seen it before, of course, when they were kids and still threw fists to settle arguments. And once in middle school, when Toby's dad came home from the Deuce smelling like cheap whiskey. They'd broken a window or something. But hell, there never had to be a reason for an ass kicking in Toby's house. Still, they stood in the kitchen staring at the cracked linoleum, trying not to give the bastard a reason or the satisfaction. Luke got sent home before the real whipping started. And that wasn't really the right word to describe what happened to Toby when Luke wasn't around.

Not even close.

2

TOBY didn't remember falling asleep, only waking up when Luke opened the front door and the early morning light slipped into the dark apartment. A few moments later, Luke was gone. His runs were a morning ritual, heavy or not.

They'd spent the night watching professional wrestling, which Luke hated. But Luke still put a respectable pile driver on Petey as the television switched to a police drama, followed almost immediately by suplexing Jack-Jack onto the couch. When Luke stood up, a theatrical wildness in his eyes, Toby slapped his chest, pointed to an invisible crowd, and posed. It was enough to get Luke laughing, which was no easy feat lately.

Toby turned on the television, absently watching an infomercial for a contraption that peeled oranges. The hosts threw their heads back in laughter every few seconds, excited, as the camera panned across the crowd, all of whom seemed equally ecstatic about what looked like a giant knitting needle. Toby's stomach howled for an orange.

They'd scrounged up enough change last night for two small frozen pizzas, but even without Luke eating it wasn't enough. And now, the cabinets were just as empty, except for the same lonely can of hominy that had been there for months. When Toby finally found some cereal, it took the dust from two different bags to make even half a bowl, which he carried out to the balcony of the apartment.

He set the bowl on the railing and blew warmth into his hands, watching the cars pass on the two-lane in the distance. When Luke came running into the parking lot in a full sprint, the garbage bags he was wearing shushing loudly with every stride, Toby lifted the bowl to his lips and downed the milk, the dust, all of it.

Luke impressed everybody. Coaches, high school and college alike, teachers—even though he was barely a C student—and of course girls, who might as well be invisible for all the game Luke had. The last time a girl had talked to him, Luke had gone stupid. Mouth shut like he couldn't remember a single word.

Still, game or not, when it came to the mat, Luke was a single-minded killer put on the earth by whatever gods were in charge of taking dudes down, and hard. Watching him destroy his opponents had the same effect as a horror movie. You were simultaneously anxious for them, and unable to look away.

It would be easy to explain his dominance as simply biological. He was strong, fast, and scary. But that was only part of the story. Luke worked harder than anybody Toby had ever met. At the end of every run, he sprinted. When there was a French test (and he was shit at speaking *en Français*), he was the last guy to turn in his test. Something burned inside him, something most people didn't have. Toby had never been good at anything, not like Luke.

Luke pulled the garbage bags off his legs as he climbed the stairs, dropping them in a sweaty pile in front of the apartment's door. He leaned against the railing next to Toby, breathing hard.

"How much did you get?" Toby asked.

"Not enough. We stayed up too late. I'm tired as hell."

A car pulled into the parking lot, and both of them stared down as a twenty-something man got out holding a gallon of milk. He wore the same generic blue work shirt that everyone in this building, this town, owned. Luke stretched his back and then touched his toes. When he stood up, he shook his head.

"My entire body is off."

"I say you pack on twenty, thirty more pounds and just go

heavyweight," Toby said. "Surprise everybody."

Luke ignored him, stretching again.

Toby had tried out for football their freshman year, and even though he had made it through the whole season without getting hurt or, honestly, getting into a game, he wasn't made for sports. They'd lose a game, and it would take everything he had to keep himself from cracking a joke. If it hadn't been for Luke, he'd face an ass kicking daily, and he knew it. But it rarely stopped him.

"You already have a scholarship," Toby said. "Who cares about Connor Herrera?"

Luke stood up and kicked the wet garbage bags off the ledge. They landed on the ground with a splat. It was more emotion than Toby had seen from Luke in weeks. But then he must've caught himself, because he looked down for a second, and when he spoke, his voice was even.

"I care."

Petey appeared in the doorway, rubbing his eyes.

"You guys are being loud as shit," he said, and Luke immediately cuffed him on the side of the head. Not hard, but Petey's chin trembled.

"I don't want to hear you talking like that," Luke said. When Petey didn't answer, Luke went down on one knee so he could look him in the eye. "You hear me?"

Luke always said the twins were wild, but Toby knew wild. Petey and Jack-Jack were just kids. The kind of kids who wouldn't think twice about ramming a shopping cart into your shins just for the hell of it, but kids nonetheless. Though who knew what would happen when Luke left for school next year.

Come fall, Toby would follow Luke to college. He had no idea how they'd pay the rent or buy food. Whether there were rules about first-year students living in apartments. He didn't know if the boys would come with, or if they'd see them on breaks. But he'd been building this abstract new life for them since Luke took state their freshman year. And once Luke signed the letter of intent, the faint light of hope that had gotten them through countless nights of pain and anger and desperation transformed into one word, a state he could barely even imagine—*Iowa*. But in a few months, what he could or couldn't imagine didn't matter, not anymore. They were finally leaving.

"Go wake up Jack-Jack," Luke said, and Petey paused, just a second. Like he was running the odds of his next move. Luke nudged him gently toward the door. "I'm going to get us some breakfast."

Petey went yelling into the living room as Luke sighed and started down the walkway.

Ms. Hildebran had lived five doors down since long before Luke and the boys. She spent her days watching game shows, her stories, and whatever else came on. Smoking and talking to the television. Every so often she'd call Luke and Toby in, giving them a slice of cake or a piece of cantaloupe.

Toby could barely hear what Luke was saying when Ms. Hildebran came to the door, but he knew the script well enough. She disappeared, coming back and pressing a plastic grocery bag of food into Luke's hands. Luke looked at his feet as she talked. At the end she reached out and pulled him into an awkward, one-sided hug.

They were already eating, the smell of microwaved sausage and fried eggs coating the apartment, when Doreen walked in, carrying three bags of groceries.

"Hello!" she sang, but nobody answered. The ash from her cigarette looked ready to drop until she switched all the bags to one hand and flicked the butt behind her, into the parking lot. She stood there for a second, staring at the food on their plates, her mouth open.

"What the hell?"

"There wasn't anything to eat in the house," Luke said plainly. He was eating egg whites, nothing else. And even though he was trying to play it cool, Toby could see he wasn't.

"You know I don't like you going over there," she said.

Luke went back to his eggs.

Doreen sighed and dropped the bags on the chair. "Anyway, can you get them ready for school? I had a long night. You don't even have to pack lunch. I got Lunchables."

At the mention of Lunchables, Petey and Jack-Jack abandoned their plates and ran for the bags, rifling around until they saw the bright yellow boxes. Before they could run off, Luke grabbed the boxes and tossed them to Toby.

"If you eat them now, you won't have anything for lunch," Luke said.

Toby held the Lunchables high above his head, trying to block their punches while still keeping the boxes high enough. Doreen lit a new cigarette, blowing a long string of smoke from her mouth.

"All right, quit. Go get dressed. Jesus." She swatted at the boys and they went rumbling to her room. When they were gone, Doreen took another long hit on the cigarette before she turned to Luke and said, "I'm having a friend over for dinner tonight. So I'll need you here to help."

Luke collected the dirty plates, his face still blank. When he looked away from Doreen, Toby jumped in.

"I'll come by and help too."

Nobody acknowledged him. Doreen stepped back and flicked ash out the open door.

"I'm making meat loaf," she said to Luke. "Mashed potatoes."

"I can't eat potatoes," Luke said. "I'm cutting weight. You *know* that."

"What's one night going to matter? I don't want Ricky thinking you're some kind of weirdo."

Toby knew the look Luke gave his mother right then. He'd laid the same one on his old man countless times, despite knowing it would mean the belt or the replacement power cord for the dryer that hung purposefully in their trailer's kitchen. The meaning couldn't be clearer.

Fuck. You.

Toby flinched when Doreen picked up the bags of groceries in a huff and started slamming cabinet doors until everything was put away. She didn't say another word as she breezed back through the living room to get her cigarettes. The last sound either of them heard was her yelling at the boys to hurry up so she could go to sleep.

"Well, this guy Ricky sounds like a real winner," Toby said, forcing a laugh. "What are the odds the dude is rocking a mullet?"

Luke stood there grim faced, holding the plates.

"And what grown-ass man still goes by *Ricky?*" Toby continued. "Not Rick. Or Richard. Might as well call him Sparky. Or . . . fucking . . . *Tiger.*"

Luke cracked a smile.

"I bet he'll show up in the back of his mom's station wagon or something."

Finally it worked. They both died, laughing until it hurt. Until the twins came tumbling into the living room, demanding to know what was so funny.

November 12

T—

Man, when Sister came by today I had myself all puffed up—just looking for a fight. As soon as she saw me she was like, "Luke, I brought you something." Held out a brand-new journal and pen, which must've been hell to get approved, considering they don't want us to have anything. That's how it is too. This place is designed to remind us again and again that we're not really human. Not anymore.

I don't know, man. As soon as I saw that pen and journal, everything fell apart. I started wiping my eyes real hard, like that time you got pepper in your eye when we were kids. Dude, you screamed so loud I thought for sure somebody had set your ass on fire.

I'm cracking up right now. For real.

Anyway, Sister isn't dumb. She saw right away what was happening and she took me to one of the visitation rooms, away from everybody. Told me I could be honest with her. That I didn't have to keep everything inside.

But you don't survive in a place like this being honest. Hell, I could be honest all day long and what does that get me? A beating. A reputation. And then suddenly every guy in here is giving me the eye, just waiting to jump.

The only way you survive is by wearing a mask. All the time, no matter what. You go out in the yard and watch dudes play basketball—better put on that mask. That's how you laugh, how you can bring yourself to joke with them. Talking about how they wouldn't know what to do if I ever decided to take a step on that court.

That's the carefree mask, the one that every person in this place wears. It screams: "Is that all you got?" It promises that no matter what you do or say, it isn't going to affect me.

I know you know all about that one, T.

Sister doesn't want to hear that, though. She wants me to be open, to be honest. But I can't interact with people the same way I could before. I can't open up or tell anybody how I'm feeling or what scares me. Because that shit will get you killed. Yeah, maybe your heart won't stop beating. Maybe you won't see any blood on the floor. But you're dead all the same. The only way to live in here is to be completely walled off, to live solely on the inside. That way nobody can take anything away from you ever again.

Of course as soon as I got in that room with Sister, I dried my shit up quick. Started joking around. She sat there staring at me, like she knew every single thing I was going through.

She was all, "You don't have to hide from me."

And I said, "Who's hiding? I'm sitting right here."

But honestly? It was like a bomb went off inside me.

Sister's always saying how nobody can live alone. How people still care about me. Still love me. Whenever she gets going on that, I always laugh and say something like, "Oh yeah? Who?" But I already knew she was talking about herself, which is fine. I like the Sister. She's one of the only people who doesn't treat me like some kind of animal. She touches me—and ha-ha, don't even get thinking about *that*, because I'm talking about on my arm. And it's not just me. Sister hugs every dude in here, even though the COs are always giving her hell for it.

Do you know what it's like to go through day after day never touching another person? Being touched? I never thought about that before, not even once.

Anyway, when Sister reached for my arm, I pulled back. The last thing I needed was to walk back into the pod all boo-hoo again, so I sat there staring at the table until I could look her in the eye. When I did, she said, "You don't have to show me the letters. But I think you should keep writing to Toby."

That's the first time anybody's said your name to me in almost a year, man. And goddamn. All I wanted to do was punch the wall until my hand disappeared. Until I couldn't feel it anymore.

Luke

3

LUKE was holding a worksheet up against his locker, trying to finish a line of math problems, when Toby shot down the hallway like he was being chased. He was always wearing on someone's last nerve. But most people knew at this point it wasn't worth the effort. Luke was always there to save him.

"She's from Chicago," was all Toby said, trying to breathe.

Luke barely looked up from his worksheet. "What?"

"Annie," Toby said. "She's new. Wears this jean jacket, which, like, I never thought denim could look that good just hanging from somebody's shoulders, you know?"

Luke gave an affirmative grunt, but he had already stopped listening—especially when Toby began dissecting the girl's jacket further, her hair, which Toby described as "messy but in a hot way." Luke had nine problems and four minutes to do them, already an impossible task even without Toby yammering. He stared at the worksheet, supposedly remedial, and tried to wrap his mind around the shapes and angles.

"And then she kind of told me to go fuck myself," Toby said.

"I already like her," Luke said.

Toby pushed him against the locker, which only made Luke laugh.

"We definitely had a connection," Toby said. "I think the whole 'fuck off' thing is more a general posture, rather than an actual, you know, feeling toward me specifically."

"Don't sell yourself short," Luke said. "It could totally be both."

Toby leaned against the bank of lockers, as if in mid-swoon, and wiped his forehead. Luke sighed and started to put the worksheet in his backpack unfinished when Toby snatched it from his hands.

"Just let me do them for you," he said.

Luke shook his head. There had to be some grace in honesty, some benefit to coming to class defeated and looking for help. But Toby had already written in the answers to four of the problems, even showing his work. Despite himself, Toby was smart. He had breezed through calculus his junior year. Could recite the date and year of not only Abraham Lincoln's assassination, but the name of the farm where they found John Wilkes Booth twenty-four hours later. All of it like it was the day of the week too. Of course, none of that made him any more socially appropriate. In fact, it made people hate him all the more.

"You should play hard to get," Luke said. "For once."

Toby shook his head. "You're good at a lot of things," he said, handing the worksheet back to Luke. "Like rolling around with other dudes in tight outfits. But when it comes to, like, matters of the heart . . ."

Toby started dancing, a kind of dirty two-step that drew comments and stares from everybody passing in the hallway. Toby ignored them, nearly floating as he singsonged his love and intentions for everybody to hear.

Three hours later—Luke and Toby hadn't had a class together since sixth grade—Toby walked into the lunchroom, cool as anything. A girl in a jean jacket, built tall and solid, like she could hurt you, followed right behind him, looking pissed.

"What's up, man?"

Toby said it casual. Like this girl wasn't following close enough to know what kind of shampoo he used. Toby dropped his bag, barely sitting down before she grabbed him by the collar and pulled him back up.

"What the hell is your problem?" she yelled.

It got everybody's attention. Like, *everybody*. Luke didn't know whether to stand up, hide, or laugh with the rest of the cafeteria. The only thing he did know: this girl was serious. Even the normally unflappable Toby seemed momentarily panicked.

"You told that guy I was your *girlfriend?*" The volume, in Luke's opinion, was impressive. Her voice seemed to come from her knees, from the dingy floor of their cafeteria, gaining more and more power until finally exploding from her mouth. Toby, recovering his cool, only shrugged.

"Annie, I didn't say you were my girlfriend. That would be ridiculous." He looked back at Luke and winked. "I *said* you were girlfriend material. That's a compliment."

Annie grabbed him by the front of his shirt this time. Toby looked weightless in her grip. Luke couldn't stop watching her.

"You realize I could fold you up and put you in my pocket, right?" she said.

That got some laughs. Enough that Luke stood up. It was one thing for Toby to get some needed humility. But this was quickly approaching humiliation. Luke waved his hand in her direction, hoping to make eye contact. The look she gave him was broken glass.

"And who are you, the fucking bodyguard?"

Luke opened his mouth, like he had something to say back to her. But he just stood there, frozen and stupid. She stared at Luke, finally determining that he was just as hopeless an idiot as Toby.

"I am not your girlfriend," Annie said, turning back to Toby. "Say it."

She made Toby repeat it back to her twice, because the first time was an unconvincing mumble. When appeased, she let go of him and—as if suddenly realizing she was in the middle of a crowded cafeteria—looked around, her eyes widening. She scuttled away from the table to a chorus of laughter and cheering. Toby sat down and gave Luke a look like "Whatcha gonna do?"

Toby opened his milk without a word, downing the whole carton and wiping his mouth before he finally said, "That means she's into me, right?"

Luke knew he was kidding, but still.

"She'll kick your ass if you even glance in her direction. That's the only message she was putting out."

Toby opened a second milk and shrugged.

"Well, I've been through worse."

They didn't say anything after that, the cafeteria like a wave of sound rising and falling every few seconds. Luke tried to focus on the carrots and celery he had on his plate.

Eventually Toby cleared his throat and said, "Here's the thing. I like me a powerful woman."

"God, you're stupid. You know that, right?" Luke said, shaking his head. "Just plain old *stupid*."

Toby finished off the carton, smiling.

The next time Luke saw Annie, she was climbing into a shitty compact car at the edge of the school parking lot. Luke was walking to the gym, and actually, he more heard her than saw her. The car sounded like a toy that needed a new battery, and her music—loud, aggressive rock—blared through the open windows. She nearly hit Ms. Hoffman, the ancient English teacher who once told Toby he was *nothing* when he got caught stealing chocolate milk. Not good for nothing, or even would amount to nothing. Just *nothing*. As if he was something too low to consider. It still rose up into Luke's throat every time he saw her. Of course it slid right off Toby.

Annie roared out of the parking lot, oblivious to Ms. Hoffman's finger wagging. When she disappeared in the distance, Luke turned in to the gym.

The freshmen were already rolling out the mats. Once they were taped and wiped down, the coaches would show up to unleash whatever hell was planned for the next two hours. And that was exactly what the coaches would call it—*hell*. They weren't too far off. But Luke lost himself in the work, the fatigue. When the younger wrestlers complained, he stared. When they weren't pushing themselves hard enough, he got in their faces. Coach O told them to leave everything they had on the mat—blood, sweat, all of it—and Luke treated it like gospel. He never left the room anything short of spent.

The scale stood in the corner of the room, like a silent heckler. Luke ignored it and soon enough was deep in his warm-ups—somersaults, cartwheels, front handsprings—only stopping when Coach O came up beside him.

"Simpson wants to challenge again today," he said, rubbing his eyes. Anybody could challenge the A wrestler before the next meet. Tyler Simpson challenged Luke every week.

"Okay," Luke said, rolling his neck. He knew the next question would be "How's the cut?" So he asked, "Is anybody else challenging?"

Coach O pulled out a well-worn mini notebook from the pocket of his T-shirt and flipped pages until he found the right one.

"Carter at 106. Phan at 132. Simpson, like I said. And then Fisher at heavyweight."

At an actual meet, Luke's routine began as soon as the

126s started—slowly transforming into a workout probably more vigorous than his coach liked. The object was to hit that mat just as everything in his body really got firing. To drop the jump rope and sprint onto the mat, ready to go.

For a guy like Simpson—a fellow senior who'd been stuck behind Luke for three years—he could go half speed if he wanted. Last week Luke had pinned him in a matter of seconds. Picked the ankle and *boom*, it was over. This was the first year they would've actually been in different weight classes, had Luke decided not to cut. When Simpson first heard, he lost it. Even had his dad up at the school, complaining to Coach O. The answer they got was the same as it had always been in the wrestling room: work harder and win.

To make things worse, he had history with Toby.

Tyler was Patty's brother, a girl who'd nearly gotten Toby killed last summer. They'd met at the pool and maybe it was the sun, the heat, but she had invited Toby to her house. The way Toby told it, he was in Patty Simpson's bed—itself inconceivable to Luke—with his pants half off when her father came home and Toby went for the window. Thinking about Toby running bare-assed through the street cracked Luke up, true or not.

How Tyler found out, Luke couldn't say. But Toby never had a problem reminding him.

"You still over?" Coach O asked.

Luke nodded.

He didn't look at Coach as he slipped to the mat, feigning a single leg and then immediately spinning, ready to break his opponent down. Every movement fluid, practiced. When he was back on his feet, Coach O put a hand on his shoulder and said, "You can go 182 for this meet. Call it a tune-up for Herrera."

"But how would that make Tyler feel?" Luke said, and Coach O smiled uneasily.

They'd spent the preseason slowly bringing his weight down, cutting pound by pound until he was light enough to be pushed around by even marginal 182-pounders. He was supposed to be at 170 by now, one match before Herrera. *That* was the tune-up. Take down whatever fish Bunker Hill put in front of him, just like he'd planned.

"I'll make weight," Luke said.

"How's everything else?" Coach asked.

He was always having Luke over for dinner. Always springing for new wrestling shoes, even as Luke outgrew two pairs in one season. And when Luke needed money to pay the electric bill last year, after days calling it "camping" so the twins wouldn't worry, Coach paid it without question. If Luke had to count the truly decent people in his life, it would be a short list. And Coach O would top it.

"They want me to come visit Iowa," Luke said. "After Herrera."

"You should," he said. "You're going to be living there for the next four years. I can help you get up there, if you want."

Luke nodded, but the trip wasn't likely. He could barely rely on his mom long enough to get to practices and meets, let alone a trip to a state that seemed halfway around the world. Besides, what would they show him? Yes, Iowa had a great wrestling team. And yes, Luke was excited to keep wrestling—to see how far he could go. But he didn't need to see the facilities. He didn't need a free T-shirt or a night out with the team. All he needed to know was that he and Toby would have a place to go once they stepped off that graduation stage in May.

Coach stood there a few more seconds before popping Luke on the shoulder.

"Take it easy on Simpson," he said. "And don't worry about the scale. Got me?"

Thirty minutes later, Luke was standing in the middle of the mat, ready. He cleared his mind and dropped his hands—loose, low—and as soon as the coach's whistle rang out, he smiled.

Simpson stalked toward Luke, hoping for a tie-up. Before

he could do anything, Luke snapped him down to the mat. The rest of the team was trying to hide their laughter as Simpson got up, wiping his nose and looking for blood. Once he was close, he shot for Luke's legs. Luke saw it coming— let it happen, even—and sprawled back effortlessly, pushing Tyler's face hard into the mat.

Luke barely heard the yelling, the way Coach O shouted instructions to Simpson—to do anything besides sit there as Luke spun around him for two points. He snaked an arm under Tyler's head, wrapped up one of his legs. All he needed to do was shift his weight and sink the half nelson.

Seconds later, Coach slapped the mat.

Simpson went stomping out of the wrestling room, something that happened often after a challenge. Coach O never said a word about it, because that meant they were competing. So nobody thought anything of it when the first sounds came from the hallway—like a stack of lunchroom trays falling to the ground. It was Simpson dealing. But the clattering kept on, followed soon enough by two voices yelling.

Luke didn't rush toward the sound with the rest of the team. He dropped down and started doing push-ups, trying to keep these hours holy. Then Fisher yelled for him. Luke reluctantly stood up and walked into the hallway.

He didn't quite register what was happening when he first

saw Simpson pointing his finger past the two teammates who were holding him back. And there was Toby, leaning against the wall and holding his eye, wearing a stubborn smile Luke'd seen on his face a hundred times.

"You want your ass kicked a second time?" Luke yelled, trying to push through the crowd. Fisher grabbed him at the last second. But Luke didn't want to be held back. He wasn't trying to put on a show for anyone. If you messed with Toby, Luke came for you.

Tyler didn't back down. "I'm so sick of his shit."

Luke broke away from Fisher and went straight for Simpson. Coach O stepped through the crowd and grabbed him. The man was old enough to be Luke's grandfather, but Luke couldn't move once Coach pinned him to the wall.

"Enough. Everybody back in the room."

The rest of the team slowly started moving, but Luke's brain was cooked. All he wanted to do was make Tyler Simpson hurt, a kind of singular purpose that he rarely felt outside the mat. Of course, when he was wrestling, it was never about causing pain—only winning. This was different.

Coach O got in Luke's ear.

"Get back in that damn room. Right now." Any other kid, any other day, and that would've been enough. Luke tried to take another step as Simpson slipped past. Coach pinned him even harder. "I swear you'll never wrestle in this school again. State champion or not."

Coach had a reputation for two things. You worked your ass off in class and on the mat. And if he made you a promise, he kept it. Luke knew this better than anyone. After his freshman season, Coach had pulled Luke out of the hallway and taken him to the teacher's lounge. For a long time, Coach O had sat there, working a toothpick from side to side in his mouth, not talking. And then all of a sudden, he'd said, "Do you want to go to college?"

Luke hadn't thought about it before. College was a vague thing, a concept he understood but couldn't visualize in any concrete way. Did he want to go to college?

"I guess."

Coach pulled the toothpick out of his mouth and pointed it at Luke, eyes hard.

"*You guess?* Son, do you want it or not?"

He made Luke say exactly what he wanted—to leave. Or to be more precise: to escape. It was the first time Luke had really said those words. With Toby, it was a shapeless dream. But once Luke said it, it felt real for the first time. And every moment from then on—whenever Luke started to stray in school or in practice—Coach O would remind him of the promise he'd made.

Coach stared Luke in the eye. "Are you going to end this or am I?"

Luke nodded, but Coach wouldn't budge. "I need you to say it, son."

"It's done," Luke said.

Coach held him against the wall a second longer before finally letting him go.

They ran the rest of practice, until nearly everybody in the room had either puked or seriously considered the possibility. When Luke tried to throw up, nothing came. He heaved in the corner, his entire body trying to expel something invisible inside him. When he stood up to keep running—one of the assistants told him to take it easy—his legs wobbled. But hell if he was going to stop. He pushed back to the front of the group as they circled the mats again and again and again.

"I won't tolerate bullshit," Coach said. "I don't care what somebody says to you or about you. You. Walk. Away. You are disciplined. You are machines. Do you understand me?"

Luke was the loudest voice in the room.

As soon as Coach blew the whistle, Tyler ran to the locker room. Luke sat in the corner, sipping water and trying to will his body up. Before he could move, Coach O came over and sat next to him, mopping his own forehead with a damp towel. They both stared at the room silently.

"Listen, I get it," Coach O said. "Simpson can be a little prick sometimes. But . . ."

Luke started taking off his shoes as Coach O searched for words. Luke could finish the sentence. But . . . *there's so much riding on this year . . . don't let people make decisions for you . . . you have a special gift.*

"Sometimes you have to let people fight their own battles. I know you and that kid Toby are close, but you aren't doing him any favors by stepping up to every guy who wants some."

Luke leaned forward, once again feeling like he was going to throw up. Like everybody, Coach only saw one part of the story. And Luke had stopped trying to fill them in a long time ago. He nodded and went to stand. Coach stopped him.

"You understand what I'm saying? You can't protect him from everything."

Luke forced a smile. "Like you said, Simpson's a prick. I won't let it happen again."

Coach O hesitated. "If you need something, let me know. Okay?"

When Luke went into the hallway, Toby was still leaning up against the wall. That same shit-eating grin on his face.

"I really, really hate that guy," Toby said, pulling tissue

from his nose. The blood was dry, almost gone

"Just ignore him," Luke said. "And try to stop being an asshole."

Toby looked offended.

"He grabbed himself and told me to use my mouth for something useful," Toby said. "I told him I'd stick with his sister."

It took a second, but they both laughed. It was enough to make Simpson come after him, sure. But something didn't add up. Throwing a punch—or a few, if Tyler's face was evidence—wasn't Toby's style. He didn't mix it up, especially with a guy Tyler's size.

"What else happened?"

Toby tried to laugh off the question, the concern. Normally, that would be enough for Luke to let it go. They both had enough embarrassments; not everything needed calling out. But the longer they stood in the hallway, the more Luke saw past Toby's I-couldn't-give-a-damn attitude. Something panicky and feral pulsed underneath every word, every subtle movement. Luke had seen Toby this way too many times to ignore it.

"You don't look okay," he finally said.

"Shit, man." Toby didn't say anything else for a second. But then he looked Luke in the eye and sighed. "When I punched him back, he laughed and said he thought my dad would've taught me better. Happy?"

All the anger, all the rage came flying back. Every piece of dynamite in his body told him to run to Deerfield, where Tyler lived. To pull him out of his house and beat the ever-living shit out of him until he cried, until he couldn't cry anymore, because Luke was sure that was the only thing that would make this feeling go away.

4

TOBY followed Luke outside in the cold, trying not to think about his throbbing lip, or the way Tyler had smiled—like he knew exactly how to hurt him. It wasn't even the words that shook Toby now as much as his own reaction. Fists flying without a second thought. His dad's blood, rising up.

So instead he focused on Annie. That denim jacket, the T-shirt for an obscure band (at least he thought it was a band) he'd never heard of before. The way she stomped through the hallways. And not least of all, the fuck-off eyes she painted on with thick black mascara. Every single part of her cut through his body like a hot bullet.

That's why he went to talk to her, why he had told Terrence Guthrie that he needed to meet that girl. Of course, that's where he should've stopped, should have never mentioned anything about girlfriend material. So when she had grabbed him by the collar at lunch—he swore he could still feel the material bunched between her fists—something inside him had been altered.

"Oh, shit," Luke said, under his breath.

Toby barely had time to look when he heard a familiar whistle. And then his dad's voice, calling out to the new Spanish teacher, a pretty woman who'd almost made Toby toss three years of French in the shitter so he could be in her class. Luckily, she was too close to her car for his dad to offer anything beyond the catcall.

"You okay?" Luke asked.

"Yeah," Toby said, watching his dad walk toward them with his arms spread wide. Like he wanted a hug. Jimmy was thin, but put together like wire cable. The kind of guy who would still be smiling as he punched you, as he went for your throat. He lit a cigarette and took a long drag before saying, "What the hell happened to your face?"

"I got into it with somebody," Toby said.

"Well, I hope he looks worse than you do," he said. Jimmy faked a punch at Luke. "Damn, son. Look at you. Like a brick fucking wall."

When Toby was a kid, he had assumed everybody lived the way they did. Moving from house to house, once even staying in a cheap motel for a few months. The room had HBO and marked the first time Toby saw a naked woman, a late-night soft-core experience after his father had passed out on the bed next to him, both of them surrounded by empty boxes from the five-dollar pizzas they'd been eating for every meal. There was a sense of adventure in the constant moving, the transient life they led. Toby couldn't say he didn't enjoy it, if only because he didn't know any better. For the last five years, they'd been in the same single-wide, the result of a landlord who owed Jimmy something.

"You hit the gym, maybe people will stop fucking with you." Jimmy flicked Toby's ear playfully. Put up his fists like they were going to box.

"The ladies like me this way," Toby said.

Jimmy snorted. "Well, that's some positive thinking right there."

Who knew why his dad was here, let alone how many beers he'd already put away. Negotiating even the simplest deal with him was more complicated than anything Toby did in trig, so he spoke in open statements, "I was thinking . . . I might . . ." Always waiting for an opportunity, a way to navigate the minefield. His dad was staring at the parking lot, the thin blue smoke from his cigarette surrounding his head like a halo when he said, "All right. Let's hit it."

Toby flinched, opened his mouth. Luke met his eyes and shook his head quickly.

"I was going to have Toby help me with my math tonight," Luke said.

"Yeah. And we're watching the boys for Doreen," Toby added.

Jimmy shook his head, not unkindly. The way someone might if they saw a young child being mischievous.

"Nah, I've got a surprise for the boy." When he faked a punch at Toby this time, Luke jumped. Jimmy smiled, looking Luke up and down.

"Look at you. Mr. Big Time."

Luke had squared up to Jimmy only once before, and nothing had happened. Jimmy had cuffed him and gone back to his beer, laughing. They took off, waiting hours and hours until they were convinced he'd cooled off. Toby had seen his dad challenged enough times to know that Luke had gotten off light. It was either courage or stupidity that took over his father's head in moments like this. He never showed weakness, never backed down. Jimmy cocked his head and looked at Luke long and hard.

"I'll give you the answers tomorrow morning before school," Toby said quickly, starting toward his dad's beat-to-shit truck. Hoping Jimmy would follow.

They drove down River Road, toward their trailer, with the windows down, the heater cranked, and Waylon Jennings pumping loudly through the speakers. The truck didn't have air conditioning and barely had heat, but the radio was top-of-the-line. You could hear it two counties away.

"Waylon was supposed to die on that plane with Buddy Holly," Jimmy yelled. "But God was like, 'Shit no. This guy is special.' Listen—right there. You hear that note? Damn, boy."

Some families had religion, Toby's had Waylon. His grandfather—Toby had only met the man a handful of times before he ended up on the wrong side of a knife in a bar in Startown—had taken his chances in Nashville. Even opened for a few big names in the early seventies. Names that meant nothing to Toby. There were still people in this town who would stop Toby and comment on the way his grandfather could sing and play—like an angel or a devil, depending. But he had also been a notorious drunk, meaner than Jimmy, if that could be believed. After he didn't make it in Nashville, they had moved back to North Carolina so he could work in the furniture mills.

Jimmy sang along with Waylon as he took the turn into the plot of land that held their trailer. His voice was a high tenor that faltered at the top of his range. As if he was so brokenhearted he couldn't bear to hold the notes any longer. One of the best memories Toby had was hearing his dad—drunk, Toby now knew—softly singing to his mother over the phone. Convincing her to come back.

When the trailer came into view, a car was parked sideways in the turnabout that circled their front lawn. The paint shone under the single bulb of their porch light. When Jimmy saw the car, he slammed on the brakes.

"Whose car is that?"

Toby's heart started pounding. He squinted into the darkness, trying to see if he knew the car. Hoping he didn't. Jimmy didn't like visitors, even when it was Luke. Toby knew Jimmy was involved in some petty criminal activity—selling stolen cell phones, the occasional scheme. He knew about the revolver wrapped in a T-shirt and stashed in the back of the closet.

"Whose fucking car is that?" his dad asked again.

"Maybe Silas got a new car," Toby said. Silas was one of Jimmy's oldest friends from high school, two-thirds of a group of hell-raisers that were still legendary in Catawba County. Most of the stories ended with somebody going to jail. Bo, the third, had been in prison for close to six years.

"Hell no. Silas couldn't handle a sexy-ass car like that. Look at it. That kind of car is guaranteed to get a dude some ass."

Toby looked at his dad for a moment. Maybe he was

high. The car—an El Camino with a wolf mural on the tail-gate—might as well have a blinking caution light. NO LADIES ALLOWED.

"Yeah. I don't think so."

A flash of annoyance crossed Jimmy's face. Toby instinctively scooted back as his father reached into his pocket, struggling to pull something out. He cussed once, finally producing a set of keys.

"You always got something to say, don't you?"

Jimmy held the keys out to Toby, who didn't take them.

"What is this?" Toby asked.

"You are just like your damn mother, I swear." Jimmy pushed the keys into Toby's hands. They were heavy, which may have been the resin-skull key chain that now dangled from his hands. Toby wasn't sure what to say.

"It's . . . mine?"

Jimmy laughed once. "Shit, if my dad ever gave me a car I would've been out the *door*. Not sitting around asking questions. Do I need to rethink this?"

Toby shook his head and jumped out of the truck. He didn't have any more questions. Didn't need to hear another word.

November 17

T—

The first time I saw Eddie, he was dunking on this guy everybody calls Simon because he repeats every damn thing you say. You'll be like, "Can I borrow a piece of paper?" And he'll say, "Can you borrow a piece of paper." Not a question, either. He'll just say it, like he needs to think on it really deeply.

Anyway, I was standing there watching them play ball, and this old dude just takes off. One second he's standing there and the next he's in the air looking like he could jump over those razor fences, the walls. Anything they put in front of him.

Every dude in the yard went nuts. Hands in the air like Jesus himself had thrown down that dunk. From what Sister told me, Eddie was nothing short of God when he played basketball. Had a scholarship to every school in this state until he got a taste for drugs—for robbing gas stations. One night, blasted out of his mind, Eddie killed two clerks at a store. Shot another woman as she was walking in to buy lottery tickets. Everybody in here has the same story, T. Just the details change.

But Eddie's different. You'll never hear him say he was innocent. And trust me, every guy in this place is innocent. Just ask them. They're always talking about how the Supreme Court's going to free them. How the governor's going to see the light. But not Eddie. What he did hangs over him like a cloud, a constant presence. Guys will press him like, "Yeah, but they had it coming, right?" And he'll get really quiet. Like he's trying to remind himself of something.

He never answers, though. Never gives one excuse for what he did.

The first time I met Sister, I told her I was guilty. I thought she'd appreciate me owning it, because that's all you hear once you get inside. Accept. Repent. Wait. I'd already said the words a hundred times to lawyers and judges and newspaper reporters. "I am guilty." But here's the thing: everybody expects the next part of that sentence to be ". . . and I'm sorry."

But man, I'm not.

So my first lawyer never had a chance. I wouldn't say a damn word to help him or me. We set a land-speed record getting from that night to sentencing. I just wanted it over. I didn't want to give cold feet a chance to show up. Didn't want anyone telling me I was innocent. The last time I saw him was right before they sent me here. He looked me in the eye and said more lawyers were coming to help.

And sure enough, a few months later, Marilyn showed up. That first time, she lit into the CO when he didn't get me into the room quickly enough. I tell you what, they don't waste any time now. My ass is in that chair before she even walks into the room. Every week she's here too. Talking strategy and breathing fire.

Whenever she comes in, it's always the same thing. Telling me how I didn't do myself any favors. How everything from my child-hood, everything about you and me, should've been presented to the court.

She's always like, "This *matters.*"

But confessing was the end for me. Lock me up. Let me just be. But I guess that's not Marilyn's style. Today, when she was here, she was especially fired up. Huffing as she paged through my files. Glancing at me every few seconds like she was reading a bad report card.

The more she looked at me, the more I knew what was coming next. The frustration would turn to anger at the cops, the lawyers, the judge. Anybody who had a hand in me sitting here. It always ends with her trying to get me to believe that telling that story one more time will make some sort of fucking difference.

I turned around in my chair and yelled at the CO, this big-ass dude everybody calls Sasquatch. "Take me back!"

Marilyn stood up and touched me on the shoulder, saying, "Luke, Luke, *Luke*." And of course Sasquatch was like, "No touching!" in that gruff voice they think makes them sound hard. Marilyn pulled back her hand like I was a burning flame.

Everything was rushing past me like I was standing in traffic, T.

I stood up, probably too fast, because Sasquatch put me up against the wall. His mouth went to the microphone clipped to his shoulder, saying he needed assistance. And I don't know what happened, but something snapped. I started pushing against those bricks like I was trying to keep myself alive. But that fat ass put his weight against the back of my knees. After that, I went slack and all I could say was, "I'm done. I'm done. I'm done."

Marilyn lost her mind. Her screaming at Sasquatch was the last thing I heard before they started pushing me through the pod, which is about the worse situation you can ever find yourself in, man. That means isolation. It's silence and four walls that, after a few hours, might as well be infinite. Being alone like that works its way inside you, burrows deep into your bones, your brain.

Doesn't matter if it's a day, a week. When you come out, you're different. Bent in a direction you were never meant to be.

Luke

5

LUKE walked home slowly, his legs heavy and his stomach hollow, staring at the sky. Trying to catch stars behind the cloudy darkness. Anything to keep his mind from playing out what could be happening with Toby and Jimmy.

When they were kids, Toby had come into a set of walkie-talkies. Sometimes Jimmy gave Toby things, never wrapped—always thrown at his feet like something he'd killed. Still, the walkie-talkies were quality, the sort of thing used on construction sites. Sometimes in the middle of the night, Luke's would chirp and he'd hear Toby's cracked voice, asking him to come to the plane. It was never good, but something about the memory made Luke wish he could rewind time. Could go back to one of those moments when he and Toby spent the night huddled together in the husk of that plane, barely saying a word.

Luke tried to push the memory away, but it was pointless.

Scene after scene from their childhood played in his head until he was in the parking lot of the complex.

The apartment door was cracked open and his mom was on the couch, sitting on the lap of a man wearing a sleeveless camouflage T-shirt. They were sharing a cigarette, neither noticing Luke standing in the doorway. It wasn't until Jack-Jack came running toward him that his mom looked up.

"Luke!" She was drunk, stumbling sideways and laughing as she sloppily embraced him. "We've been waiting for you!"

She laughed again when the man pinched her on the ass and said, "Aren't you going to introduce me?"

"Stop it," she said, playfully swiping at his hand. He passed the cigarette up to her. "Luke, this is Ricky. He's a supervisor down at the Pepsi plant."

Ricky stood up and reached his hand toward Luke, not taking his eyes off Doreen. Luke shook it limply, and Ricky turned to face him.

"I thought you were some kind of badass wrestler," he said. "What kind of handshake is that?"

"Luke, shake his hand properly," his mom said.

Ricky clamped his hand on Luke's, this time grinning and looking Luke square in the eye. He wasn't a big man, a good six inches shorter than Luke. He had the look of a football player a few years past his prime, the type of guy who ate at buffets. Ricky considered Luke for another second before glancing back to Doreen, a pandering smile on his face.

"I'm going to shower," Luke said.

His mother lit another cigarette, yelping when Ricky dropped onto the couch next to her. They both ignored him.

Luke let the warm water fall over his body. Normally he looked forward to his time in the shower. The twins weren't constantly running to him for food or attention. He could think, jerk off—disappear as the steam enveloped the room. This time he wasn't in the shower five minutes when Petey burst in and said, "Mom needs your help!"

He was out, dry, and dressed a few minutes later. In the kitchen, his mom was struggling to get the large pot of mashed potatoes off the stove.

"Help me with this," she said.

Luke lifted the pot easily, holding it as she scooped the thick mash into a glass bowl. His grandmother had taught Doreen to cook when she was young, telling her only daughter that men didn't care about school, only a woman who could cook, clean, and keep her mouth shut. Doreen had jumped in his father's Camaro when she was fifteen and, not a year later, had Luke bouncing on her knee. They'd only been back to the small Virginia coal-mining town of Doreen's youth once, maybe twice in Luke's life.

"You could've asked Ricky to help," Luke said.

"He's our guest," his mom said in a theatrical whisper. "Besides, he's relaxing."

Luke looked into the living room. Ricky had a beer between his legs and sat there staring past the television show the boys were watching. Every few seconds, he brought the bottle to his lips.

"He's not spending the night," Luke said. It came out more of a question than he would've liked.

"Oh, shit." She sucked a glob of hot potato from her finger, chasing it with another sip from her wine. "And of course he's not spending the night. Is that how you think of me?"

Luke didn't answer. He wanted to believe she'd wake up one day and realize how hard he and the twins had been living. When Luke was younger, sometimes they'd go on little day trips—Doreen called them vacations—to state parks that had waterfalls, malls that seemed to last for miles, and even a zoo once or twice. They'd eat at restaurants with shiny menus that promised free ice cream after the mini corn dogs or chicken nuggets. Luke would lose himself on those trips, but it didn't matter where they were, or how much fun he'd had—the same inexplicable dread slowly crept back into his body the moment they were pointed back home.

"Take the meat loaf," she said, nodding to the still-steaming pan. He followed her—mashed potatoes in one hand, pre-packed dinner rolls in the other—into the living room.

They ate on TV trays, the television now turned to bull riding. Ricky knew a guy who rode on the professional tour. Every time a new cowboy came up, the twins got really excited and asked Ricky if that was his friend. After the fifth or sixth time, he snapped at them to be quiet. Luke stared at his mom, but all she did was move food around her plate.

Luke, of course, wasn't eating. He nibbled on mini carrots that he'd sneaked out of the school cafeteria. He was working through one at a time when Ricky tapped his fork on his plate and pointed it at Luke.

"What's his deal?"

"Oh, he's trying to make weight," Doreen said. "He's . . . how much do you need to lose, honey?"

Luke ignored the "honey." Language like that only came out when she was drinking wine or there were people to impress.

"Four pounds."

Ricky took a drink of his beer but didn't say anything else. Still, every few minutes he'd look at Luke's carrots and shake his head. Every swallow brought another look, each one more amused than the last. Finally he cleared his throat.

"Look at these guys." Ricky pointed the tip of his bottle at the television screen. "Those are men. They don't eat fucking *carrots*. That's real cowboy shit, right there."

One of the riders in the chute reworked his grip around the rope. Once his hand was in place, he started nodding like he was trying to convince himself it was a good idea to be strapped to a thousand pounds of muscle. Then they released him into the arena. The entire ride took five seconds, ending with the cowboy running for the fence as the bull bucked itself around the arena.

Luke ate another carrot and didn't say a thing. He had nothing to prove to Ricky and was more than willing to drop it. To go back to vaguely ignoring him the way he'd ignored all of Doreen's other boyfriends.

"Now, I played football," Ricky said.

"Of course you did," Luke muttered under his breath.

Ricky stopped chewing. "What's that supposed to mean?"

"Nothing. I just know a lot of football players."

Luke smiled. He knew exactly how Ricky would react. His mom wasn't blitzed enough to be blind to what was happening. She laughed nervously and put a hand on Ricky's forearm.

"He takes wrestling really seriously, that's all." She shot a look at Luke. "Right, honey?"

Luke didn't answer, kept smiling at his plate of carrots.

"You really think you're something, don't you?" Ricky asked.

"He's won three state championships!" Jack-Jack said, excited. Ricky didn't even turn toward him, which was probably for the best. Had he gone at either of the twins, it would've been over. Instead, he laughed.

"Hell, if you want to spend your time playing grab ass . . ." He grabbed Doreen's thigh.

"Stop!" she said, giggling.

Luke got up and told the boys to take care of their plates, to brush their teeth and get ready for bed. As soon as he said it, his mom stood up and followed them into the kitchen.

"What do you guys think about a slumber party in the living room?"

Of course Petey and Jack-Jack lost their minds. Sprinted to the bedroom to pull their blanket and pillows out of the room. When they were gone, Luke made a point of only staring at the sink as he washed the plates.

"Listen, I don't need your permission to have somebody spend the night," she said.

"Do whatever you want."

"Ricky's a good guy," she said. "He's really funny. He's got a house near the lake. He said we could all . . ."

Luke tuned her out. Fifteen minutes later, she led Ricky

to the bedroom, carrying the box of wine and two red plastic cups. Luke turned off the lights and switched the television to a cartoon, and soon the boys fell into the sort of deep sleep he hadn't experienced in years.

In the dark, with only the television on, the apartment looked like an aquarium. A place he'd been before, the memory buried under years of anger toward his mom. They'd gone to Atlanta. Visited the Coke museum. And then the aquarium, the entire ocean spread before him like a moving painting.

Doreen had met the man online, a car salesman who turned out to be nice but married. They stood in the back, with the shadows, reaching for each other. Giggling like little kids. The same laughter—and other assorted vague sounds—slipped through the apartment's thin walls.

Luke grabbed his shoes and the heavy-duty garbage bags he'd kept stashed behind the couch, and checked on the boys one last time before he quietly stepped outside onto the walkway of their apartment. The wind blew leaves across the nearly empty parking lot. In the corner, a person was smoking, the gold cherry pulsing like a lightning bug. Luke locked the door behind him and pulled the bag over his head as he went down the stairs, punching holes for his arms on either side.

In the distance he could hear the country highway that, if he ran far enough, would take him all the way down to Charlotte. He and Toby had made half-hearted attempts at running away before, never making it more than a few miles down that road.

He sat down on the curb and rubbed his legs, trying to work out the post-practice stiffness. People assumed he ran to keep in shape. They'd see him going demon down the road and honk their horns. Yell out encouragements. It did help him stay in shape, of course. But nights like tonight, after a brutal practice, he ran to empty himself. To push himself until the entire world looked different, until he couldn't feel anything and his whole body turned heavy, like a water-soaked log. Until even the plane looked alien as he passed it. At enough speed, in the right kind of light, it became the plane of Luke's childhood fantasies. The one that could still carry them away, just like that.

His eyes were closed when a voice called out. At first he thought it was his mom, and he stood up quickly—too quickly. His legs screamed in protest and he groaned. Annie appeared out of the shadows, dropping a cigarette onto the concrete.

"Please tell me you didn't follow me here," she said. "I swear to god, if your little friend pops out, I'm going to get my stepdad's tire wrench."

Luke was suddenly awake. Every part of his body alive.

"I live up there," he said, motioning to his apartment. "And Toby's not here. But he is most days. So . . . I don't know. I'd buy some repellent or something."

Annie smiled, just barely. Luke couldn't tell if she was amused or, maybe, had already entertained the idea of incapacitating his friend.

"So what's with the garbage bags?" she said. "Is it some kind of perverted sex thing?"

"What? Oh my god, no."

Luke tried to smooth the garbage bag, which suddenly seemed impossibly wrinkled. And why did he care? He dropped his hands away from the bag immediately. This time Annie didn't try to hide her smile, and her laughter rang across the parking lot.

"I was kidding," she said. "But, you know, I am interested in what's . . . happening here." She wagged her finger at the garbage bag.

"I need to lose weight," he said. "So I can wrestle."

"And you do this often?"

"Well, the running. The garbage bag is new. I've never been heavy before. They say this will work."

He was rambling and he knew it. Annie yawned, rubbing both hands through her hair.

"Who's *they*?" Annie asked.

"Oh, my coach. The internet."

That same unreadable smirk. It unnerved Luke.

"Well, as great as this has been . . . I need to go to bed. Until next time?"

"I'm Luke."

"Until next time, Luke."

When she turned to leave, without thinking, Luke said, "Hey—do you live here?"

"Yep. And as shitty as you might think this place is, it's the Hyatt compared to where we lived in Chicago."

And then she was gone.

6

TOBY had never listened to Elvis before, but he had that mess cranking not five minutes after he'd bought the tape at the truck stop off of I-40. Because of course the El Camino had a tape player. And of course the only tapes he could find were *Elvis: The Hits* and a collection called *1970s Truck Driving Classics*. He bought both.

He had to admit, the El Camino was a nice car. Aftermarket leather interior. Not a scratch on it, inside or out. The manual gearshift was a metal skull with eyes that lit up whenever Toby hit the gas. He didn't know a damn thing about engines, but when he pushed the pedal down the car jerked forward with such muscle, such elegance, he had to use every bit of willpower not to open it up on the empty highway.

There was a bigger question Toby was avoiding, of course. Where did Jimmy get the car? And when Jimmy stuffed a wad of twenties into his hand . . . where did the money come from? That wasn't walking-around money, and this wasn't the sort of car you got from a country lot. But Toby didn't care. Not today. He flew out the door before Jimmy could take either back.

Toby turned the radio up, letting Elvis pour through the open windows as the predawn light began to fill the horizon. After two or three songs, he almost switched to *1970s Truck Driving Classics* because, honestly, he wasn't feeling the King. But then "Burning Love" came on, and he didn't stop rewinding the tape until it was time to pick Luke up for school.

When he turned in to the apartment, Luke was sitting on the steps waiting for him. Toby threw the shifter into park and jumped out, singing the last words of the song loudly into the parking lot. Despite the performance, Luke's eyes never left the car.

"Please tell me you didn't steal this."

"If I was going to steal a car, it wouldn't be an El Camino," Toby said, reaching in and turning down the radio.

Of course Luke would want more. Or, more precisely, he'd keep asking questions, keep sighing and staring at the car like it was a hand grenade, until Toby finally told him the truth. When he looked at his friend again, Toby smiled big and easy.

"Jimmy gave it to me."

"T . . ."

Luke trailed off, looking at the car again. Toby understood. He could wake up tomorrow morning and the car might be gone. And it would somehow be Toby's fault. Nothing came free, not from Jimmy, not once in his life. Toby knew this better than anyone, Luke included.

All he wanted was to enjoy the car, if only for one day.

"Just let me drive us to school," Toby said.

Luke still looked conflicted, as if Toby was asking him to choose between life and death. And for a second, a lick of anger flared up inside Toby. Why couldn't Luke just pretend, even for a few minutes, that they were normal? When he was younger, Toby had coveted the expensive basketball shoes everybody else wore. The houses they lived in, with pools and windows that weren't clogged with ancient air conditioners. A life where his and Luke's only worry was getting twenty dollars off their parents so they could waste it at Applebee's after the football game. The injustice stuck in his throat, even now.

And if the car disappeared tomorrow, fine. If Jimmy threw a beating his way, whatever. That was tomorrow. They had the car today, and Toby wasn't going to waste it.

"You can run your ass to school if you want," Toby finally

said, moving to the driver's side door. "But I'm driving."

Luke grabbed his backpack off the ground, eyeing the car and then Toby.

"Is it a car or a truck?" As soon as Luke said it, he smiled. Quick, nothing more than a flash. It was the most real thing Toby had seen from him in ages.

"It's both. That's what makes it so damn amazing," Toby said. "Not to mention the wolf mural on the tailgate. What else do you need?"

Before he could answer, the apartment door flew open and a man in his underwear was yelling down to Luke.

Toby laughed and whispered to Luke, "Oh shit, is this *Ricky*?"

The man stomped down the stairs in only his work boots. He was short but looked strong. Like a mechanic. Luke shouldered his backpack.

"Those boys aren't ready for school."

"Mom does Wednesdays. She's off and I have practice."

"Well, your mom isn't feeling well—"

Luke laughed, and Ricky took a step closer, smiling as if he'd enjoy mixing it up with Luke. Toby ran over and stood between them.

"We can get them ready," he said to Luke. "I'll drive them to school too. It's fine."

Luke was staring hard at Ricky, who smiled and scratched himself. "Listen to your boyfriend."

Toby leaned his head back and groaned. "Really? That's your move? I don't know why I'm surprised, but I am."

Ricky looked confused for a moment.

"You called us gay. That's your go-to put-down. It's basic, which whatever. But putting that aside, it loses some teeth when delivered by a guy who chased us down in the parking lot in his underwear. You know?"

Luke said his name, but Toby was already rolling.

"Like, seriously. This isn't hard. Take Luke. His eyes are so far apart, they're almost on the sides of his head. He looks like a fish you see on nature shows. A flounder or some shit."

Luke shook his head, but Toby didn't care. The dumb look on Ricky's face was enough to keep him going forever.

"And what about me? I look like the kid in the movie who dies of cancer. Shit, I'm nearly eighteen years old and I shop in the kids section at Super Mart. But you trot out gay. Jesus, it's just depressing."

Ricky adjusted himself. "I call it like I see it."

"Well, if that's the standard, I'd hate to tell you what I see."

Ricky sprang forward, a finger pointed at Toby's face. Before he got two steps, Luke had him against the hood of the El Camino. A small voice floated above them, loud and panicked. Petey, wide-eyed and wanting to know if everything was okay.

"Everything's good, buddy," Luke said, still holding Ricky down. "Get Jack-Jack up. Toby and I are taking you guys to school."

The boy paused before padding back into the apartment. When Doreen appeared on the balcony, she was naked under a thin robe. Toby caught a flash of her breasts as she came running down the stairs, yelling Luke's name.

"What are you doing?" She pushed Luke hard until he released Ricky. "Jesus, baby, are you okay?"

Ricky got off the hood and wiped his mouth.

"No big deal. Luke was just showing me a few of those wrestling moves." But his eyes were daggers on Luke, who only smiled.

"Luke, apologize to Ricky."

"Apologize?" Toby said.

"Luke Teague, I swear to god, if you don't apologize, I'll call that school and get you yanked off that wrestling team quicker than you can spit."

Luke's eyes never left Doreen's as he said, "Ricky, I'm sorry if I hurt you."

"Hurt me?" Ricky laughed. "Okay . . ."

Luke just stared at his mother until Doreen and Ricky disappeared back into the apartment. When they were gone, Toby still didn't know what to say to Luke. So he turned to the four or five people standing, watching. Waiting for the fireworks.

"Show's over. Go back to your lottery tickets."

A man gave him the finger; another woman laughed and triumphantly stuck her phone into her pajama pants. When he turned back, Luke was leaning against the bumper of the El Camino, staring at the asphalt parking lot. Toby walked over and stood next to him.

"I'm sorry," he said.

Luke was silent, but then he glanced over at Toby. "Do you really think I look like a flounder?"

Toby laughed. "It was a moment of inspiration. But now that I've said it . . . I'm not sure I'll ever be able to unsee it."

The spark of amusement faded from Luke's face and he sighed, pushing himself off the hood of the car. "I got to get the boys ready. We're going to be late."

Toby reached out and stopped him. "Are you, you know, okay?"

Luke stared right through him, suddenly unreadable.

"Yeah, man. I just need to get them ready."

December 25

T—

You can always tell when someone just got out of isolation. There's a hollowness to them. Everything about this place is designed to break you down until you're nothing but a number. Because you can erase a number, and what does it matter? There's always another one to write down.

My first day out, Sister came to see me—Eddie right behind her. Both of them wanting to know how I was doing.

Neither of them sat, and I didn't say a word, because what am I supposed to say? I felt like a rug had been pulled out from under me and I was still falling. When Sister reached over and touched me on the shoulder, I jerked. Every CO in the place went stiff.

The first time I got solitary was a month or so after I'd gotten here, and at first I was like, "Is this all you've got?" Because it doesn't seem like much until maybe the second or third day. That's when everything starts crawling. Everything gets dark and dizzy. Like you've been hit in the head a hundred times. And it doesn't matter if it's a week, a month, or longer—it breaks you.

We're not supposed to be alone like that, T.

Anyway, Eddie sat down next to me and starts saying, "You know they put me in solitary for a solid two months once?"

But I didn't give him nothing, man. Of course, he kept on talking in my ear like a gnat. Telling me how he about lost his mind. How I was probably feeling the same way right now.

I wasn't about to get real with everybody watching us, so I shrugged. Pulled out my pen and paper and started writing this letter—trying to tune them out. Eddie kept on with the "you'll be okay" line, which was bullshit. In here you learn that a moment might be okay, but eventually everything falls apart. You are never okay, no matter how much you try to keep it together.

Remember when we were trying to fix the plane and we propped it up on those sawhorses we lifted from the road crew down on Highway 321? You were underneath it, really thinking you would be able to find a way to patch all those holes. Solve that rust. And then it snapped. Split down the middle like a pair of secondhand pants.

How you got out with just a scratch, I'll never know. But that's the best I can describe what it felt like sitting there, T. Like thousands of pounds of rusted-out metal were falling on top of me and I couldn't get out of the way.

Sister stopped my hand from moving. "We can talk about it, Luke. You're not alone."

And man, I just had enough. I was like, "How can you say that? All I am is alone. And there's no use in talking about it, because soon enough, Eddie, me—all of us are going to be gone. It might not be today or tomorrow, but it's going to happen. And there's not a damn thing you can do about that."

I didn't blink once, T. Let them have every one of those words like it was a fist. Sister looked like I'd really hit her too. Her eyes were wide and she kept opening her mouth like she wanted to tell me I was wrong. But she didn't. Hell, she *couldn't*.

I stood up and walked away. Every ounce of energy I had was gone. I couldn't have said another word to them if I tried. So I went back to my cell and fell asleep. I didn't care if I ever woke up again.

I avoided Eddie for a few days after that. But today, we had a special dinner and I couldn't duck him. I was sitting alone—enjoying the silence—when Eddie walked up. He was already done eating too, so I knew why he was there. Before I could say a word, he was like, "Nope."

Then he stood there, wiping his hand up and down his face.

Not saying a damn word. When he finally looked at me he was all, "You aren't dead yet."

That stopped me, T. Like getting hit with a brick.

I guess Eddie saw it as an opening, because he just kept talking about how nobody wants to be in here. How we all need to accept the things we can't change.

That's when he lost me.

I accepted this shit a long time ago. It's everybody else who's pretending it isn't happening. Pretending that some court or lawyer or, hell, Jesus himself is going to swoop down and save me. Everybody plays their game until there's no game to play anymore. Until the rest of the world takes notice and it's like, "Shit, that one's been alive for a little too long. Let's put a stop to that."

A few weeks later, the machine starts moving. They set a date. And then you're being wheeled into that room as your family tries to hear you through thick glass. Screaming or praying or crying out those last words.

Every single guy in here is going out that way. Yeah, sure—there's some hard exceptions. Dudes who use those final words to hurt somebody, to kill one last time. But that's the exception, T. There's no dignity lying on that table. Most of us will meet it crying, the most alone we've been in our entire life.

Anyway, I told Eddie to get out of my face and he lost it. All,

"You think you're hard? You think I haven't seen this shit a hundred times before?"

Every word came out louder than the last. Telling me how it took him ten years to get his head right—ten years, gone. Just like that. Sister had told me that Eddie spent more time in isolation than anybody she'd known. That when she first met him, he spit on the glass. Said things she wouldn't repeat. A living, breathing monster.

Anyway, Eddie must've been looking a little too much like his old self, because one of the COs said his name from across the cafeteria. It seemed to snap him out of it too. He nodded at the guard, holding up his hands to show we were cool. As he sat down across from me, everything about him was calm as a Sunday morning. Except for his eyes. They were on fire.

He talked out the side of his mouth, each word hard as rock.

"You think I want to be happy all the time? You think I don't want to burn this whole place to the ground?"

When I didn't say anything, Eddie reached across the table and grabbed my hand, which would be trouble as soon as the guard saw us. But Eddie didn't care, wasn't even pretending to look in his direction as he talked to me. Fast. Like I was standing on the edge of a cliff.

I didn't want to hear another word he was saying, but then he was like, "You get to choose if you care. They can't take that away from you. And you get to choose if you're going to walk through the rest of your life like a dead man. I've made my choice."

After that, he stood up and stomped off like he was mad at me. It's a good thing too. Because what Eddie and Sister—everybody in this place—doesn't realize is, you and I never had a choice. There wasn't a single moment when we weren't risking something. Every minute, every second. An anxiety that never leaves. Struggling for breath my whole fucking life.

And that's supposed to change in here?

Luke

7

LUKE barely spoke to Toby on the way to school, staring out the window and trying to quiet the howling anger inside him. To forget how his mother barely came out of the room as he got the boys ready for school. When they got to the parking lot, Luke jumped out of the car without a word, pretending not to hear Toby call his name.

The wrestling room was empty, save Coach O and Seth, a former college wrestler who came in every week to help Luke work out. He laced up his shoes as Seth jogged around the mat. Luke fell in behind him, nodding to Coach as he passed.

ONE PERCENT IMPROVEMENT, A HUNDRED PERCENT EFFORT. He'd taken those words to heart from the moment he saw the poster in the room. As he ran, he could feel the sweat tracing a line down his back, every single drop representing the work he'd been putting in since that very first win years ago. Despite everything. Because of it.

His entire first season, people penciled in an automatic win. Luke Teague? Never heard of him. As far as they knew, he was just another kid wrestling in busted-up Nikes because he couldn't afford wrestling shoes.

And then he ran the table.

The first few wins were easily explained. Anyone who followed high-school wrestling could tell you: a couple of wins didn't mean much. Something like that could be cultivated. There were plenty of wrestlers who hit the district tournament only to discover they were soft as cotton. Wrestlers Luke ran through like a buzz saw.

He pushed himself harder and harder, trying to empty his mind as he circled the small wrestling room. Every time he thought he was free, Ricky would pop into his head. Or his mother. Toby and that damn car. He'd done close to a hundred laps when Coach O called him over to start seven-minute live sessions with Seth.

Most days, Seth could barely keep up with Luke. But as soon as Coach told them to start, Luke couldn't find the groove. Everything floated by him seconds too late. Seth had his legs and was driving him to the mat, controlling him in every way.

Coach O was shouting instructions and encouragements

as Luke slowly pushed himself up to his hands and knees. Seth tried to drive him back down, but he was too high, and Luke spun away. Coach clapped. When they were both standing, Seth winked at Luke. It was nothing, a head game that a lot of wrestlers played. Some blew kisses or whispered in your ear when they had you down. It rarely bothered Luke, but today the way Seth did it got under his skin.

Luke shot toward him, but the entire move was undisciplined. Seth hit him with a crossface and wrenched Luke down to the mat. For a second, Luke was on his back— the first time in years. He bridged and got to his stomach, but it rattled him. For the rest of the seven minutes, he wrestled safe. Enough that by the end, Seth was cussing him.

"Do you want this or not?" he asked.

Luke took off his headgear and tossed it to the corner. Coach O moved Seth off the mat, whispering something to him. Before he left the room, Seth held out both his arms and said, "He won't get there wrestling like that."

Coach O came over to Luke when Seth was gone. "Off day, that's all."

"I'm still over," Luke said. "I can feel it."

Coach waved it away. "Don't worry about that. Are you doing the work?"

"Yes," Luke said.

"Then that's all you can do."

Luke nodded, and Coach O took him by the shoulders. "You're going to go to class. Eat a good lunch. Go home and get a full night's rest. And then you're going to come in here tomorrow night and take care of business."

Luke tried to object, but Coach held up a hand. "Match by match, Luke. Stop worrying about the scale. Just come here tomorrow, ready to kick some ass, and I promise you'll be ready for Herrera next week."

Relief flooded him. It wouldn't last, he knew, but for a moment Luke felt calm. Like the world wasn't spinning out of control. Coach O's face went stern.

"You still owe me twenty minutes," Coach said, checking his watch. "I'll take it in laps. And stop eating all that pizza. Okay?"

Luke smiled and started running. He circled the mat as fast as he could until Toby burst through the doors, looking annoyed.

"Jesus. It smells like ass and cat food in here," he said. Luke slowed down but didn't stop running, and Toby came up beside him, jogging.

"You know most people would think this isn't normal."

"Okay," Luke said. It was all he could say. He could already feel something bubbling up in his stomach. Sometimes when he trained, it almost became a game in itself. How long could he last before he had to retch?

Toby kept talking.

"Not me, of course. But other people. I hear words like 'freak.' But I've always got your back, as you know."

Luke ran to the corner of the room, to the garbage can. There wasn't anything in his stomach, but he still managed a sickly green slime that was neither solid nor liquid. He spit into the can a few times.

When he stood up, Toby said, "That's exactly the smell this room needed."

Luke shook his head. "I'm going to be here for a while."

Toby didn't look shocked, but he didn't look as if he was going to leave the room anytime soon, either. He stood there like he wanted to say something before hesitantly reaching into his pocket and pulling out a wad of bills.

"You want to skip and go somewhere? Do something?"

"Where did you get the money?" Luke asked.

"I found it in the car."

"You expect me to believe that?"

Toby grinned. "Well, you caught me. I've been selling my body to the women of Catawba County. Big demand."

Luke didn't laugh. They both knew Toby was lying. They both knew where the money had come from. When he realized the joke had failed, Toby's face went hard.

"What do you want me to say?" Toby dropped both his hands and stared at Luke, not waiting for him to answer. "What do I care how Jimmy got the money? It's mine now. Shit, it's ours."

Luke didn't want to argue with him, but even if Toby didn't care about the money—Jimmy would. They might not see the strings attached to this, but there was one on every single bill Toby held.

"I can't skip," Luke said. "They won't let me wrestle."

"Fine. Whatever," Toby said, stuffing the money back into his pocket.

Luke looked at the mat. He didn't want to disappoint Toby, to be the one always holding up the caution light. But they'd been waiting so long to get out of Hickory. Somehow it seemed worse to mess up, to ruin everything months, rather than years before they could escape.

"Maybe we could take the boys out for ice cream," Luke finally said. Now Toby was looking at the mat. He nodded, obviously happy but not wanting to show it as he kicked his heel against the wall.

"If you're lucky, I'll buy your ass a diet ice cream," he said.

"I'll make sure I run home this afternoon, just in case."

Toby nodded but didn't make to leave. He looked Luke in the eye.

"I know I shouldn't take the money," he said. "But sometimes . . ."

Toby stared up at the ceiling in frustration. The truth was, Luke didn't need him to finish the sentence. He knew every word of it by heart. Sometimes you didn't want to struggle for every inch of your life.

"Don't take anything else from him," Luke said.

Toby smiled. "What? Do you think I'm stupid?"

The smile faded as quick as it appeared.

The rest of the day was a blur. By the time the final bell rang, Luke felt good. He went to the regular team practice and Coach O told him to take it easy, a comment that got Simpson and his friends laughing on the other side of the mat. Luke worked out with the assistant coaches, both of them quitting before he needed to. At the end of practice, he felt strong.

He started the long, slow run down the highway toward his apartment. As he ran, the usual people passed him. Men coming home from work in loud, jacked-up trucks. Tired moms in minivans. Every so often a kid from school would honk, wave—neither of which Luke acknowledged. He ran blindly, only focused on each step that hit the pavement.

So when the rusted hatchback slammed its brakes and then backed toward him with an unhealthy whirring sound, Luke almost kept running. It wasn't until Annie said his name that he stopped.

"Do you ever walk?"

Nobody understood cutting weight. No matter how many times he rationalized it, explained that he didn't mind the discipline. And that's all it was: discipline. He didn't care about not eating a slice of pizza or skipping the doughnuts his English teacher sometimes brought for their first-period class. In some ways, his entire life had prepared him for it. But it wasn't only about not having enough to eat. It was a sacrifice for something bigger than him. Something that was close to holy.

Still, all he could manage was, "I'm still trying to lose weight."

This time Annie laughed without hesitation. "Yeah, I can tell."

Luke's entire body went flush. He wanted to clarify, to channel Toby for a moment and say something smooth. Something like, "Well, I can tell you're beautiful." Even thinking it, the words were dull and clumsy. But he did think she was beautiful, a fact that suddenly embarrassed him.

"When can I actually see you wrestle?" Annie said. "From what I hear, you're kind of a badass."

"I do okay," Luke said. It came out unintentionally cool.

"I'll judge that for myself," she said, hanging her arm out the window and pointing as she talked.

It should be so easy: ask her to come to the match tomorrow. To cheer him on. Shit, Toby had done as much a hundred times over the years, inviting girls to watch Luke wrestle. None of them came, of course—wrestling wasn't the sort of sport that naturally attracted spectators other than parents—but the invitations always came so effortlessly from Toby's lips.

"So . . . do you want a ride?" Annie finally said. "It's pretty cold."

Luke hadn't felt it until he stopped, but now his skin was suddenly puckering in the sharp air. He imagined sitting in the car, the heat hitting his skin. How his legs—his entire body—would collapse into the seat next to Annie. That was enough. He opened the door, squinting into the sudden bright light, and flopped down into the seat. As soon as the door was closed, Annie turned up her music and spun the tires until they were back on the road.

She drove fast and sang loudly, only looking at Luke when she took a turn at light speed and he instinctively grabbed the seat cushion below him.

"Doing okay over there?"

Luke nodded, picturing them flying off the road, hitting cows or trees or anything else that would kill them.

"You're just going . . . fast," he said.

"Ugh, that's the problem with this whole state. Everything's moving in slooooow motion."

"Except you," Luke said without thinking. Annie smirked, conceding the point with a nod. Was it that easy to be smooth? Was it more comfort and confidence than anything else?

"You're probably one of those North Carolina Forever types, aren't you?" Annie said.

"No. I'm leaving as soon as I can," Luke said.

Annie studied him, totally ignoring the road. As if she was searching for a clue. "Yeah, I don't believe you. You've got good ol' boy written over every square inch of that body."

She poked him in the leg for emphasis, and they both froze at the contact.

"Well, I'm going to Iowa. In August."

"Iowa? Oh my god, why?"

"Wrestling."

Annie laughed once. "You couldn't pay me to go to Iowa."

Luke turned and looked out the window. Going to Iowa never felt like a choice. It was a culmination, an ending. He had no idea what happened after they drove across the state line. And he wasn't sure it mattered *what* they were doing, as long as they were gone.

"I was just kidding," Annie said, reaching over and touching his shoulder. The same spike of cold excitement shot through him. He turned and stared at Annie, her face animated as she spoke. "But seriously. Why *do* people love this place so much? So far, I've seen nothing special. Just a bunch of good ol' boys in trucks chewing tobacco. And by the way, what's that about?"

Luke had nothing. "I've never chewed tobacco."

"Good. Because, *nasty.*" She made the turn that would lead them back to the apartment complex. Luke felt the impending good-bye in his gut.

"So how much do you have to lose?"

"I'm almost done, I hope. It was four pounds."

Annie's eyes went wide. "Four pounds! Jesus, where are you going to lose it? You're already nothing but muscle!"

"Well . . ." Luke wasn't sure what to say. They could see the apartments now. Could see the lights lifting above the darkness that was the parking lot. He wanted to tell her to keep driving. To extend this any way he could.

Instead he said, "I wrestle tomorrow. If you want to come."

Annie pulled into the parking lot, shooting him a sideways

glance. At first Luke was nervous he'd misread something—that she really didn't want to see him wrestle. Before she could say anything, Annie cussed loudly and slammed on the brakes. The entire car jumped.

"What the hell are you doing?" Annie yelled.

Toby was standing in front of the car with his hands on the hood, as if he'd stopped them himself. He looked from Luke to Annie and then back to Luke as they got out of the car. Without a word, Toby broke into a smile—big and forced.

"Well, this is . . . unexpected." He stepped away from Annie's car, still smiling. "Are you on the wrestling team?"

"Don't be a dick," Annie said. "I saw him running and asked him if he wanted a ride."

"And he . . . stopped? Damn, you must have superpowers. I've never seen anybody or anything get between Luke and a workout."

Luke tried to conjure an explanation. He should've been straight with Toby as soon as he'd seen Annie in the parking lot. As soon as he felt that twinge of expectation in his stomach. He knew Toby liked Annie. And even if that infatuation only lasted two or three weeks—because they rarely lasted any longer—Luke should've said something.

Basically, he was a coward and he knew it.

"She lives here," Luke said.

"What!" Toby shook his head in mock amazement.

Annie smiled at Luke. It was quicker and grimmer than any smile he'd seen before. But it still rolled through his body like a cannonball.

"Well, I'm here all the time," Toby said.

"Oh joy," Annie said.

They stood there in silence. Luke searched Toby's face for any sign of hurt. Some kind of clue to what he should say next. But when Toby turned to Luke, he was still guarding every emotion he had behind a big, fake smile.

"I told the boys I was taking us out to eat." He flashed the money again. "They picked Olive Garden."

Luke nodded. Of course they did. Doreen had taken them for their birthday last summer, and it had been a life-changing experience. The singing. The free dessert, complete with candle. They talked about it constantly, screaming every time Doreen drove by the restaurant.

Toby motioned to Annie. "You should come too. It's on me."

He shot Luke a look like, "Don't say a word," so Luke didn't. He let Toby have his moment.

"Uh, thanks. But no."

"What? You don't like Olive Garden?" Toby laughed, as if she didn't believe in gravity.

Annie gave Luke a quick look and then said, "I'm good."

"Are you kidding?" Toby was full-on once again. "Free breadsticks! *Salad*."

It struck Luke that he knew nothing about Annie. They lived in the same apartment building—but what did that mean? People moved in all the time, new to the state and not informed on where they should or shouldn't live. A month, maybe two, and the families with their out-of-state plates and minivans that were a tick too nice for the parking lot would disappear like a magic trick. To houses on the lake or one of the manicured subdivisions miles from here. Maybe she didn't understand what it meant to be hungry, not even to care when the server gave you a look as he brought the eighth, ninth basket of breadsticks to the table. Eating them, sure. But wrapping them up in the napkins you asked for earlier—extending this meal for days, if possible.

Not that Luke would be taking a bite of the breadstick. Still, he knew.

Annie kind of smiled again as she said, "I'm going to pass. But thank you."

She glanced back at Luke before hurrying through the door of her apartment. When she was gone, Toby stood next to Luke—both of them staring at the empty parking lot. Everything about Toby was now muted.

"I didn't know she was going to drive me home," Luke said.

Toby looked at Annie's apartment but didn't say anything at first. When he spoke, he sounded tired.

"But you knew she lived here."

Luke didn't say anything, because he knew he was wrong. Toby had every reason to be angry with him. So he dropped his head and stared at the asphalt. Toby sighed and started walking toward the apartment.

"I'm going to go get the boys."

8

THE Olive Garden was just off the interstate, a few blocks away from every other restaurant in town. When they walked in, loud and presumably Italian music pumped through the speakers. The hostess, a smaller blond woman, reached toward the stacks of menus next to her and asked if the boys wanted crayons. They grabbed the menus and crayons from her hand, their eyes wild. No part of this experience would be taken for granted.

Toby wasn't going to take it for granted, either. Even if he was mad at Luke, as soon as he stepped inside, he was swept away by the reminder that they didn't get to do things like this. And fine, he shouldn't have taken the money from Jimmy. But they would deal with that later, just like they always did. So if Luke wanted to sit there and silently object, Toby would let him. He would eat and have fun and use every smile as a thorn, reminding Luke that he wasn't the only one who was struggling to understand recent decisions.

As soon as they sat down at the table, Toby waved the server toward them.

"Salad and breadsticks," he said. When the man tried to ask another question, Toby shook his head and repeated himself. "And four waters."

The man walked away, grumbling. Toby snapped his menu closed and put it on the table.

"Tour of Italy. That's the business, right there. You can't go wrong with something called Tour of Italy."

Luke's menu was sitting in front of him on the table. "I'm going to gain weight just breathing the air in here."

"Maybe if Annie were here, she'd be able to get you to eat," Toby said.

"What's that supposed to mean?"

The waiter walked up and began arranging the salad bowl and breadsticks on the table, saving Toby from having to spell it out for Luke. He wasn't angry, not really. It was more shock, a weird surprise that Luke would be bold enough to go behind his back on anything—but especially with a girl. Toby grabbed a breadstick and took a bite, trying to lose himself in the garlic and butter.

The boys grabbed two breadsticks each, and the basket was empty. Luke gave the server a sympathetic look and said,

"We'll probably need lots of bread."

When he was gone, Toby said, "Why are you apologizing? That's his job."

"We're acting like a bunch of assholes."

"I'm being an asshole?" Toby laughed. The dart hit home, closing Luke's mouth. Toby wouldn't keep it up much longer; he just wanted Luke to acknowledge that he'd done something shitty. And so far, all he seemed concerned with was Jimmy's money and how the waiter would feel when they left.

He turned to the boys. "What if we could eat here every night?"

They cheered and asked Luke if people actually ate at the Olive Garden every day.

"No," Luke said, which deflated their excitement.

"But what if you *could*?" Toby said, not looking at Luke as he spoke. "What would you eat?"

The boys began listing off every item on the menu, including the calamari, until Toby told them it was squid. Luke and Toby spent more time talking to the boys—telling them to sit down or not to throw ice—than talking to each other. And when the food arrived, it was like a miracle. Appearing from the back, steaming. Chicken fingers for Jack-Jack. A cheese pizza for Petey. And Toby's Tour of Italy.

As they ate, Toby caught Luke looking around the

restaurant nervously. As if he was waiting for cops to come breaking through the windows. Every time Luke's head twisted because of a falling plate, a shrill voice from the kitchen, it grated on Toby. All he had to do was relax, for one night. Forget everything and, even for a moment or two, take normal breaths. Act like the sky wasn't crashing around them.

"I don't know why you're doing this to yourself," Toby said, holding up a steaming forkful of lasagna. "Because this? This is the best thing I've ever eaten. Like—"

"I'll take your word for it," Luke said, holding up his hand.

"Just take a bite. See what I'm saying." Toby held the lasagna toward him.

"Stop," Luke said. Forceful enough that the boys stopped chattering and looked at the two of them. Toby put the fork back down on the plate and asked the boys, "Who wants dessert?"

The twins were near catatonic when the server finally brought the check, pausing momentarily as if he had just realized they were a table full of kids. They couldn't possibly afford everything they'd ordered.

Toby took the check and looked at it, whistling long and slow.

"Tour of Italy comes at a price, I guess." He peeled off

a few twenties and stuffed them into the black puffy folder that held the check. Luke was staring at him, the money.

"Jesus, calm down," Toby finally said. "What do you think is going to happen?"

"Why did he give it to you, though? That's all I want to know."

"Because he was drunk? Because one of his loser friends finally paid him back? Hell, I don't know. And I don't care."

Luke told the boys to get their jackets on, standing up like the conversation was over. This was his regular move, a kind of holier-than-thou decision process that drove Toby nuts.

"I just think it's weird," Luke said. "That's all."

"Yeah? You want to know what I think is weird?" Toby was being loud now. The boys were watching, but he didn't care. He was already wound too tight. "That you would go out with Annie like that. All you had to do was say something. You know I wouldn't have said a damn thing. You know that. And yet?"

Luke's body slumped, and even though Toby knew he'd won, he still stormed out of the restaurant, already in the car with the engine running when Luke and the twins came outside.

The drive back to the apartment was quiet. By the time they pulled into the parking lot, the boys were asleep. Toby helped Luke carry them up the long stairs. Once they were on the mattress, Toby turned around and started for the front door. Luke stopped him.

"Hey, wait a second." Luke closed the bedroom door. "I wasn't trying to make you mad."

"I'm not mad," Toby said.

Luke rolled his eyes. "Okay."

"I'm not," Toby said.

And he wasn't, not really. Luke should've told him about Annie, but it wasn't like they were getting married. If anything, Toby was annoyed that Luke couldn't get past the money. He wanted Luke to trust that Toby would see the line way before it got crossed. But he couldn't, and that was the story of Luke's damn life. And it burned Toby up.

"Are you spending the night?" Luke asked.

Toby had never been stubborn, not when it came to things he really wanted. He could be tempted into second-guessing just about any decision he made. Of course Luke knew this. But maybe this was his way of apologizing. Sweeping it under the rug and pretending it had never happened. A convenient absolution.

Before he could say a word, Luke said, "And I know. You get the couch."

* * *

Toby was asleep when the knock came, two times like a shotgun. Luke was already up and looking through the blinds when Toby stood up. He didn't even need to ask who it was. Luke's hands were already fists. Toby touched him on the shoulder and shook his head, opening the door.

Jimmy stumbled into the living room, the boozy sweat filling the room like cheap cologne. He took a drink from his beer and tossed the can behind him, onto the landing. The tinny clatter made Jimmy laugh. He raised a finger to his lips and pretended to tiptoe the rest of the way into the apartment, dissolving into even louder laughter a few seconds later.

"Where you been, boy?" he said to Toby. It sounded almost jovial, as if they'd been playing hide and seek. But tone didn't mean a damn thing, and Toby knew it. "I need you to get me to the Deuce. Pronto."

"It's like four o'clock in the morning," Toby said. "The Deuce is closed."

"Well, if I come around," Jimmy said, "they open that door. So let's go!"

"How did you even get here?" Toby said, looking into the parking lot. "And where's the truck?"

"The truck is . . . indisposed," Jimmy said, chuckling to himself. "In. Disposed."

"What the hell does that even mean?" Toby didn't like that his voice broke with frustration, but he was tired and confused. And he wanted Jimmy to get the hell out of there.

Jimmy reached for Toby's arm.

"Let's go. Time to roll."

Toby stepped back, even though he knew it was a mistake. "I want to go back to sleep."

When Toby was a kid, he'd seen two cats get into a fight. They were a whirling mess of claws and spit and teeth. Jimmy took a broom handle and smacked one of the cats hard, skidding it halfway across the yard. The thing yowled as it ran under the car, a sound Toby couldn't get out of his head for weeks.

He waited for something just as fast and vicious. He'd take it without flinching if it meant Jimmy would leave. Instead, Jimmy grabbed his wrist and yanked him toward the door. Toby half expected Luke to jump toward them, but he stood there, a strange "I told you so" expression on his face.

Toby shook free of Jimmy's grip once they were outside. Jimmy lit another cigarette and began wobbling down the stairs. For a second, Toby reached out his hands. Pushed the air. He imagined his father's temple hitting the side of the concrete steps. The life going out of his eyes. Nobody would say a thing.

Toby wasn't sure if it was fear or the stupid baked-in love kids have for their parents that stopped him, but they both got to the bottom of the steps, and neither one of them spoke. His dad dropped some ash on his shirt and cussed.

"We don't have much time," he said.

Toby couldn't help himself. "The Deuce is closed."

Jimmy stopped and pulled the cigarette out of his mouth. He seemed completely sober as he stared at Toby. Jimmy's anger didn't go away, not like most people. He held on to it for weeks, months—longer. A beating could come for things Toby barely remembered doing.

"Sometimes you're too smart for your own damn good."

"It's just . . ." Jimmy cocked his head as Toby spoke. All Toby wanted to do was get him home, so he held up his hands like he was pacifying one of the twins. "Never mind. You're right."

They weren't a mile from Luke's apartment when Jimmy fell asleep. Toby drove slowly, like he was trying to keep a baby from waking up. When he came to the intersection that would take them to The Deuce, he sat there for a long time. There was no reason to go. The bar had been closed for hours and the only thing waiting for Jimmy would be trouble. What kind, Toby didn't know. And he didn't want to find out.

He turned toward their trailer. Toby could only hope that, when Jimmy woke up in the morning, the booze would cast a dark shadow over this part of the night. Still, he took the long way home. The moon lit the trees and the empty buildings as he drove through downtown. The entire time, Jimmy was slumped against the window—out. But as soon as the tires hit the gravel road, his dad jumped.

"What the—" He grabbed the seat belt. "How . . . why am I in this car?"

"You told me to take you home," Toby lied.

"What?" Jimmy shook his head, still trying to get his bearings. "No, I wanted to go to the Deuce, goddammit. What time is it?"

Toby looked at the clock. It was almost five.

"You told me to—"

Jimmy's punch only grazed Toby's cheek, the seat belt holding him back. He scrabbled to get it off as Toby threw himself out of the car. Toby ran for the front door, but Jimmy grabbed him just before he got to the cinder-block steps and tossed him to the ground. Toby instinctively shielded his face with his arms.

"All you do is talk. And now I fucking missed it," Jimmy said, standing over him. He was trying to take off his worn leather belt but fumbled with the buckle. Toby spun onto his stomach and tried to crawl away. He only got a few feet before Jimmy tackled him. Toby couldn't help himself, he started crying.

"Just take the car and go!"

But Jimmy was blinded. By whiskey or anger, Toby didn't know. The belt caught him on the back of the neck. Then his shoulders. Then his neck again. As Jimmy raised it once more, his weight shifted and Toby kicked his body up, sending Jimmy to the ground.

Toby didn't run immediately. Instead, he swung—as hard as he could. The first time he'd tried in years, and he knocked the shit out of his old man, right in the eye. It even shocked Toby, who froze long enough to let Jimmy get back to his feet. The belt swung almost playfully in his hand.

"It isn't fucking *open*," Toby hissed.

Jimmy cracked the belt, the buckle catching Toby right above the temple. Toby dropped, his vision doubling. The tickle of blood dripping down on his cheek. And then he wasn't sure whether he passed out or just forced himself to separate from his body until it was finally over.

They were flying.

It was him and Luke and the boys and it was glorious. They sped across the state of North Carolina, across the oceans. Below them, people laughed and waved—look! As the countries scrolled by, they crossed mountains, wonders of the world, going faster and faster until monsters appeared far below them. Creatures they'd never seen, snapping their teeth and running their claws against a stone floor.

Toby kept them in the air. Kept them moving at the speed of light, the speed of sound—faster than anybody had ever flown before. And soon the sun came up and there was nothing below them, above them, no ground or water, just a never-ending sky.

Toby woke up cold and in pain, the side of the plane bruising his ribs. He didn't remember walking to the plane or much else that had happened. His head throbbed and his entire body was raw. He was too cold. Too tired. But—reaching out to touch the rough metal of the plane—safe.

He slumped down, trying to use the crumpled leaves as a blanket. Curling his body until he was asleep again.

January 11

T—

I spent a lot of time thinking about what Eddie said about getting my head right. And man, I wish I could tell you that one of those little light bulbs popped above me, the way it happens in cartoons. How all of a sudden, I was happy and started feeling good.

But hell no. The more I sat there, the more I got angry. I tried writing you a letter about it, but I couldn't get more than one or two words down before I'd get pissed and crumple the paper up. By the time I finally blew out of my cell for lunch, looking for Eddie or Sister, I ran straight into this dude everybody calls Jokes. Here's the thing: Jokes is one of those ironic names. Because this dude will light you up, even if he only thinks you're talking sideways to him. He's been here a few years longer than me, but has probably twenty or thirty more infractions. Talking shit to guards. Having something that looked enough like a weapon got him to iso for a solid month. And of course, beating on dudes like it was his job. So when I ran into him, he puffed up.

It was like I had never left the mat, T. I had that dude sized up and was about to take him down when Eddie pulled me outside, stopping once he got to the basketball courts. He picked up his ball and tossed it to me. Eventually, I gave it a couple of dribbles. The last one hit my foot and went rolling into the grass.

Eddie shook his head and laughed. Told me I played ball like every other wrestler he'd ever known—poorly. Then he picked up the ball and tossed it lightly into the air, nothing but net.

What was I going to say to that? You and I both know I couldn't catch a ball or swing a bat. Wrestling is one of those sports designed for people who've lived tough lives. People who know how to endure.

He walked over, got the ball, and cool as could be, said, "We'll go to ten."

But I wasn't about to get embarrassed like that. Before I could walk away, he shot the ball toward me, a chest pass like a bullet. I barely got my hands up.

In here, anything can be a challenge—even the smallest thing. Which meant that anything could be seen as weakness. You didn't have to be a damn detective to know what he was doing. Everybody was watching us, so I fired that ball right back at him.

Hard as I could. Eddie caught it like it was a stuffed animal, barely a sound from the leather hitting his hands. He nodded, impressed.

But man, I wasn't falling for it. I didn't want to play basketball. All I wanted to do was wander around the yard until they blew the whistles. Eddie must've seen it too, because all of a sudden, he started talking trash. For everybody to hear.

Like, "I'm gonna take it easy on you, young buck." I might be shit at basketball, but I wasn't going to let him stand there and burn me. So I said, "You sure you aren't going to break a hip or something?"

That was a *mistake*, T.

I knew Eddie could ball, but I swear he had two baskets on me before I even got a chance to move. The next time he started toward the basket, I dropped back and jumped just as he let the shot go. Grabbed that thing out of the air like I owned it!

You should've seen Eddie. He had this look on his face like he'd never seen such a thing in his life. I dribbled to the top of the key and got to thinking I was going to hit a three-pointer. Before I even got the ball up in the air, Eddie was in my face talking about, "That's a man's shot." And "Ain't nobody to pass to up in here."

He kept dogging me, kept talking. And man, did I ever want to shut his mouth. So I threw the ball in the air, trying to make the shot with him in my face. All the dudes watching us let me hear it.

"Supposed to put the ball in the hoop!"

"Maybe he thinks he's playing volleyball!"

It was rough, T. But I wasn't even thinking about them. All I wanted to do was beat Eddie. Hell, even score on him. He got the ball back and asked if I was ready. I didn't answer him and he just smiled. When he went to shoot, I jumped. When I did, he dribbled underneath me and dunked.

Even the guards lost their minds at that.

I didn't see the ball again. Maybe when I was wrestling, I would've at least been able to keep up with him. But even then, I don't know. When Eddie had that ball in his hand, it was something else. It was like he was *somewhere* else. I never had that sort of effortlessness on the mat. Not the way Eddie played.

Afterward, we were sitting in the sun—it was warm for January—and I was still sucking air. He wiped sweat off his forehead and was like, "I hope you were a good wrestler, because you sure can't hoop."

Man, it reminded me of you.

After that, they blew the whistles and we had to line up. When I got back to my cell, I had all this energy and I wanted to write to you, but I couldn't sit still. It was like my heart had finally started beating again and now it didn't want to stop. So I knocked out ten push-ups, then ten more. I had it in my head I was going to do a hundred. I got thirty, maybe, before everything started feeling like Jell-O.

I was still shaking when I picked up the pen to write you.

Luke

9

LUKE was still awake when the sun finally started to peek above the clouds. He woke the boys up, got them dressed and on the bus. And then he sat in the parking lot, waiting for Toby to show. Every time a car came around the corner, he stood up. But it was always some busted-up truck, a half-restored Trans Am.

He tried to not think about last night, how he had let Jimmy pull Toby out of the apartment without so much as a word. That's what Toby wanted, right? And hadn't Toby said he could handle it? Luke believed that he could. Despite his size, he'd always been tough. Yet the real reason why he didn't step to Jimmy was gnawing at him.

He wanted to prove a point. He wanted Toby to come back this morning without the El Camino, telling Luke how his dad was a bastard. That same old story. But sitting here now, Luke could kick himself for being so damn stubborn.

He didn't know whether to run to the trailer, to sit here on the curb, or to go to school and find Toby first thing. So when he started jogging, it was simply out of habit. Something to focus on. He wasn't even out of the parking lot when he heard his name. Annie waved from her front door. Luke reluctantly jogged toward her.

"Trying to run off those breadsticks?"

Luke was confused at first. "Oh, the Olive Garden."

Annie looked to the side, like there was somebody else who could validate Luke's weirdness. He tried to rally.

"I always run the morning of a match," he said.

That was the truth, and it hit him like a revelation. Toby knew Luke was still over. He always ran to school on match mornings. Relief inched into his body.

"I'm not sure I believe that," Annie said with a smirk. "I think you went overboard at the O.G. and now it's pudgy city."

She reached out and poked his stomach, making him jump. Annie seemed equally surprised by her action, because she pulled her finger back so quickly, Luke swore he'd hurt her somehow. The awkwardness of the moment took over, and Annie started walking to her car as quickly as she could.

"Okay . . . well, I'll see you at school."

"Hey, hold on."

Luke ran to catch up with her, opening the passenger door. Annie stared at him like he'd just stripped and run across the parking lot naked. He was just as surprised, honestly. But he forced himself to believe Toby would be waiting at school. Ready to give him shit for taking another ride from Annie, who already had her sunglasses on. Who was smiling so big, she looked like one of the twins—goofy and excited. Without a word, they took off.

For a few moments, Luke was at ease.

But the farther they got from the apartment, the more he started watching the roads. Hoping he'd see the El Camino tearing toward his apartment. Toby, late as hell because he'd overslept. Anything to bring back the assurance he'd felt in the parking lot only a few minutes earlier.

Annie sighed and turned off the radio. "That's another thing I hate about North Carolina—terrible radio stations. How many times can I hear the same twenty-year-old grunge band?"

Luke didn't even realize she was talking to him until she said his name and snapped a few times in his face.

"Sorry, what?"

"I was *trying* to get your opinion on Nirvana, possibly the most overrated band of all time?"

Luke was clueless.

"Okay, well, just trust me on that one," she said. "Um, let's go with something different. Are you excited about your match tonight?"

"Excited? Not really."

He was blowing it, but he had no idea how to tell her about Toby or begin to explain the constant fear he carried with him at all times. Even the glimmer of hope he felt when they finally pulled into the parking lot required a history he didn't want to tell. So he said nothing as Annie parked in the farthest corner from the door, letting the car idle as they sat in silence.

Luke scanned the small parking lot for the El Camino. It wasn't here.

Annie followed his gaze. The parking lot was slowly filling with other students, cars spanning from brand-new SUVs to a Dodge pickup that could've been in this same parking lot twenty years ago and still been the oldest thing on four wheels. Dread hit him at a sprint, seizing his entire body.

"Is everything okay?" Annie asked.

Luke nodded, looking again for the El Camino. He unbuckled his seat belt, as if that would help. When it didn't, he fell back into the seat.

"Toby," Luke finally said.

"Ah," she said, biting her lip. "He looked kind of pissed at you last night. Did you guys have a fight?"

"No." Luke had to force himself to say the next part. "Well, kind of. It's complicated."

"And you thought he'd be here," she said.

Luke nodded, and Annie scanned the parking lot with him. He was trying to hide the growing panic. To forget all the times Toby had gone missing before, because this could be nothing. But the way Annie was staring at him, her face looking more and more worried, he knew he wasn't hiding anything.

"Do we need to go find him?" she asked.

"You'll be late."

Annie gave the school a side-eye. "You vastly overestimate my commitment to academics."

Luke nodded absently at the joke, refusing to stop his futile search of the parking lot. Annie reached over to touch Luke on the leg. He didn't feel a thing.

"Hey. We can go find him. Right now. Okay?"

They were moving before Luke even answered.

Luke had Annie stop fifty feet before the gravel driveway. It was about a quarter mile back to Toby's trailer, and it wouldn't take him two minutes on foot. But more importantly, leaving Annie at the mouth of the drive protected both her and Toby from whatever Luke would find.

"It's right down there," he said. "I'll be back in a minute."

Annie gave him a suspicious look, but she nodded. He jumped out of the car and started down the driveway, trying to jog away the same feeling of anxiety he'd felt every time he'd come down this road.

When they were twelve, maybe thirteen, Luke had made the same walk. He hadn't known then what he was walking into. Toby crying, huddled behind the cracked underpinning of the trailer. Luke heard the whimpering and thought it was a stray. It wasn't until Toby called out that he'd realized what had happened.

This time, there were no sounds except the birds, chirping happily and flying patterns around the trees. Luke knocked on the thin door of the trailer and waited. The El Camino was behind him, parked in no particular way. Normal, he told himself. He knocked again, louder and harder. Still nothing. Of course Toby could sleep through a damn tornado.

A shadow shifted toward the back of the single-wide. And for a second, he had hope. When Jimmy opened the door, though, the nasty black circle shadowing his right eye surprised him. Luke couldn't remember the last time somebody had gotten a punch in on Jimmy. Or more relevantly, the last time Toby had tried.

"Yeah?" Jimmy spit once and wiped his mouth. Luke's eyes watered from the smell of him.

"I'm looking for Toby."

Jimmy rubbed his good eye. "He's at school."

When Jimmy tried to close the door, Luke blocked it with his foot. A twitch of muscles tightened in Jimmy's face.

Jimmy pretended to be this happy-go-lucky guy, playing around with the bartenders and waitresses. But everybody knew he was an asshole. Hell, they were scared of him. He never let the other side of himself show until it was too late to do anything about it. So people played along, hoping they didn't stumble into Jimmy's bad graces. Luke was just as guilty as everybody else, never saying a word whenever Jimmy started talking about wrestling. But he wasn't playing the game now.

"He's not at school."

"Well, then maybe he's off chasing skirt. A dog will hunt."

"Yeah, I don't think so."

Luke shot another look at the trailer, trying to decide if he should push past Jimmy. He didn't hear anything, but the black eye worried him. Luke glanced at it, and Jimmy groaned.

"You got something to say, or can I go back to bed?"

Luke listened hard, just in case there was a sound or a

muffled cry. Any sort of message Toby might be sending. But there was nothing, so he stepped back off the cinder blocks.

"No. Just tell him I was looking for him," Luke said.

Jimmy turned around and slunk back into the trailer. "Will do, superstar."

Luke waited. But the only sound was Jimmy closing the bedroom door and falling on his old mattress. When it was just the birds singing once again, he walked back to the car, conflicted. Annie had let him walk down the driveway alone without a question. But would she be just as understanding when he asked her to pull off the side of the road? As he disappeared into the woods? Luke opened the door and sat down.

"He's not here," he said, erasing the panic from his voice.

Annie, to her credit, didn't ask for details.

"We can keep looking for him," she said. "All day, if we need to."

Of course, other people knew about the plane. Every few weeks—especially when they were younger—they'd come on a Sunday morning and find empty plastic bottles of vodka, crushed cigarette butts. A condom once. But they didn't bring friends, dates, or anyone in-between. It was an unspoken rule. And Luke had to break it.

"I know where he is."

"What?" Annie's face lit up with excitement. "Well, let's go get him!"

Luke hesitated, and then he told her how to get to the plane.

They parked on the side of the road, and Luke fought the urge to go tearing off into the woods. Annie looked up and down the empty road, to the patch of trees that had somehow survived the farms that bordered it on both sides. She thought it was a joke.

"So he's . . . here?"

"Yes," was all Luke said. Annie nodded, but Luke could tell she wanted him to say more. He took a deep breath, ready to see if he could trust Annie. "This is something I need to do alone. It's weird, I know."

"No, no. It's fine."

But he could see that she was confused and maybe a little bit angry. His and Toby's backstory was a web. He never had to explain the rules to anyone else.

"I just—"

"It's okay," she said, smiling. "Really. Go find him."

Luke intentionally went a hundred feet to the right, not taking a direct line to the plane. Maybe it was stupid to still keep it private, but he didn't care. When he finally broke into the stand of trees, he called out Toby's name. As kids, being covered by the branches and the leaves always made him feel invisible. Or maybe invincible. How many times had he come in here and completely lost himself?

The plane sat as it always did, cocked slightly to the left. Ready to fall apart. Through part of the rotting body he saw a shoe, a busted Nike Toby had been wearing for years. The sense of relief returned immediately.

"Hey, Toby."

Luke was still saying the words as he stepped around the plane, noticing how the leaves had blown around Toby's body like he'd been in that spot for weeks. And when he saw blood on the collar of his shirt, Luke panicked.

"Toby! Shit. *Toby.*"

Toby groaned and turned over, revealing a deep cut drawn above his right eye. The rest of his face was swollen, blue with the cold and bruises. When Toby finally opened his eyes, he saw Luke and tried to sit up.

"I'm fine," Toby said, pushing himself up to one elbow.

Luke wanted to go back to the trailer and match the damage on Toby's face, bruise by bruise—worse, more—until Jimmy couldn't stand. To let every second of pain and anger come out of him in one moment of glorious, almost beautiful, violence.

"Fuck him," Luke said. It was all he could get out.

"Fuck him?" Toby managed. ". . . barely know him."

Toby laughed once, then clutched his side in pain. Luke was about to help him up when his friend's eyes went wide. He spun around, trying to hide himself so fast Luke was sure it was Jimmy. But Annie stood there, face white. Her mouth opened, but none of them said anything until Luke stood up.

"We need to get him home."

They drove silently, the only sound coming when a sheriff's deputy pulled out of a gas station and Annie gasped, repeatedly checking the speedometer the entire mile he cruised behind them. Luke prayed those red and blue lights would start rolling. He wanted to explain why they weren't at school. Why his friend was broken in the back seat. But when they reached Propst Crossroads, the deputy peeled off onto Highway 10 and was gone seconds later.

At the apartment, Luke opened the car door before Annie even parked. Once his feet hit the asphalt, he stopped. Ricky and his mom were probably inside, doing god knows what. A new, deep panic swept over him. When they were kids, it was easy enough to hide Toby from any adult. Build a pillow fort or pretend they were camping in the closet—Doreen never complained they weren't around. But now he had no idea what he should do or where he could take Toby.

Annie came up behind him, her face mirroring everything Luke was feeling. "Let's take him to my place."

"I don't want to explain it to anybody."

Annie looked confused, but then waved the comment away. "My stepdad is a trucker. He won't be back until next week."

Luke tried to anticipate the consequences of each action. Of each decision he needed to make. He put his hands on the hood of Annie's car and dropped his head.

Annie touched the small of Luke's back.

"Help me get him inside."

Annie's apartment was bare. There wasn't even a couch, just a folding chair and an air mattress in the living room. A small television sat on a TV tray, a game show playing silently. If Annie was embarrassed by any of this, it didn't show. She disappeared and returned with a pillow and blanket. As soon as they lowered Toby down, he startled awake—nearly jumping off the mattress.

"Where am I?"

"You're okay," Luke said.

"Where am I?"

He was breathing hard, exhaling three times for every

breath he took. Luke held out his hand, the way he'd approach a wild animal.

"You're at Annie's apartment," he said. "I didn't know where else to take you."

"Annie?" Toby searched for Luke's, and then Annie's, face before swallowing. He licked his lips and then said, "I should go home."

"No way," Luke said.

"You can stay here as long as you need to," Annie said. "Whatever you need."

The shame was thick on Toby's face, and he barely looked at either of them. Annie cleared her throat before going to the kitchen. Luke heard her open a cabinet, followed by some running water.

"Can you take me home?" Toby said softly. *"Please."*

Whenever a beating happened, they rarely talked. Instead, they watched television and ate ramen or canned soup as the hours and days slipped away like water. Toby would sleep and Luke would stare out the window, primed and ready if Jimmy showed up. Simply put: they always hid.

Luke shook his head. Toby cussed.

"Then take me to school," Toby said.

"What?" Luke bent over, like he didn't hear him correctly. "Are you kidding me?"

125

"School. Please."

"I'm not taking you to school," Luke said. "But I'll be here with you. All day."

Luke went over to the ancient television and turned the knob, hoping it would endear Toby to the idea of staying put. Before he could find anything, Toby pulled himself up.

"You've got a match today."

"I'm skipping it," Luke said.

"Fuck that."

Luke pretended to not hear him as he fiddled with the knob, coming back to the same grainy game show. He couldn't give a damn about wrestling right now, and if Toby didn't realize that, he didn't know Luke at all.

"What about Herrera?" Toby said.

"What about him?"

"All I'm going to do is sleep. You know that."

"I could go get the VCR from the apartment," Luke said, continuing to ignore him. "There's nothing on."

Toby's voice spiked. "Why don't you ever fucking listen to me? I don't *need* you here. *Damn.*"

Luke stopped messing with the television. Leaving Toby right now meant going against every instinct he had. And this had never been a question before. Luke stood there, silent.

"Look at me," Toby said, his voice still tense. When Luke turned around, Toby sat up completely, flinching. He rubbed his ribs gingerly as he spoke.

"It's going to be fine. I'm just . . ." Toby took a breath and finally met Luke's eyes. "This shit can't change anything. You know?"

"I don't know what you want me to do," Luke said.

"Go to school. Go to the match."

Luke reluctantly nodded. "I'll come back right after it's over."

Toby, exhausted, nodded and then lowered himself back on the air mattress. They stared at the silent television for a few minutes before he was asleep again.

Luke was watching him when he noticed Annie standing in the doorway. She motioned to the front door and Luke followed her, looking one last time at Toby before he stepped outside.

"I'm sorry," she said, closing the door until it was just a crack.

As Luke was opening his mouth to downplay it, to tell her it wasn't a problem—that Toby was as tough as he was annoying—Annie leaned over and kissed him. It was awkward, mostly her lips on the side of his mouth. As if she had missed. His entire body froze, and then an explosion of energy shot from his toes to his ears to his stomach. He wasn't sure if he was going to throw up or kiss her back.

"I'll take care of him," she said. "I promise."

He nodded. And still feeling frozen inside—or was it fire?—he grabbed his bag and started sprinting toward the road.

It was the fastest he'd run in years.

10

TOBY woke up confused, calling into the alien apartment. It smelled like Italian food. Or maybe it was burgers. And in the vague darkness, a shape moved. Toby instinctively pushed himself against the wall until he heard a girl's voice.

"It's okay. It's Annie."

Toby was still up against the wall, fighting the impulse to jump off the mattress and sprint out the door. Even if he wanted to talk to Annie, a wave of shame swallowed him whole. And right below that, something new surfaced: a weird fury. Luke shouldn't have brought him here.

"I made you some food," she said.

Beside her was a paper plate covered in aluminum foil. Toby was still trying to calm down, but Annie stood up and brought him the plate anyway. She was inches from him, looking both embarrassed and unsure of what she should do.

"Luke went to school, for his match."

"I know."

Before he knew what he was doing, Toby stood up. Annie took him by the shoulders, gently trying to guide him back down to the bed. How many times had he wished for something like this to happen? But now he shrugged her off. All he wanted to do was get out of there. He was at the door when Annie said his name.

"Where are you going?"

"Outside," he said, hoping the cold air would shock his lungs.

He fumbled with the lock until she came behind him and let him out. Walking through the door felt like breaking through the water after a long dive to the bottom of a lake. He dropped to his knees and nearly choked on the gulps of air he took in.

"Are you okay?" Annie asked.

"I'm fine," Toby said, sounding so desperate and fragile he could barely stand to hear himself.

"Are you sure? I don't want you to get sick or—" Annie stopped herself. "I don't know. It's just really cold out here."

His mind raced—how long had he been out? What had Luke told her? Probably the highlights. And she'd never be able to erase it, making him forever something to pity. That, more than anything else, brought the sourness to his lips.

"Just leave me alone," he said.

"I'm trying to help you."

"No!"

It was all Toby could come up with. The pale yellow lights of the parking lot were too bright. The ground too hard. And Annie's voice was worst of all—dripping with a concern Toby had learned to live without. All he wanted to do was lie down and close his eyes until there was nothing left inside him. But he couldn't, not here. Not with Annie watching him like some kind of wounded puppy.

"I'm sorry," she said. "But you need to come inside, because sitting out here is stupid."

She smiled. It was almost enough that Toby wanted to accept the apology. Not to run off—the way he already knew he was going to—but instead to sit on the couch, watching the shitty television until Luke came back. Same as always.

But he couldn't.

It was cold and it didn't take long for Toby to start shivering. But he couldn't move fast, so he focused as far ahead on the road as he could see. Everything hurt. His head felt like it had a ditch running through it. He couldn't open one of his eyes completely. And the stiffness he had first attributed to sleeping on the cold ground now showed itself as pain.

Bruises he didn't remember receiving.

He walked the road, not even glancing to the trees when he passed the plane, until he came to the long gravel driveway that led back to his trailer. He stood there, staring at the blurry collection of lights. From this distance, the five or six trailers set back in the road looked almost inviting. Of course, the closer you got the more reality came into focus. Everything here was falling apart.

When he got to the trailer, his stomach jumped. It was anger, he told himself. He forced it to be. Whatever waited behind that door wouldn't bring another stitch of fear.

At first he didn't think anybody was home. The kitchenette's light was on, shining down on the hot plate that Toby didn't remember ever using. He relaxed—which he hated because he kept telling himself he wasn't tense. And then there was a cough from the bedroom.

"That you?" his dad asked.

If Toby came across a rabid dog, if it bit him, he wouldn't stand there and take it. He would run. Wouldn't ever walk that way again. But here he was, searching for something to do with his hands. Like every time before this.

"Yeah," he said.

His dad stumbled into the living room. Toby's stomach turned again when he saw the damage he'd done. Jimmy's eye was black and there was a long cut across his eyebrow. He wanted to feel proud, but he couldn't muster it. The strange concoction of fear and anxiety pushed into his bones, bled through his skin.

"You didn't go to school."

"What?"

They didn't have a phone and it wasn't like Jimmy worried about his attendance record. But then he remembered Luke. He would never forget seeing Annie appear on the tree line, the way Luke didn't even think about it.

"I don't need people bothering us," he said.

"Nobody's coming out here," Toby said.

"Well, Luke did." Jimmy paused a full five seconds after he said it. "All I'm saying is, I don't need anybody with a reason to start sniffing around right now."

"It won't happen again. Don't worry."

And then what? He had nothing left to say. Not: "Hey, Dad, why did you beat the shit out of me earlier?" Or even: "I spent the night in the woods." It was pointless. And Toby was tired. He sat on the couch and had started peeling off his shoes when Jimmy stopped him.

"What are you doing?" Jimmy asked. "You owe me a ride to the Deuce."

Toby dropped his head. He didn't know if he could take

another beating, physically or in any other way. He threw up his hands and waited as Jimmy retreated to the bedroom, returning with a duffel bag, stuffed full. Jimmy set the bag at the front door and went to pull on a shirt and jeans. When he came back, he smelled like cologne and cigarettes.

"Better late than never," he said.

The Deuce was just outside the city limits, not to mention the interest of the city cops, who were more than happy to let the sheriff's deputies handle the brawls and occasional knife fights that broke out in the parking lot. It was home to bikers and metal concerts and the type of person who couldn't give a shit about microbrews. Cheap beer ruled, the sort you could drink fast and, later, throw up without regret.

Toby had been to the Deuce a hundred times. When he was younger, he'd sit at the bar and eat tater tots or grilled cheese while his dad laughed and held court for hours at a time. Back then, he thought it was the greatest place on earth. A place where his dad smiled and laughed and never laid a hand on him. In truth, it wasn't much: a bar, a recently constructed stage in the corner, ten small tables, and five or six booths against the far walls.

You couldn't call it a biker bar anymore, even though that's how it had gotten its start and there was certainly that population in the room most nights. In recent years, the scene was a weird mix of drunks, derelicts, and the occasional college students who showed up because the risk of getting a knife pulled on you sounded fun. A story to tell friends.

Toby helped Jimmy carry the duffel bag into the bar, fully intending to turn around and leave, until a voice—female and familiar—rang across the busy room.

"Oh shit!" It sounded if she had a cigarette between her lips. "I remember when you were knee-high to a grasshopper. Get over here, boy!"

Val was probably the same age as his dad, but had the look of most of the people in the Deuce. She could be fifty as easily as she was thirty. Her bleached hair had grown out enough that it looked as if she'd dyed just the tips. Skinny, but not in an athletic way. She motioned to Jimmy.

"Put those in the back."

"Roger that, General."

Val turned to Toby. Nodded at his face. "What happened to you?"

"Nothing. I had an accident."

Val nodded. "Good boy."

It was a test, a kind of perverted brotherhood. The way soldiers and cops and firefighters seemed to have each other's backs, no matter what. Except this didn't have anything to do with honor or courage, just silence.

Val filled a glass with beer and put it in front of Toby. "Take the edge off that eye."

Toby stared at the beer. Once he had gotten old enough to see what the Deuce really was, he'd promised himself he would never end up here. Losing his nights to cheap beer and the nameless heavy metal band setting up in the corner. How many times had he and Luke had this exact same discussion?

He picked up the beer and downed it, fast. It nearly made him throw up, and Val laughed.

"Slow down there, champ." She took the glass and, with a wink, filled it back up. "Better nurse this one until your dad's done."

Toby did drink the second one slower. He told himself every sip was the last, that he'd stand up and leave. But when he finished the second glass, he didn't stop Val from filling it up again.

Across the bar, the bathroom door opened, and Toby looked. A woman—younger than Val and pretty in the neon bar light—barely noticed Toby as she came up to the bar and asked for a pitcher of beer. It might've been the weird lights, or the fact that Toby's heart was bouncing, but he couldn't stop staring at her. She was beautiful in a way that was incongruent with the dingy Deuce. As if she had wandered in accidentally.

She sighed and turned to Toby, smiling.

"What's your name?"

"Toby," he said. "But my friends call me *Toby*."

"Can I ask you a question, *Toby*?"

Val shook her head and started washing glasses behind the bar. Toby was all in. He smiled, nodded. Ready for anything.

"Of course you can."

"Why *the fuck* are you staring at me?"

Toby immediately shrank. Val was chuckling as she handed the woman her pitcher. "He's just a young buck, Lily. Don't kill him too quick."

"Young bucks don't live long when they stare like this guy," Lily said, not looking at Toby.

"I just—" Before Toby could say anything else, Lily walked away to a booth at the back.

Toby was afraid to turn and look at her, but she was gravitational. When he worked up the courage to glance in her direction, he figured the booth would be full of people—all of them laughing, with Lily at the center. But she was alone, staring at her phone. As if she could feel his eyes on her, her head popped up, and Toby nearly fell off the bar stool trying to turn around.

"Lily's a piece of work," a man said to him. "Don't worry about it."

He wore crisp new blue jeans and an equally new white T-shirt that still had the lines from being folded into its package. Standard prison issue. A present given upon release.

"I should go," Toby said, standing up. But the beer was already working against him. He stumbled a step backward, and the man smiled. A single gold tooth glinted briefly. It sent Toby back in time, when his mom was still around. It was her and his dad and another guy drinking beer and playing cards. Disappearing together, still laughing, into the back of their house—they had a house then—leaving Toby alone sometimes for hours.

"You ain't got no idea who I am, do you?" the man said.

Toby didn't say anything. He glanced over at Lily, still interested only in her phone.

"You're Jimmy's kid?" the man said. Toby didn't acknowledge the question, and the man laughed. "He do that to your face?"

"Did somebody do that to yours?" Toby fired back.

"Shit. You and your old man really are two knobs on the

same tree. Biggest smart-ass I know." The man held out his hand. "You know me. I'm Bo."

Toby had heard his father described in any number of ways, but smart-ass was never one of them. Still, Toby knew Bo from the sort of beer-riddled nostalgia that Jimmy sometimes used as a replacement for throwing his fists around. Stories about Jimmy and Bo in high school. Playing baseball together—his father had been one of the best pitchers in the state until he got a taste for raising hell. Bo had gone in on a burglary charge, five, maybe six years before.

Toby shrugged, ignoring Bo's hand. Tried to make it all as badass as possible.

Bo laughed and slapped Toby on the shoulder. "Listen, me, your old man, and Lily . . ." He paused, raised his eyebrows as Toby tensed. "We're going to drink some beer. Celebrate my release and *rehabilitation*."

Toby shook his head. "I . . ."

"Shit, when I was your age, I would've killed to get a beer any way I could." Bo called out to Val. "I need a couple more glasses. And besides, where else you going?"

The question rang in Toby's head. Not to Luke's match. This would be the first one he'd missed. He closed his eyes and imagined Luke's hand being raised in victory for the hundredth time in the last four years. Toby usually sat at the top of the bleachers, giving him the best view of every girl who walked into the gym. Throwing Luke a nod when he looked up to Toby after a win. What would Luke think when he looked up tonight?

Val handed Bo the glasses and he stood up, pausing and nodding toward Lily. "I promise the claws go away once she's got a few drinks in her."

The bar had been slowly filling with people and, as Bo and Toby walked back to the booth, a terrible Metallica cover band started playing "Ride the Lightning." They whipped their hair vigorously, hands flying up and down the necks of their guitars. Toby couldn't decide if playing with such passion for a bunch of drunks was inspiring or depressing.

When they got to the booth, Lily said, "Did you make sure these glasses were clean?"

She glanced up and, seeing Toby, leaned her head back.

"This is Jimmy's boy," Bo said, sliding next to Lily and dropping an arm across her shoulders. Toby's heart sank.

"Of course he is," Lily said, shrugging off Bo's arm. Without looking at Toby, she said, "Well, are you going to sit down or not?"

Toby sat on the very edge of the booth, afraid to risk even a look at Lily. Bo laughed as he poured everyone a beer.

"Shit, Lily. This boy is terrified of you."

But it wasn't terror. The public takedown she'd executed on him, if anything, would embolden Toby—make him like her more. This was an emotion of a different stripe. The kind that sent heat up his neck.

"Tell him about the time you Tasered that dude in the Carowinds parking lot." Bo turned to Toby, laughing. "I never saw anything like it. Shit, I don't even remember why she did it. Just that dude on the ground."

Bo pretended to get Tased, shaking the entire booth. Toby took a chance and looked at Lily, hoping she'd fill in the story. When she met his gaze, an invisible current nearly put him on the ground too.

"He tried some lame-ass pickup line on me," Lily said.

Toby smiled, which was admittedly a risk. Lily could be packing a stun gun right now and Toby had no doubt she'd use it. Instead, she reached for her beer and Toby caught the briefest smile cross her lips in return. He was about to say something—"You can knock me out anytime," perhaps—when Jimmy fell into the booth. Bo drummed the tabletop excitedly and poured a beer. But Lily froze. Nobody but Toby noticed.

"True friends, right here. Not even going to wait for a man to finish his business before they tie one on," Jimmy said, shaking his head. When he noticed the glass in front of

Toby, he laughed. "Oh shit, are you drunk too?"

"I wanted to get drunk with *you*, dickhead." Bo pulled Jimmy's neck close to his body in a half-hearted headlock. They wrestled briefly for a second. "But turns out your son's an apple off that same tree. So now we're all celebrating!"

Toby stole another look at Lily. The tension was gone, and she was hiding behind her phone again. He must've stared a few seconds too long, because she sighed and dropped the phone.

"What?"

Jimmy laughed and grabbed Toby by the shoulders. "Careful with this one, son. Won't think twice about using your pecker as target practice."

Lily rolled her eyes and emptied the pitcher into her glass. Bo was about to stand up when Jimmy stopped him.

"Hold up!" Jimmy yelled out Val's name and held the empty pitcher in the air. When he looked back, it was to Toby first. Grinning like he was in a parade. When Val brought the beers, Jimmy handed her a hundred-dollar bill and told her to keep them coming until it was gone or somebody hit the floor.

Then he lifted his beer in the air and said, "Drinks are on me tonight."

January 13

T—

I woke up yesterday feeling like somebody had taken a pipe to my entire body. My legs, my arms—hell, even my damn *elbows* hurt. I hadn't been that sore since those first couple of wrestling practices freshman year, when I'd come home and the boys would jump all over me. The whole time I was just dying. Forty pounds of little kid can mess you up, T.

Shit.

I wasn't even trying to talk about them. But that's how it happens. You think you're coasting, that somehow being in here has become normal. You start forgetting about time. There are dudes in here who look that comfortable too. Walking around like they're in a retirement home. Always doing the same thing, laughing at the same bullshit with their friends. I have to believe they have these moments too, when a picture of what life is supposed to be comes floating into their heads out of nowhere. All of a sudden you're thinking about your first-grade teacher. Hoping your face behaves, not letting it betray anything. Trying to stay hard.

But like I said, I'm not even trying to talk about the boys right now.

Anyway, I was supposed to meet with the lawyer again, so I was surprised when Sister showed up a few minutes before and asked if she could talk to me. Usually she carries on whether I like it or not. This time it was like she was choosing her words. The same way I'd get when I had to explain something the twins accidentally saw on TV. Or why Mom's "friends" sometimes spent the night.

So I was like, "Just say it, Sister."

That's all Sister needed, I guess. Because she started saying I needed to give Marilyn a chance. Getting worked up about how I need to give myself a chance.

I checked out, T. Stared at this crack on the wall in the visitation room until it started looking like a spider. Then a bridge. A few minutes later, I swear I could see a face with these big-ass eyeballs. But man, like I told Sister—Marilyn, everybody—if I don't care, why should anybody else?

I barely said two words to that first lawyer. When I confessed in the police station, he tried to get me to take it back. He asked for the recordings, anything he could get his hands on. But it didn't matter, because I didn't want to walk it back. I didn't want him to stand up there and tell people I was innocent.

Do you understand? If anybody could, it would be you, T.

Grand jury. Sentencing. All of it. I didn't say one word. I stood before all of them, blank. Nothing left inside me.

Here's a word that Marilyn likes to bring up: "mitigating." That lawyer tried to get me to give him a name, anybody who would come in and make an excuse for what happened. What I did. To soften the scary pictures everybody in our town now had of me.

I made that lawyer's life hell. And he was doing it for free. So by the time they got around to sentencing me, I don't think anybody was surprised when the judge put me here. A few people even cheered.

Marilyn wants to bring it all back up. She wants me to have another chance to stand up in front of everybody and talk about how we grew up so shitty. How nobody took care of me or you. How we were basically alone since we were kids.

But goddamn, that just isn't true, is it?

You and me were never alone, T. Not when we had each other.

Nobody understands it, not even Sister. But I still nod. Tell her I'll give it a shot. I already know that nobody—not her or Marilyn or anybody—will ever understand, but I'm hoping you do. You know?

Luke

11

THE referee watched the scale's weigh beam teeter up, then down, before stopping perfectly balanced.

"One seventy, exactly."

A collective sigh went across the locker room. Coach slapped Luke on the shoulder, followed by a few teammates. Luke stepped off the scale and disappeared back to his locker. It probably looked cavalier, almost cocky. Or maybe it would come across as confidence, portraying a mystical belief that the scale wouldn't betray him. In truth, he couldn't shake visions of Toby sitting in Annie's apartment. Beaten and broken and more angry than he'd ever let Annie know.

Usually Toby showed up at his apartment, rubbing at his stomach or arm like he'd run through a patch of poison ivy. Trying to hide the damage. Doing anything he could to keep himself from crying, screaming—grabbing a baseball bat and going back to the trailer to finally let that bastard know exactly what it felt like to run. To fear. To hurt.

Instead, they watched television. Went down to the Wilco to steal some candy bars, doughnuts, whatever they could get their hands on, to eat on the curb outside of Luke's apartment. That's how the healing started, wordlessly. They didn't need to talk about it because it was just another part of life, like school or trying to pick up girls at the mall.

Finding him curled up in the belly of that rotted-out plane shook Luke, more than he wanted to admit. Luke had lifted him up so easily, as if Toby had already lost something permanent. He knew he'd made a mistake bringing Annie. And an even bigger one taking Toby back to her apartment. But what else was he supposed to do?

The kiss zipped through his brain too, darting between the legs of every other emotion. He could still feel her lips on his own. He should have kissed her back.

Coach O came walking toward him, a huge smile on his face.

"Lucky bastard," he whispered, snapping him with the small towel he always carried. "Get this one out of the way and then next week you get to put Herrera straight on his ass, okay?"

Luke nodded.

Once Coach was gone, he shook his arms, his legs, and

put on his singlet. When he jogged into the gymnasium, a few people clapped. Even with Luke, wrestling didn't exactly draw a crowd. Every so often you'd see a coach from another school and, before he signed with Iowa, there would be small pockets of older men with notebooks, writing down every single thing Luke did. Tonight, though, he didn't notice the crowd. He jogged around the gym, trying to empty himself of everything but the mat. His opponent, a kid named Davis Lowry, watched his every step.

When they called his name, he stripped his warm-ups and jogged straight onto the mat. Lowry looked too small to be a 170. And maybe he was. It wasn't uncommon for teams to move a warm body—a JV sophomore—up for the match. They were already going to lose the points—why risk losing a wrestler too? Luke never hurt them too bad physically. He was rarely even on the mat more than a few minutes. But sometimes it only took seconds to break an opponent mentally. Something that kid would remember every single time he saw Luke.

Davis Lowry was looking to his coach like he'd been lied to. Luke already had him, and everybody in that gym knew it.

The referee blew the whistle, and all the sound sucked out of the room until it was just Luke and Lowry circling like a couple of dogs itching for a throat.

Luke shot, took the legs, and slammed the kid to the mat. Two points, raised in the air.

Beneath him, Lowry's breathing changed into panicked, shotgun spurts. But he wasn't giving up. He was trying to create a base, pushing back against Luke with an unexpected determination. Then he reached back, presumably trying for some kind of reverse, and Luke hammered the kid.

Lowry whined like a kicked dog as Luke drove his shoulder to the mat. From here, it was an easy headlock into an even easier pin. Coach O was already clapping. Instead, Luke let him up.

The referee held a single finger in the air, one point for Lowry.

A few people cheered, assuming Davis had escaped his fate momentarily. Just getting a point on Luke was an accomplishment, something to be proud of. The kid was rubbing his arm and looking over at his coach. As soon as he dropped his hands and got into his stance, Luke attacked and drove him down hard.

Luke let Lowry up again, giving up another point before throwing him back to the mat almost immediately. Lowry mouthed breathless cuss words that sounded more like prayers. But there was a wall around Luke, shielding him from the glares of Coach O. The other coach, yelling. Luke let Lowry up one final time. By then everybody in the gym knew he was playing with the kid. And for the first time in many years, Luke didn't give a damn.

When he finally pinned Lowry, nobody clapped. Coach O's eyes followed him all the way into the locker room. Once he was alone, all of the feeling came back to Luke in one sudden rush. He couldn't sit down, but he couldn't stand either. Every fiber of his body was alive. Luke was so angry he could barely see straight. All he wanted to do was go back on the mat and keep on hurting that kid.

Because that's what he'd been doing. Humiliating him, yes. But hurting him too.

Luke punched the locker in front of him, the pain jolting up his arm. He paused for a second, looking at it. And then he hit it again. A third time. Four, five, six—until his hand was bleeding and the red metal locker was bent nearly in half.

Nobody came over to talk to Luke when the meet ended. He didn't even look up until his coach came and sat across from him. Only then did he notice that the locker room was empty. Coach sat in front of him, working his gum and sighing heavily every few seconds. He pointed at the locker behind Luke.

"That doesn't look very good."

Luke didn't turn around, just stared at his hands. "And your hand?"

"It'll be fine."

Coach nodded. "You want to tell me what that was about?"

Luke shook his head, which he knew Coach would respect. And he didn't ask again, just sat in front of him working that gum. Even if Luke wanted to tell him more, what would he say? In movies and in news stories, people said, "Something snapped." But that's not what had happened. Instead, it had been a slow burn. So slow that he didn't even see it creeping toward him. All of a sudden—like a quick-moving tide—he was knee-deep. Then up to his neck. The anger drowned out everything else.

And even sitting here now, he couldn't calm down. He couldn't get it to recede.

"Do you want a ride home?" Coach asked. "We can talk about it in the car."

"I'm okay."

"You don't look okay, son." He bent over and forced eye contact with Luke. "You look like somebody fighting his way out of a corner."

Luke barely moved. They sat that way until it became evident Luke wasn't going to accept any help. Coach stood up and put his hand on Luke's shoulder before walking back to his office and, eventually, out the door. Once he was alone, Luke expected all the nervous energy—the anger—to drain out of his body the way it always did. But the longer he sat there, the more tense he grew.

Toby could move in with them, he told himself.

Or he could move in with Toby. Pull him away as soon as he smelled trouble.

Hell, they could grab tents and camp, finding showers and food when and where they could. Living transient but free. Every single solution rose up quickly, its hand in the air—promising to be the answer. But none pulled their weight. They never did. More troubling was what popped into Luke's head next.

He still wanted to beat on something.

Luke stood up and ran out of the locker room like something was chasing him. When he was a kid, before the twins were born, he would have moments of complete terror that overtook him. He could be sitting alone, watching television, and a shadow would settle on him without provocation. And that's how he felt now, as if he was only steps ahead of something monstrous reaching, grabbing for his shoulders.

He pushed through the doors and sprinted across the empty parking lot and didn't stop until he saw the lights from his apartment building. He ran all the way to Annie's door, pausing only right before his hand raised to knock—suddenly optimistic that they could figure it out. Bashful for the kiss. Hoping Toby was okay, calm and sleeping so it could all happen again.

He stood there for another second, the cold catching up to his warm body, before he rapped on the door. It was silent. So when the door flew open, he jumped. Annie was wearing pajamas and a T-shirt.

"Is he with you?" Annie said, looking past Luke.

"What?"

"Toby. He ran off. I tried to stop him, but . . ." She looked down at the pavement. "I'm sorry."

Luke turned to the parking lot. As if Toby would be sitting on the steps. As if Luke had somehow missed him when he had barreled through moments ago. Maybe Toby'd gone up to his apartment, knocked on the door until Doreen answered. Maybe he was asleep on the couch right now.

"Did his dad do that to him?" Annie asked.

Luke should deflect, because Toby was already mad. But he was tired of pretending. Tired of telling people that it wasn't a big deal. All he wanted was somebody who would listen and, maybe, understand.

"Yes. But it's not like this is a surprise. If you know what I mean."

"I think I do."

Annie reached for his hand, and he flinched. When she saw it, bulbous and bloody, she bent down. "Jesus, Luke. What happened to your hand?"

"Wrestling."

Annie looked at his hand again, suspicious. "We can go find him. It's not a big deal."

Luke didn't think Toby would go back to the trailer, but he didn't know for sure. They'd made plenty of revenge plans on nights like this. Finding the revolver Jimmy kept wrapped in a T-shirt in the back of his closet. But the plans never had real teeth. The next morning, the bruises didn't seem so bad. Now Luke wondered if that was ever really the case.

"Maybe he went upstairs," Luke said. "I should probably go check."

"When he left, he was . . ." Annie stopped herself, but Luke already knew.

Betrayed. Angry. Panicked.

"Hey," Annie reached out and grabbed his good hand. "It's going to be okay. Whatever you need, I'll do it."

She moved to come even closer, and Luke's stomach flipped.

"He just needs to cool off," Luke said. "But could you stay here, in case he comes back?"

Luke didn't want to leave Annie, but he was relieved when she nodded. Part of it was knowing, if he found Toby, he'd need to smooth things over. Having Annie standing next to him wouldn't help. And maybe he wanted to give Annie a reason to find him later, once Toby was safe. He allowed himself one second to think about her and him sitting close to each other, whispering as Toby slept.

She smiled and squeezed his hand once before letting him go.

When Luke opened his apartment door, the lights were on, and at first he thought that had to be a good sign. Toby wouldn't be asleep yet, but it was way past bedtime for the boys. And when his mom was home, she put them to bed even earlier. He heard a glass clink against the kitchen sink.

"Is that you, baby?" his mom called out. Luke walked into the kitchen, and his mom's face fell. "Oh, Luke."

"Have you seen Toby?"

His mom looked confused. "No . . . I'm waiting for Ricky. He's planned a surprise for me tonight."

Years before, Doreen had started calling Luke her "partner." They had an equal responsibility for keeping the apartment clean, for cooking, and for taking care of the boys. By Luke's math, this partnership wasn't close to equal. He didn't mind watching the twins. He didn't mind being the one who showed them how to grow up. But he always expected that she'd reciprocate when he needed it.

"Something happened to Toby," Luke said.

"Something's always happening to that boy." His mom laughed.

"No. Mom. Something, like, *happened* to him." When Luke said it, his mom reached for a cigarette and lit it without looking at Luke.

"Well, that has nothing to do with us. I don't need to know about other people's laundry."

Luke couldn't believe it.

"Jimmy beat the shit out of him," Luke said.

These were words he never said. Words Doreen didn't want to hear. Luke let them push down on her until the front door opened and Ricky's voice rang across the apartment.

"Doreen! Bring that fine ass this way!"

"That's enough of that," Doreen said, smoothing her shirt as she walked into the living room. When she saw Ricky, her face lit up with a smile so big, Luke couldn't tell if it was real or not.

"Look at you," Ricky said. "Fine as *hell*. You ready?"

"You know it, baby," Doreen purred.

Luke grabbed his mom's arm and she laughed nervously,

tapping him on the hand like he was one of the boys, not wanting her to leave for work. But he wouldn't let go. How many times had Toby spent the night on their couch? How many times had he made them laugh over dinner, stopping only when Doreen couldn't breathe? And now none of that mattered.

"Didn't you hear me?" Luke said, his voice rising.

Luke could see the embarrassment on Doreen's face slowly becoming annoyance. It was in her voice when she said, "Luke, calm down. I'm sure he's fine."

"Calm down? *Calm down?*"

Ricky stepped up and put his hand on the small of Doreen's back, directing her away from Luke. They only got a few steps before Luke jumped forward and blocked the door. Ricky shook his head.

"I'm sure you think this is worth it," he said. "But son . . ."

"Just help me," Luke said, ignoring Ricky. "Please."

Help could be anything. Driving him around to find Toby. Saying they would postpone their plans. Or even something as simple as telling him it would be okay. That Toby would be okay.

Doreen seemed to be weighing the request when Ricky said, "Okay, enough of this shit."

He marched toward Luke and tried to bully him out of the

doorway. At first Luke didn't even acknowledge the attempt. He rooted himself into the carpet and stared at his mother, hoping she'd make the right decision. But when Ricky grabbed Luke's bad hand, trying to force his arm behind his back, instinct kicked in. Luke drove the man hard away from the door.

Whether it was Luke's unchecked momentum, or Ricky's diminutive stature, Luke lost leverage almost immediately. Before he knew what was happening, Ricky improvised a hip throw and Luke landed on top of the flimsy coffee table, splintering the wood and glass. The sudden shock took his breath, and he lay there for a half a second, envisioning what he was going to do to Ricky.

Every movement. Every punch.

As Luke got to his feet, somebody knocked on the door. Doreen's face tightened immediately. Maybe she thought it was Ms. Hildebran, or one of the other nosy neighbors, because she stomped to the door and threw it open, her mouth ready to cuss out whoever was standing there.

Annie's eyes darted around the room, as if she'd heard the entire fight from downstairs. And maybe she had. She looked at the broken table and then to Luke, still standing in the pile of wood and glass.

"Hey, I was just . . ."

Annie's voice trailed off as Luke started walking.

Doreen's voice jumped as she spoke. "Luke . . ."

He didn't look at his mom or Ricky. He didn't ask for their permission. No more talking. When he got to Annie, her eyes were wide.

He gently took her hand and led her to the door like this was homecoming, prom, and the only problem was his mom bothering them for one more picture. And when they stepped outside, the cool night on him like a moment of grace, Annie's hand firmly in his, he wanted to keep walking with her forever.

12

TOBY couldn't feel his face, not after the second or third pitcher. By the time they'd dropped the fourth on the table, he was just as loud—just as ecstatic—as any regular. Jimmy was loving it too. Slapping him on the shoulder and yelling out, "That's my boy!" and "Like his old man!" As if they'd crossed an invisible line. Into a new place where they could respect each other.

Toby lifted his glass high, burped loudly, and downed the beer like he had the last two. The more he drank, the easier it went down. All he wanted to do was laugh and dance and spend the rest of his life feeling exactly this way.

Until his stomach reached up and grabbed his throat.

"That ain't good," Bo said, laughing.

"Don't you let him puke out here," Val yelled. "Get him to a bathroom."

"You heard the lady," Jimmy said, pushing him in the direction of the bathrooms.

As he walked, Toby was either floating or sinking. He couldn't tell. Couldn't give a damn, honestly. The entire bar was a beautiful blur of lights and music and laughter. He almost fell, and a faceless person caught him by the arm. Toby thanked him sloppily and pushed the rest of the way through the crowd.

The first thing he thought when he found the bathroom: this is surprisingly clean.

Two steps later, his stomach pushed everything up.

He threw up in the toilet, on the floor—painted the entire stall. In a brief moment of calm, he slipped and fell to the floor, the smell making him retch again. This time he didn't even try for the bowl.

He either passed out or fell asleep, because he woke to a shrieking "What the hell!" Followed by the thud of a body hitting the floor. The next thing Toby noticed were shoes squared up and pointed at him.

He wanted to stand, to open the door, but it was like four different people were trying to operate his body at the same time. The stall door opened and Toby saw her—Lily. He laughed. Hard enough that he threw up again. When he looked back up at Lily, he couldn't keep his face from going goofy.

"God, you're drunk off your ass."

"I'm fine. Great, even. *Great!*"

"Yeah," Lily said, reaching down to pull him up. "That's why you're passed out in the women's bathroom, covered in your own puke."

He reached for her hand and nearly slipped back down to the floor before getting upright. He wavered for a second, holding himself against the stall. She let him stand like that for a few seconds before she said, "How old are you?"

"A dick hair away from eighteen," Toby said, laughing.

Lily blinked. "Charming. How about we get your dad to take you home?"

She started pulling Toby toward the door, the entire world still spinning. Once they were back in the belly of the bar, it wasn't much better. The band was rolling. Toby did a little dance as they walked, cracking himself up again. Lily jerked him toward the booth. Toby was still laughing when Lily deposited him in front of Jimmy and Bo.

"Damn," Bo said, shielding his nose with an arm. "I was thinking he could rally, but I don't know."

"He was passed out in the women's bathroom," Lily said to Jimmy, who took another drink of his beer and shrugged.

"Classic," Bo said. Lily turned on Bo, cocking her head to the side. She didn't say anything, but Bo's stupid smile faded. She turned back to Jimmy.

"Well?"

Jimmy barely looked at Lily. "Well, what? I didn't pour the beer down his throat."

"He's your kid, isn't he? *Underage* kid, I might add."

"Why don't you give it a rest, Lily?" Val had been standing nearby, but now she was right in front of them. "As I remember it, you spent a lot of time in this bar when you were his age, and nobody said a word."

"Yeah, that totally makes it better."

Val looked as if she could take Lily's head off, but Jimmy pushed a twenty-dollar bill across the table and asked for some shots of tequila. When Val disappeared to pour them, he turned back to Lily.

"Like she said, I remember a time when you spent a lot of time in this bar."

"Time I'd like to forget," Lily said.

"Maybe," Jimmy said, smiling. "And shit, he's basically an adult."

"*A dick hair away!*" Toby yelled, getting a laugh from the people in the immediate area.

"So you're not going to do anything?"

Jimmy slammed his hand on the table and stood up.

"Let him do what every other fucker in this place does when they have too much. Sleep it off in the car. Jesus, Lily.

I never took you for a goddamn mother hen."

Val put two shots down in front of him, and Jimmy slammed both. Toby had a vague notion he should respond. But then something deep inside him—something unaffected by the alcohol—told him to shut up. Lily grabbed him by the arm and pulled him toward the door. People hooted and hollered as they walked away, but Lily didn't let go until they were in the parking lot.

Outside, two guys were arguing loudly, seconds away from punches being thrown. A couple was making out in the shadows of the building. Everything made Toby giggle. "Those guys are going to fight—get it! Get it!"

Lily blew air between her lips. "Please shut up," she said, scanning the parking lot. "Which one is your car?"

Toby burped sourly. "That fine-ass El Camino over there. Did you know El Camino means 'the road'? I like that. The *road*."

"Fascinating. Give me your keys."

She unlocked the driver's-side door and helped Toby in. She pocketed the keys but didn't close the door. She stood there looking at the parking lot and then down at Toby, who was still giggling. She cussed under her breath.

"Fuck you, Jimmy. *Fuck. You.*" She nudged Toby. "Get in the passenger seat. I can't leave you here."

Toby scrambled between the two seats and spent a solid two minutes trying to find and buckle the seat belt before Lily reached across him to help. For a second, Toby was stone-cold sober. It was the brush of her hair against his chin. Her smell . . . a sweeter version of the bar they'd just left. But she didn't pay him a single bit of attention. She fired up the El Camino's engine and let it idle in the cold for a few seconds.

"Where are we going?" Toby asked.

Lily stared at the bar for a long second before pulling out of the parking lot. "My house."

Toby wasn't sure how long they'd been sitting in front of the small white house when he woke up and scrambled out of the car to throw up. When he got back in, Lily was crushing a cigarette into the ashtray—the fourth.

"Feeling better?" she asked.

Toby's head was throbbing, and his entire body might have been run over by a dump truck. "Jesus," was all he could manage.

"In my experience, he can't help you with this."

"Seems limiting," Toby said, cradling his head. "You know, for the Lord."

Lily laughed and reached for her pack of cigarettes, which was empty. She tossed it back into her purse and stared into the night. Whatever humor Toby had pulled out of her disappeared. Outside, the darkness hummed around them.

Toby was sobering up quicker than he thought could happen. Or maybe he'd been asleep longer than he assumed. He'd never been drunk before. Barely had anything more than a Mountain Dew because—as Luke put it—he was stupid enough sober. No need to mix alcohol into the equation. And as sobriety creeped up on him, the sickening feeling of betrayal returned. His stomach grumbled again.

He stole looks at Lily. She was beyond him in all ways—age, looks, no matter what metric you used. She was early twenties and what he'd call North Carolina perfect. Nobody would confuse her for a model, but what did that matter? Toby liked the imperfections. He liked the way her eyes already crinkled in the corners. Her hair, growing out of a bad dye job. The way she smoked, even. As if she dared people to tell her it was unhealthy.

"Why were you even in there?" Lily asked. "The world has plenty of assholes. Like your dad. So maybe stay away from the Deuce?"

"You think I'm an asshole?"

"You puked all over the women's restroom," Lily said, giving him a look. "I don't think that qualifies you as a saint."

He didn't want to be an asshole. He didn't want to be like his dad.

"I guess you're right."

"Don't worry—I have a *lot* of experience with assholes," Lily said. "You were only at about a four tonight. I don't tend to find assholes attractive until they reach a seven or eight, easy."

Toby shrank a bit. Lily closed her eyes and leaned back, absently fishing for a cigarette again until she remembered the pack was empty. Toby watched her, hoping she wouldn't suddenly open her eyes and catch him leering. But he couldn't turn away.

"What."

"Nothing."

"I can feel you staring at me."

"How is that even possible?"

Lily opened her eyes and sighed.

"If you take your clothes off, you can come inside."

Toby stiffened.

"Calm down, cowboy. You're covered in puke. There're some clothes in the spare bedroom, left over from a missionary family my dad hosted. I'll leave them by the front door. When you get dressed, come inside and I'll make us something to eat."

* * *

Toby waited an extra five minutes before he got out of the car and stripped off his clothes. Even his underwear smelled like puke, and once everything was off, he was embarrassed to have been in the car with Lily in that state. He grabbed the hose and gave himself an impromptu wash. When he went to the porch, covering himself the entire time, he found the clothes Lily had left for him.

"Oh hell no," Toby said.

The shirt was ten, twenty years old, and covered in Pokémon characters. The pants weren't much better: corduroys, worn at the knees with a patch on the ass. But he was naked and—dammit—the clothes pretty much fit him. The shirt was a little tight, the pants showed his ankles. He looked like a fifth grader on his way to a sleepover.

The house smelled like cigarettes and scented candles, a mixture that almost immediately made Toby want to puke again. He called out for Lily, who didn't answer. Everything inside was meticulously arranged. There were angel statues delicate enough that Toby didn't want to go too near. On the corner table was a candy dish filled with butterscotch hard candies. An afghan was folded across the headrest of a plastic-clad recliner. But most fascinating were the Jesus pictures. The Jesus books. The Jesus *everything*.

"Be careful or you're liable to get saved," Lily said, making Toby jump.

"It's an impressive collection," Toby said.

"My dad's. This was his house."

Lily had on new clothes and her hair was wet. It struck Toby that she probably had smelled as badly as he did. He was going to apologize when she said, "Are you hungry?"

Toby followed her into the small kitchen. It wasn't much bigger than the one they had in the trailer, but once again it was very neat and very nice.

"More Jesus," Toby noticed, pointing to a particularly somber picture of the Lord right above the sink.

"There's a whole lot of Jesus here," Lily said, pulling a carton of eggs from the refrigerator.

"So your dad is religious."

"A pastor, actually. And he *was* religious. He died a few months ago. Hence . . ." She waved her hands in the air. "My reappearing act."

"I'm sorry."

"Don't be."

She said it with a casual disregard most people didn't have when it came to parents. Particularly dead parents. Toby caught it immediately.

"So where were you?"

"Seattle." Lily looked over her shoulder as she talked. "You been?"

Toby laughed. "Is that near Charlotte?"

Lily smiled and turned back around. "Something like that."

She didn't say anything else. The only sound was the eggs being cracked and then, slowly, the hiss of the pan. She kept her back to Toby the entire time she cooked. Once the eggs were finished, she put a plate and a large glass of ice water in front of him. Toby eyed the eggs. The smell already had his stomach churning. When he brought the fork to his lips, he gagged and pushed the plate away.

"Not the reaction I was expecting," Lily said.

Toby clamped his mouth shut. If he opened it, he would throw up again. But the walls had been breached. The smell of the eggs, the milk. The butter in the pan. This wasn't going to be pretty. He stood up and ran back to the front door, getting outside just before he puked.

Lily brought the glass of water to him. "I'm sorry, I wasn't thinking. Eggs were probably a bad idea."

Toby sipped the water and leaned his head against the wooden railing of the porch. Lily sat next to him.

"So I'm assuming you didn't do that to your face in the bathroom?"

Toby took a long drink. Lily stared into the dark yard as she spoke.

"I'm sorry. About that."

Toby finished the water without a word. Then he sat there silently holding the empty glass. When he finally opened his mouth, the truth spilled out.

"You said it best," he said. "Jimmy is a huge asshole."

"I know you're joking, but . . ." Lily bit her lip. "You know this is fucked up, right? Like, he shouldn't do that."

Toby looked at her, trying to figure out if she was joking. "Of course I know that. Who wouldn't know that?"

"I wasn't trying to—shit, I don't know. I'm sorry."

"The problem is, it *is* normal. At least for a little longer. And then . . ." Toby shot his hand to the sky like a plane taking off, framing it against the moon. "I'm gone."

There was a time when this conversation would've excited him. To tell somebody besides Luke the truth about Jimmy. About leaving this town behind until the memory was as disposable as a piece of gum. Something you spit out the window.

Of course leaving meant making up with Luke. Forgiving him or forcing him to apologize. Either way, he'd have to swallow down everything—no matter how bitter it tasted—so they could get back to the dream that had sustained them for years. Him and Luke in the back of a Greyhound bus—hell, in the El Camino now—following whatever highway would take them out of Hickory, North Carolina, fastest.

He wasn't ready to do it yet, though.

"Listen, you can sleep on the couch. It's comfortable and much better than sleeping in your car. Okay?"

Toby shot up too quickly. He probably would've fallen over into the grass if Lily hadn't caught him.

"Whoa there," she said, close to his ear. When he was steady, she chuckled and said, "You going to make it, or am I going to have to make your bed up out here on the porch?"

Toby nodded and Lily led him inside. She pulled a pillow and blanket out of a corner bench and handed them both to Toby. The couch was softer than the one he slept on in the trailer, which was more springs than cushion at this point. Toby woke up most mornings feeling like a stuck pig. And on the rare nights when he could arrange his body around the springs, he still woke up sore and twisted. When he laid down, something occurred to him.

"Why not just take all the Jesus stuff down?"

Lily sat next to him on the couch and stared at the wall.

"Let's just say I never planned on staying long enough for it to matter. And besides . . . me and Jesus have been ignoring each other in peace for a long time now."

"How did your dad feel about that?" Toby asked, his eyes already feeling heavy.

She patted his leg gently and said, "I don't want to talk about it, okay?"

That was the last thing he remembered before he fell asleep.

January 17

T—

I went outside today, ready to bring it to Eddie. You should have seen me. As soon as I got on the court, I had the ball in my hand and started working. The whole time thinking, Eddie doesn't even know about *this*. I was throwing up shots—hitting a few too—and running around like I was on scholarship.

Here's the thing about being inside: you're not supposed to let anything affect you, T.

So when Eddie didn't show up after five minutes, ten . . . fifteen . . . I just kept playing. Working my ass off too. But the whole time I was checking the yard, trying to see if Eddie was hanging by the weight bench or around the fence. Punking me in front of everybody, you know?

Because that's the other thing about being in here: once you step through these doors, people drop you.

Friends, family—it doesn't matter. Nobody's scaling these walls. Nobody's coming on visitation day, talking about how much they miss you. Crying for you. That's one of the subtle tortures of this place. It doesn't involve needles, or getting jumped. Just the deafening silence of everybody you know forgetting your name.

So when Sister came walking up, I already knew what she was going to say. I didn't stop playing, though. I was throwing that ball as hard as I could against the backboard. Not even trying to make it in. When she finally told me to stop, it took everything I had to not punt the basketball over the fence. To the moon, if I could.

She looked sad standing there watching me. I threw up another shot—missed—the whole time trying to build a wall between me and her. Trying to pretend it didn't matter that Eddie had ditched me. People get frozen out all the time in here. But that's the problem. I never saw it coming from Eddie. And I should have.

She tried to say something but I was like, "Whatever. I know all about Eddie."

That stopped her, T. Looked like she was about to fall over right there on the court. But man, I don't know why. Everybody leaves you. Every single one. So when she asked how I knew about Eddie, I shook my head. Put another brick in that wall. It was bound to happen, I told her. And then I cemented the whole thing together with four words: "What do I care?"

Her mouth dropped open when I said that, and pretty soon, I felt pretty stupid standing there with the ball in my hand, so I tossed it behind me and tried to walk away. Make that cut clean. Honestly, though? I was surprised Sister didn't say anything back.

She was staring up at the sky, her lips moving like she was praying.

When she looked down, there were tears in her eyes. They blew the whistles and just before I lined up, Sister reached over and squeezed my shoulder so hard that I felt her fingers on my skin for ten minutes after I was inside.

Luke

13

LUKE was halfway down the stairs when his mom followed him outside and called his name. Behind her, Ricky was telling her to let Luke go.

"Luke. Please, stop. *Stop.*"

Luke obeyed but didn't turn around. Annie stood next to him awkwardly, eventually offering Doreen a quick wave.

"Hi. I'm Annie."

Something inside Doreen lit up, incongruent to the situation, because her voice dripped with excitement. "Are you a friend of Luke's?"

"We go to school together," Annie said. "And I live here. In the apartments. We moved in a few weeks ago."

"Well, don't think all this yelling is normal for us," Doreen said, laughing. "You know how boys can be."

Luke spun around. "Are you kidding me?"

"Luke, not in front of your friend . . ."

"I tell you Toby's dad beat his ass, that he's missing, and all you care about is what *Annie* thinks?"

"Luke, it's okay." Annie touched his arm, but he barely felt it.

"Why don't you two go for a walk?" Doreen said. "Let everything calm down and then—"

Luke didn't wait for her to finish. He stomped down the stairs, hoping Annie would follow him. He was halfway across the parking lot when she caught up. She didn't tell him he was being rude. She didn't tell him his mom was nice, or pretend that she hadn't just seen the definition of dysfunction. She walked beside him silently, eventually grabbing his hand and squeezing warmth into his whole body.

Having Annie with him, feeling her hand in his, threw him off balance. Usually he would sprint to the plane and knock out fifty, sixty push-ups before the exertion slowly siphoned away the anger. But he was already dead tired, and the anger was still begging to be fed.

They were half a mile away when she nudged him with her shoulder.

"You got a plan?" she asked. "Or is this purely a symbolic march?"

"I need to find Toby," he said half-heartedly. He didn't know what he needed.

"Or . . . maybe we could go to Wilco," Annie offered. "Get some snacks. Figure out a plan?"

Luke didn't answer, and she brought both of them to a stop. When he looked into her eyes, she smiled.

"Listen, he didn't want to be anywhere near me or you," she said. "So maybe we give him a chance to cool off. And you too."

Luke opened his mouth to object, but Annie shook her head. When he tried again, she refused him again. Why it worked, Luke didn't know. But when he opened his mouth a third time, she smiled and slowly started walking, dragging him behind her.

They walked down the dark road, accidentally bumping into each other on the uneven road. When a car passed, Luke dropped behind Annie and instinctively grabbed her shoulders to steer her away from traffic, the way he did with his brothers. Sometimes even with Toby, because in all honesty he was less aware than either Petey or Jack-Jack. Every time Luke came up next to her, she retook his hand.

Slowly he felt the edge beginning to dull.

"I'm going to get a doughnut and some hot chocolate," Annie announced. "And I don't want to hear anything about making weight tonight. Life's too short to be on a damn diet all the time."

Luke laughed. Tried to hide it. He didn't know why.

"Well, guess what," he said. "I made weight."

Annie slapped him on the shoulder. "Two doughnuts for you!"

Luke wrinkled his nose. "Or maybe a candy bar."

A truck rumbled past them, and when Luke took Annie's shoulders, she turned and faced him. She was taller, maybe just a half an inch. They stood there staring at each other until Annie said, "Please tell me you aren't hating on doughnuts. Doughnuts are the shit."

Luke shrugged. "They're too sweet. I don't know."

"This is . . . shocking."

Neither of them moved, their breath visible in the air. Finally Annie shook her head and spun around.

"Let's keep this show moving. I don't have all night."

Luke held the door, and they both squinted into the bright halogen of the store. Annie rushed inside, rubbing her arms as she shot toward the empty doughnut case. Unfazed, she turned around and began stalking the aisles, indiscriminately pulling candy bars and bags of chips off the shelves.

Luke stood near the cash register, unsure whether he should follow her. On the mat, he was polished and exacting. He seemed to know what his opponents were going to do before they did. But that was drilling. Constant repetitive motion. With Annie—if he was being honest, any girl—he second-guessed even the simplest movements. The most innocuous words. He didn't have the time in. And more importantly . . . a wrestling mistake could be fixed. There was always another point, another match. He wasn't sure if the same could be said about her.

Annie came to the front of the store, her arms full of cellophane and plastic. She had candy and potato chips, a bottle of soda and a large water. The clerk looked baffled by the sheer amount of junk food on his counter. She smiled at him and—with a grand consideration—grabbed a pack of sugar-free gum from the stand right behind his register.

"And something for my friend here," she said. Then she stage-whispered, "He's working on his figure."

"Is that everything?" the clerk deadpanned.

"Now that you mention it," Annie said, tapping a finger on her chin. "We'll take one of those nudie mags too."

"For your friend?"

"Trust me. He needs it."

Luke wanted to shrink into the walls as they shared a laugh. But the joke never went any further, because Annie didn't have an ID and the strangely principled clerk wouldn't even pull it out from behind the counter for her to inspect.

By the time everything was bagged and in Annie's hand, Luke was running out the door.

"Hold up," Annie said, rummaging in the bag. "Here."

She tossed him a candy bar. Luke caught it and didn't hesitate for a second. He opened it and took a big bite. Annie applauded and then sat on the curb and opened a package of cupcakes.

"Back in Chicago, I used to hang out at a lot of gas stations."

"Really?" Luke asked.

"Yeah. I mean, not professionally or anything. But me and my friends would go to shows and afterward there wasn't much else to do. So we'd do this, you know?"

She smiled, her teeth black with frosting and cake. "Hey, sit. You're making me nervous."

"I've never been to a concert," Luke said, dropping next to her.

"What!"

Luke didn't want to tell her that he barely listened to music. Part of it was practical: without a phone or even the internet, there weren't many options outside a dusty zipper case of CDs his mom had from high school. But it was more than that. Music worked you up. It brought you down. He saw it with the guys on the team, hip-hop or metal blaring, and it felt like a liability. He wanted to stay flat and even keel.

Once, last year, the language arts teacher assigned him a poem about this rough-and-tumble guy who couldn't let people see the bluebird that lived in his heart. How it would ruin everything. It floored Luke. Sometimes, when Luke least expected it, he'd think about that tiny bluebird and wonder if his was still alive.

"Oh my god!" Annie said. "We should go to a honky-tonk show."

Luke laughed.

"What?"

"Honky-tonk show."

"There's that place right past the school. The Silver Bullet," Annie said. "And we should totally go."

"Is that the kind of music you normally listen to?"

"Well, no. But you probably wouldn't know any of the bands I like."

"What? Like rock and roll?"

This time Annie laughed. "Yes, I love the rock and roll. It really swings. . . ."

Luke shook his head, making Annie laugh even harder.

"Japandroids. Beach Slang. At the Drive-In, if I'm feeling old school. Stuff like that."

"Are those . . . bands?"

Annie nodded, taking a drink of soda. "Next time you're in my car, I'm going to blow your mind."

Relaxation, familiarity, had snuck up on Luke. The fight with his mom and Ricky temporarily masked the bottomless anxiety he always felt. But now that the anger had burned away, Luke was left with an inescapable feeling that, in one blink, he'd managed to ruin everything between him and Toby. The questions launched through his mind like bottle rockets. Could he have rescued Toby without Annie? Would Toby trust him again? And of course . . . where in the hell did he go?

He couldn't answer a single one. He slumped on the curb.

"Are you okay?"

"I'm just thinking," Luke said.

"About honky-tonks?"

"Uh, sure," he said.

Annie put an arm around Luke and pulled him close to her. He could feel her heart beating hard through her chest, either excited or nervous—Luke couldn't tell. Or maybe she ran hot all the time, like an engine racing. The bag of chips dangled in her other hand. She stared at him, eventually rolling her eyes.

"You're not very good at this," Annie finally said.

And then she kissed him. As her lips moved over his for the second time, he wanted to give himself completely to her. She pulled away briefly and put her forehead against his, a move that felt strangely intimate to Luke. He had no choice but to look her in the eyes.

"Thank you," he said.

"My pleasure," Annie said. "Think you're ready to go back?"

As soon as the words left her mouth, Luke froze, suddenly conscious of what she'd seen. The broken table. Doreen and Ricky. The total chaos of his life.

"I don't care, you know," she said. "About any of that stuff."

She reached a hand to Luke, and when he took it, she pulled him up until they were both standing. He wanted her to kiss him, but instead she led him away from the Wilco. Not letting go until they were in the parking lot of the apartment.

Ricky was leaning against the railing, beer in hand.

"Doreen, they're back," he called, watching Luke and Annie climb the staircase.

Luke's mom walked onto the landing, and the smell of perfume was immediate. Her makeup was redone, her hair now up. When Luke looked at Ricky, he realized he was wearing a pair of pressed blue jeans and a button-up cowboy shirt, complete with bolo tie. Doreen smiled cautiously.

"Ricky has a surprise planned for me," Doreen told Annie, taking her hand and leading her inside the apartment like they were a couple of friends rushing to gossip in the bathroom. Luke tried to follow, but Ricky stopped him.

Luke braced himself, but Ricky reached into his jeans pocket and pulled out three twenty-dollar bills, holding them out to Luke. "We'll be back late. Maybe tomorrow morning."

Luke looked at the bills but wouldn't take them. Ricky sighed and folded the money back into his palm. He took his hand off Luke's chest and let him into the apartment. As soon as Luke was inside, Ricky said, "Make sure you get that mess cleaned up too."

Doreen was talking to Annie in the living room. At first, Luke didn't think anything of it, but Annie wouldn't meet his eyes. She looked like she'd seen a ghost.

"Okay, okay. Do I need to bring anything?" Doreen asked, turning to Ricky. "Did you give that money to Luke?"

Ricky chuckled. "Golden boy doesn't want my money."

Doreen took the bills from Ricky's hand and held them out to Luke. "Take the boys to IHOP or something. Annie too."

Luke didn't move. Didn't say a word.

"Baby, don't worry about it," Ricky said. "Let's get out of here. Wait until you see what I've got in store for you."

But Doreen was still staring at Luke like she couldn't understand why he wouldn't accept the cash. Wouldn't bend over backward to thank Ricky for everything he was doing for their family. She shook the confusion, the annoyance, away like cobwebs and gave Ricky a faint smile.

"I assume we'll be home soon," Doreen said, hitting Ricky playfully. "But who knows with this guy? He won't tell me a single thing!"

They kissed each other, Ricky's hands inching closer to Doreen's ass. She yelped and spun away from him, grabbing a pack of matches from the kitchen.

"This is Ricky's cell, just in case." She wrote the number down and put it and the cash on the kitchen counter. She looked past Luke, to Annie. "Remember what I told you."

Annie blushed. "Yes, ma'am."

When they were out the door, Luke turned to Annie, who had started to clean up the pieces of glass and wood on the ground. "What was that all about?"

Annie froze momentarily, but then kept picking up the pieces of wood and glass like she hadn't heard the question. Luke was about to follow his mom and demand an answer when Annie stopped him.

"She told me she has condoms in her bedside table."

"Jesus Christ . . . ," Luke said. "Why would she say that?"

"Well, she specifically said she *didn't* want to be a grand-mother." Annie laughed nervously. "It was obviously no big deal for her. And that makes me think you've been messing with me. That she's given that talk before."

"What? No." Luke stared at Annie. "I can't believe my mom told you where to find condoms."

"It's, you know, fine."

Luke could hear Toby yelling instructions in his ear. Followed by laughter and the good-natured ribbing that usually followed one of Luke's epic failures on this front. All he needed to do was say something terrible like, "Would you like to accompany me to my mother's room?" Even thinking it made his skin crawl, so he stood up and got the vacuum cleaner.

When he came back, Annie was smiling. He vacuumed, trying to figure out a way to segue into sex the whole time the machine was working. When he was done, Jack-Jack came out of the room, rubbing his eyes and complaining about a bad dream. Annie pulled him onto her lap, and eventually they both fell asleep. Luke turned off the lights, knowing he should go into the room. If Petey woke up alone, he would freak out.

But he didn't want to leave Annie, still harboring vague fantasies that she would wake him up in the middle of the night, condoms in her hand. He didn't want to be in the back room in case Toby made a U-turn and showed up at the door. Eventually he pulled his pillow and blanket to the floor, lying on his stomach and watching the stillness of the late night.

14

THE first thing Toby saw was Jesus, bloody palms out-stretched as if he was welcoming him into the new day. That alone would have normally startled him, but when Lily moved behind him he nearly jumped off the couch.

"What are you doing?" she asked, rubbing her eyes.

"I have school," Toby said.

"Skip. I'm sure you feel like shit."

Toby's head *was* aching and his entire body felt as if he'd drunk kerosene, not PBR. What was one more day? If anything, it would lend credibility to the story that he was sick. Give the bruises a chance to become nothing more than whispers. Something that could've happened any number of ways.

Lily shifted behind him, her body warm against his. And it was settled.

"If you insist," Toby said, and Lily nodded absently, her eyes closed. It left Toby in a bit of a quandary. Last night, he'd dropped onto the couch without a second thought. Half drunk, half there—it was a no-brainer. But now, in the full light of the early morning, anxiety creeped into him. He didn't know how to act. Lily opened her eyes and said, "Jesus, settle down. Please."

So he did. And a few minutes later he was asleep once again.

The next time he woke up, Lily was singing softly to herself in the kitchen. Toby walked in sheepishly, not saying anything until Lily noticed him. When she did, she jumped— almost dropping the avocados she was holding.

"Shit, you scared me. I didn't even hear you come in."

"I'm a creeper. What can I say?"

The thrill of her smile shot through Toby.

"Anyway." Lily held up the avocados. "What do you think about guacamole?"

"I think I've never had it and it looks nasty."

Even Lily's mock outrage captivated him.

"I might be able to find you some cheese and crackers. Or maybe a nice Pop-Tart."

"Sorry if one of my life rules is to avoid eating anything that literally looks like shit." Toby pointed to the guacamole in progress.

Lily stood there for a second, trying to read Toby. He was stone-faced and committed until the very last second. Until the exact moment when Lily would think he was being serious. And then he smiled.

"Oh, you're an asshole. Like, seriously." She went back to cutting the tomatoes. "I know you're a North Carolina boy, but damn. Might as well say you don't like sex!"

His mind dropped to the gutter. Lily close to his face, her hands on the waistband of his jeans. The anticipation building until—he stopped himself. Lily stared at him, amused.

"Everything okay over there?"

Toby cleared his throat. "Fine. You know. Hungry."

"Okay, well. Here's the thing . . . I should've made you go to school. That was a mistake on my part. I don't want you not going to college because of me."

"This might keep me out of Harvard. Damn it."

Lily laughed.

Inside, he wasn't as cool. Every stitch of his body was screaming. Trying to come up with any kind of plan—something they could do. But every idea, no matter how good, seemed to wither on the vine of his imagination. She wasn't like the girls at school. Perhaps because he knew they didn't take him seriously. With Lily, he honestly didn't know if he had a chance, or if she saw him like a little brother.

Somebody to protect, making any advance laughable. Or worse—met with awkward pity.

But he had to try.

"We could, you know, go to the mountains." Toby said it casually. As if this was a normal option. She could either take him to school or—hey, why not!—they could shoot up the highway to the mountains together like it was nothing. Like Toby wouldn't be joyfully terrified the entire damn trip.

He tried to play it cool, but his heart was pounding. He watched as Lily went to a different cupboard and pulled out a plastic bowl and a lid.

"Well, I guess this is guac to go."

Toby drove up the mountain, a drive he'd taken countless times when his mom was still around. She would smoke with the windows down, talking to him from the front seat. He could still remember the smell of the smoke mingled with pine. The way the sun would bounce off her sunglasses and into his eyes every time she looked into the rearview mirror, telling him how she didn't have the right kind of blood for hot weather.

"Just a quick getaway," she would always say. "To keep ourselves honest."

He never knew what that meant, but it was always said with a hint of sadness. A hint of urgency.

The trees were mostly bare now, save for a few that stubbornly held their leaves. Lily said something about the fall colors, and in a moment of either inspiration or panic, he started blurting out facts.

"Did you know that fall colors have nothing to do with when fall comes? It's all about how much rainfall you get. And the days getting shorter."

Lily gave him a sideways glance. "Well. Thank you for that, Mr. Kettle."

"Who?"

"My old science teacher." Lily rolled down her window a bit, the cold air spinning around the El Camino. "He used to dress up like a ginkgo tree for Halloween. That was his thing. I don't know if that's really awesome, or really sad."

"I think there's no question it's sad," Toby said.

"I'll tell you what," Lily said, staring out the window. "I can still spot a fucking ginkgo tree like it's nothing."

Toby laughed.

"This is something I would love to see," he said. "Do you, like, get *really* excited?"

"Kiss my ass."

"Wait! Is that a ginkgo?" Toby pointed to an oak tree.

Lily refused to look. "I'm not going to play your games."

"Because you take ginkgo trees very seriously?"

Lily smiled. "No, because you're an asshole."

They didn't drive all the way into Asheville, a city Toby always thought of as being the top of the mountain. He'd never been beyond it. Instead, Lily directed him to pull off at a rest stop a few miles from the city. When they got out of the car, Toby started shivering.

"I brought blankets," Lily said. "They're in the back."

Toby found them rolled up inside a sleeping-bag sack. He pulled out the two quilts and carried them over to Lily, who had a collection of food in her arms. Chips. The guacamole. Two cans of mandarin oranges. A feast fit for a highway road stop. And from a bag she had hidden from Toby, she pulled out a bottle of cheap strawberry wine.

"Farm of the Boones," Lily said, presenting the bottle. "A fine vintage. Bottled two weeks ago."

Toby arranged one blanket on the top of a picnic table to sit on. The other they wrapped around their shoulders, the food and wine on the bench at their feet, and they watched the empty parking lot. Every so often a new car would arrive—full of traveling families, retired people—as they nibbled and drank. The wine was sweet, almost too sweet for

Toby. But he sipped it from the small waxed paper cups Lily had packed.

"So I've made you a truant, and now I've given you alcohol," she said. "I'm seriously going to jail."

Toby raised his glass. "To the correctional system."

Lily toasted him, tossed back the wine, and poured another cup.

"God, this takes me back," Lily said. "I was totally in love with this guy in high school and I brought him up here and . . ."

She took a drink of wine. Toby groaned.

"I really don't want to know," he said.

"Stop," she said, hitting him softly. "What I was *going* to say is, I didn't know my dad followed us."

"Oh, that's not fun."

"Yeah. He got out of the car and started yelling about my *purity*. My dad could've given a shit that I was drinking whiskey at the Deuce when I was fifteen, as long as I kept my hymen intact. For the Lord."

Toby didn't know what to say except, "Hymen safety is important, I guess."

Lily laughed. "And guess what? I had sex with that guy two days later. In his van, behind the Food Lion."

She raised her glass to the heavens, toasting her dad or

maybe God. It was just starting to rain, and Toby held the blanket over their heads.

"Do you think it's possible to forgive somebody after they're dead?" Lily asked.

This was a topic Toby had thought about extensively as a kid. Well, he thought about his father dying. About attending the funeral and whether he would make some sort of statement by not paying his final respects. Refusing to cry. In the end, he had decided that he would do nothing. That even a person like Jimmy deserved a final moment of respect, whether they gave it in their life or not.

"I think you get to decide whether you want to forgive them or not," Toby said. "And if you do it, then it's done, right?"

"I don't know," Lily said, cupping the wine with both hands. "I don't know."

Before Toby knew what was happening, Lily jumped off the picnic table and walked out from under the canopy of trees and into the parking lot. She had her arms spread wide and her eyes closed, face pointed to the sky. A few seconds later, she was soaking wet. Her hair streaked onto her T-shirt in dark blond strings. When Toby called out her name, she didn't answer—just stood there with her arms out, trying to catch the rain. When he brought the blanket and put it around her shoulders, he could see her skin already puckered from the cold. Her teeth chattered like a typewriter.

Toby cleaned up the food and washed out the Tupperware in the bathroom sink, bringing everything back to the El Camino, including the wine. He wrapped the bottle in an old T-shirt and hid it behind his seat. Lily was curled in the passenger seat. Toby opened the door, half expecting her to be crying. Or at least to seem distant. But when he got in—the heat glorious against his wet skin—she reached over and took the container from his hands.

"You washed it?"

"Yeah?"

She looked at the container, then back to him.

"What?" Toby said, unsure if he'd made a mistake.

"It's just not, you know, a thing you'd expect from a high-school boy."

"That's because I'm a high school *man*."

"Oh yeah. I forgot." Lily shook her head. "*Man.* Good lord."

Toby put his hand on the gear shift, not really wanting to leave this place. As they sat there, the rain slowly began to turn to snow. When there was a thin layer across the asphalt parking lot, Lily reached over and touched Toby's hand.

"I needed this. Thank you."

Toby nodded as Lily shifted in her seat and leaned against his shoulder, both of them watching the sun slip away in the distance.

Toby wanted a snapshot of this moment, something he could live in outside of time. This was the first time Toby had had *fun* with anybody besides Luke. Sure there were moments at school, passing shouts of laughter. But usually it was him and Luke, walking to the store. Him and Luke, watching the boys. Him and Luke together as the day was long. And for the first time, maybe ever, he wondered if that was strange.

Toby didn't want to think about Luke, or the fact that school was already out. Running away from Annie's apartment was understandable, something he could twist Luke's guilt into accepting. Missing school, though, would bring a reckoning. But he would deal with that tomorrow, the next day. Whenever this ended with Lily.

"I want to take you somewhere," he said, but Lily had fallen asleep.

She sighed gently, shifting her body as Toby slowly pulled out of the parking lot. He barely made a sound, ticking off every mile back down the mountain until they were parked on the side of the road, the woods barely visible in the distance. They hadn't been sitting there more than a few minutes when Lily woke up and rubbed her eyes.

She looked into the empty blackness, then back to Toby. "Are you planning on murdering me?"

"No. This would be a terrible spot." Toby motioned to a passing car as evidence.

"Not to mention that you're a skinny little fucker and I'd break you," she said, yawning.

For some reason, Toby liked that. He pushed it a little further, trying to be smooth.

"Well, you never know what will happen in the dark."

Lily rolled her eyes.

"I can tell you one thing that's *not* going to happen."

Toby took it on the chin, with a smile. When he opened the door, he reached over and brushed Lily's leg lightly, like he did this sort of thing all the time. Like he couldn't care less. Inside him, alarms were blaring. Danger, danger.

"I don't take just anyone out here," he said.

She looked to the trees, and when she turned back, her smile was like a taunt. A challenge. "I can honestly say a guy has never taken me to the woods on a date before."

He wanted to tell her that the plane was the most important thing about him, maybe his entire life. He wanted to tell her about Luke. But he didn't say any of it, because of one word—*date*.

She got out of the car without another word. Before he followed, he grabbed the bottle of strawberry wine and then ran to catch Lily.

January 21

T—

Marilyn came by today and, if I'm being honest, I wasn't in the mood to hear another speech about how I need to do this or that. All I could think about was Eddie punking me and Sister acting all boo-hoo. How I'd barely seen either of them in a week. Man, I don't know what I was even feeling. It was like somebody had reached inside me and mixed everything up. I couldn't tell if I wanted to hit something or cry.

So when Marilyn came into the room, I sat down and tried to remember how to smile. And that probably sounds stupid to you. But really, I don't smile that often. Whenever I do, it feels wrong. Too extravagant, maybe. I don't know how else to explain it except to say that whenever I smile now, it always makes me feel like I'm doing something wrong.

Anyway, Marilyn starts right in telling me she's got good news. And like always, I'm right back at her all, "You found another lawyer to deal with me?" When I said that, she took off her glasses and put down her pen, all calm, and started tapping her fingernail on the thick folder in front of her. That's when I knew I was in trouble, T. I even tried to roll it back. But she wasn't having it.

First she starts talking about all the people who work on my case. Lawyers and law students and even a few pastors. Entire buildings of people, it sounds like, all of them working too many hours to count. Calling the governor. Studying thick books. People I'll probably never meet who care about me more than . . . well, most people I ever knew.

Marilyn was like, "They think you matter!"

And all I could think was: she sounds just like Sister.

It must've been all over my face, because Marilyn stopped tapping that folder and gave me the eye so hard I had to look away. A few seconds later, she said my name, and her voice was a lot softer. I still couldn't look at her, though.

She told me that a lot of people think me being in here is "a grave injustice." That she wanted to get my death sentence reduced.

When I didn't say anything, she pulled another folder out of her bag. It was stuffed full of papers and pictures. All the work of those same people. Collected in hopes of telling what Marilyn always calls the "real" story of what happened.

Sometimes I feel so tired, T. Tired of pretending. Tired of working up the energy needed to talk to people like Marilyn or Sister. So tired that sometimes it feels like I can't move.

Because I've been through this a hundred times. Shit, a million. And I wasn't about to look at the pictures she had in that folder. No chance.

I could feel myself starting to slip. But instead of saying anything, or throwing that folder against the wall—and that's what I really wanted to do—I sat there, trying to be hard. Like whatever she could pull out of that folder wouldn't make a damn bit of difference to me.

And then she said: "I want the court to know who you really are."

Who I really am.

When the police grabbed me, I wouldn't say anything. They let me sit like that—deep in the anger. The confusion. The sadness, like a brick around my neck. For hours and hours I sat there, until one of the detectives dropped those pictures on the desk right next to me, a convenient accident.

They were all surprised when I was like, "I did it."

They asked me three more times, had me write every single thing down. By the time the lawyer got there, it was already finished. He went through the motions best he could, and to his credit, he tried to get me to help.

But nobody understands: confessing meant nothing to me. Now, then—one hundred years from today. Saying I did it—taking whatever punishment comes? That only feels like being let off a hook.

Marilyn wants to get me a new sentencing hearing. I wouldn't get out, but I wouldn't stay here either. Most guys in here would do a backflip if their lawyer even hinted at those words. But all I could do was nod, because even though I wake up at night sweating and screaming out, thinking about the day when I'm the one walked back to that room for the last time, I don't want them to take it easy on me.

I don't want mercy or forgiveness or even justice because goddamn, T. What if that erases it all?

What I did. Why.

Because that's who I really am.

Luke

15

ANNIE was asleep on the couch, still cradling Jack-Jack, when Luke finally gave up on sleeping. He stood up and quietly walked onto the landing, flexing his throbbing hand.

He'd spent the whole night staring out the window, watching for Toby. But the truth was, Luke knew he wasn't coming back long before the sun came out. He understood why Toby had run away from the apartment, even if he didn't agree with it. If Toby had gotten over his betrayal in a single night, Luke would've counted himself lucky. Still, he couldn't stop himself from watching the road.

He was lost in his thoughts when Annie came up behind him.

"Good morning," she said, ducking her head under Luke's arm and wrapping her arms around his chest. A wave of warmth washed over him. Her hair tickled him as she looked up into his eyes.

"What are you doing out here?"

Luke smiled. "Just, you know, looking at the parking lot."

"That's weird," Annie said, yawning as she leaned her head against his chest. Soon the boys would be up, needing clothes and breakfast. Luke took a few deep breaths, but it felt like he was breathing through a wet towel.

"Do you think he went to the plane?"

Luke didn't answer. The chance that Toby had left Annie's apartment, grabbed a sleeping bag, and gone back to the plane was pretty good. He might be there right now, cussing at the cold morning air. But it was clear: Toby was making a point. Knowing didn't help Luke, though.

"*Is* it weird?" Luke asked.

Annie gave him a confused look.

"Me being worried like this."

Luke didn't tell her that he'd been up all night, or that he couldn't stop himself from imagining all the terrible things that might happen to Toby. It seemed like such an easy solution, to just get over it. But he'd tried a hundred times last night, and it never stuck.

Annie squeezed his chest. "I think it's possibly the sweetest thing I've ever seen. You love him, even if he's a complete idiot."

Luke took a breath, and then another one. He wasn't sure

if he wanted to cuss Toby, or apologize to him.

Behind them, Luke heard Petey come into the living room, followed by the thud of Jack-Jack being pushed off the couch. As they started fighting, Annie pulled herself away from Luke.

"I've got a surprise for them," she said, disappearing down the stairs to her apartment.

She came back with a box of pancake mix, eggs, and a small carton of milk. As Luke got the boys dressed, Annie made them pancakes shaped like Mickey Mouse, a trick that Petey and Jack-Jack treated with the sort of reverence most people didn't show for the dead, let alone breakfast food. The entire time, Luke kept an ear open, hoping he'd hear Elvis pumping through the speakers of Toby's car.

They dropped the boys off at the bus stop and, without asking, Annie drove Luke to the plane. He hopped out and ran to it, already drumming up an explanation for bringing Annie back a second time. Practicing his apology.

But the plane was empty, and Luke's emotions went to war.

Toby was making Luke pay for betraying his confidence. Luke knew that. Hell, he would even say he deserved it. But the radio silence was aggressive and brought with it an edge of fear that Toby had to know Luke was feeling. And *that* pissed him off.

Luke kicked the nose of the plane as hard as he could. It barely moved.

He limped back to the car, trying to stay calm. Annie looked surprised to see Luke return alone. He shook his head.

"He'll be at school."

Luke leaned his head back in the seat of Annie's car, trying to believe what he'd just said. Annie opened her mouth, but closed it almost immediately. Instead of talking she leaned across the seat and planted a long kiss on Luke. He touched her cheek lightly, finally feeling the smallest amount of proficiency. She shivered once, their lips just inches away.

"I know what will make you feel better," she said, smiling. "You. Me. The janitor's closet at lunch."

"I'm pretty sure he keeps it locked," Luke said.

"Because if they didn't, kids would be making out in there all the time?" Annie kissed him one more time. "He's going to be fine. You just have to let him blow off some steam."

Luke nodded. "It's just . . . damn. He knows exactly what he's doing. He knows this makes me crazy."

"I'm filing this information away," Annie said. "In case I ever need to use it against you."

Luke tried to burrow back down into the anger, the anxiety, but it was impossible with Annie leaning on top of him. Her hair hanging into his eyes. He leaned up and kissed her, going against every grain of his nature.

Annie's eyes were still closed when he said, "I'm not going to worry about it."

And Luke believed it too. All the way up until they pulled into the parking lot and there wasn't an El Camino in sight.

Luke wanted to keep his promise to Annie, to say that he hadn't worried about Toby once when he walked into the cafeteria. But he'd craned his neck down every hallway between classes. Made it a point to go by his locker. He even got called out by Mrs. Norris in English for staring out into the parking lot. By the time he saw Annie, already at the table with a tray of food in front of her, he knew Toby wasn't at school.

"Have you seen him?" Annie asked.

"He didn't come," he said.

Other than that, Luke barely said a word for the next fifteen minutes, doing nothing but picking at a salad and casually watching the entrance to the cafeteria. When the bell rang, he didn't move. Annie had her tray in her hands but sat it back on the table and waited as the room cleared.

"You could go to the office and call him," she said.

"He doesn't have a phone," Luke said.

Luke was fighting two conflicting feelings. He *was* worried. But at the same time, he knew that Toby was somewhere cooling off. He thought about what Coach had said: at some point, Luke needed to stop trying to save Toby. At some point, he would have to let Toby make his mistakes—whatever they might be.

"He's fine," Luke said, standing up. "I'm sure."

Luke couldn't say that he didn't think about Toby the rest of the day, but by the time wrestling practice rolled around, he was at least back to letting his annoyance outweigh the fear. As he was getting dressed in the locker room, Coach O came over and sat down next to him.

"How's your hand?"

"Okay," Luke said, inspecting it. It was still purple and the cuts were still evident, but he flexed it a few times without much pain.

"How about your head?"

Luke stared at Coach O for a second before he understood he was talking about the match with Lowry. "About the same as my hand, I guess. Getting better."

Coach O cracked his knuckles and nodded to a freshman walking by. "If you try to pull that nonsense with Herrera, he's going to eat your lunch. You know that, right?"

"I know," Luke said.

Coach O leaned forward and put his arms on his knees, staring into the empty showers. At first Luke thought their talk was done, but when he was about to stand up, Coach put a hand on his leg.

"My wife and I were thinking that maybe you'd want to come stay with us," he said. "Just until the end of the year. I know your situation is . . . difficult. And I thought I could talk to your mom, get you started on a nutrition plan. Make sure you have everything you need before you head off to Iowa."

Coach didn't look at him as he spoke. And he didn't wait for Luke to respond. He stood up and said, "Just think about it. I've got an extra bedroom in the basement ready for you anytime. Okay?"

Luke nodded, trying not to let his emotions take over. He imagined waking up every morning and hearing Coach O and his wife talking over their breakfasts. The sound of the morning news just below their voices. Maybe they'd give him some walking-around money too. A car. He could spend the next four or five months doing nothing but getting ready to start his new life at Iowa.

Before Coach O left, he looked Luke square in the eye. "I almost forgot. You're going to pay for that bullshit last night. Get ready to run your ass off."

He popped Luke on the thigh with his towel and walked away.

Practice wasn't nearly as hard as he thought it was going to be. Luke suspected Coach was worried about giving him too much before Herrera. When they got done, Luke was ready to spend a little extra time running when he heard shouting in the hallway, followed by laughter. He jogged outside, expecting to find Toby talking shit once again. Instead, it was Annie—jawing at Tyler Simpson, who was red in the face and telling his friends to shut up.

"Bye-bye now," she said, and Tyler shuffled off, giving Luke a dirty look.

"What was that about?"

"He suggested my manhood was bigger than yours," Annie said, yawning.

Luke took a step toward the locker room, fed up with Tyler Simpson and all his bullshit. Simpson had spent the entire practice laughing with his friends. Whispering comments about Luke's match with Lowry and then outright saying Luke was going to get his ass kicked by Herrera. Annie stopped him.

"Hey . . . please don't be that guy."

Luke was still mad, but he stopped. "What?"

"The guy who thinks that Tyler Simpson even shows up on my radar," Annie said. "I mean, Jesus. He drives a Miata. Nobody can respect a dude in a Miata, trust me."

Luke laughed. He remembered when Tyler's dad had bought the tiny convertible for him. Toby, essentially, had said the same thing. Luke looked up and down the hallway instinctively. Annie's voice dropped a bit when she spoke.

"He's not here. I checked."

Annie walked over to him and pulled him into a hug. Then she held him at arm's length and cocked her head to the side.

"How about you and me go back to your house and watch a movie?" she said. Luke hesitated at first, and she added, "He'll show up eventually. I promise you."

Luke reluctantly agreed.

"Okay, now go take a shower because you smell like a wrestler. And despite what you might think, it's not attractive."

She pushed him away gently, smiling. Luke started toward the locker room, but he stopped.

"What did you say to Tyler?"

"Oh!" Annie laughed. "I told him we could both whip ours out and see which one was bigger. He declined."

Luke was still smiling when they pulled into the parking lot of his apartment. The lights had just turned on, and when they got out of the car, Luke was laughing as Annie finished a story about her stepfather, David. So when he heard Jack-Jack say his name, followed almost immediately by Petey's loud wailing, he wasn't sure what was happening. They came running down the stairs, both of them still holding their backpacks.

"Mo-Mo-Mom-isn't-here," Jack-Jack said, nearly hyper-ventilating as he sobbed out the words. "And-and-you-you-weren't—"

Luke swept both of the boys up in his arms and carried them up the stairs, holding them as close to his body as he could. When he got to the door, he pushed against it hard—assuming his mom and Ricky were just asleep. It was locked. He tried to set the boys down to get his key out of his back-pack, but the twins panicked and held on to his neck like he was about to drop them in the deep end of the pool.

"Can you get my key?" Luke asked Annie.

She unlocked the door and Luke sat on the couch, holding both of the crying boys. The apartment was dark, unchanged from when they had left this morning. Nobody had been here all day. Annie brought the phone to Luke, and he dialed Ricky's number from the back of the match-book. It went straight to voice mail.

"Do you guys want pizza?" Luke asked.

The twins barely responded, and they wouldn't move or let Luke find the phonebook so he could order. Annie eventually snuck out of the apartment and returned twenty minutes later with two pizzas and a two-liter of soda. Even that didn't coax the twins from Luke's lap, at least not at first. Annie made them plates and poured soda—they weren't normally allowed to have soda—and like a couple of scared but curious kittens, they slowly climbed down and began eating.

As they did, the adrenaline that had taken over for Luke started to slip away. What was left was a shaky, panicked rage. His mother had done a lot of stupid things, but this topped the list. He stood up to try Ricky's phone again, smiling at Petey and Jack-Jack when they froze, tracking him across the living room.

"I'm not going anywhere," he said. "Eat your pizza."

He called four more times before he gave up and finally left a message more desperate than he liked. It took an hour, but slowly the boys' shoulders began to unclench. Instead of hawking over the paper plates, they sat lazily in front of them, watching the television. An hour after that, they were asleep on the floor—one of Annie's hands on each of their backs.

She slowly stood up and sat next to Luke.

"I can't believe they didn't come back," Luke said. He cleared his throat, trying to hide his emotions from Annie. She leaned into him gently. "And then everything with Toby, I just . . ."

He coughed, refusing to break down.

"We could take a walk. That might help."

Luke shook his head. He didn't want to leave the boys alone.

"Why don't you go run? I mean, that's all you ever used to do before you met me, which reminds me—I have a confession."

Luke stared at her, afraid that she was about to drop another bomb on him.

"I'm worried I might ruin your wrestling career."

Luke laughed once. "Why?"

"Because I'm so awesome and you're never going to want to run again. Just hang out at gas stations, eating cupcakes and pork rinds."

"Don't forget going to honky-tonks."

"You're right!" Annie said. After a second, she pushed his leg. "Seriously. Go. I'll stay with them."

Luke ran hard, harder than he probably should have after practice. But he couldn't feel any pain, didn't feel the tightness of lactic acid coating his muscles. He ran, trying to forget. Trying to push himself past the point where he could feel anything.

He hit the road on a sprint, took the same turns he always did. Ran blind with frustration and anger until he broke through the tree line. Usually he would slow down—especially at night. There were low branches and rogue pine-cones. Not to mention the actual trees. He would've run straight through, trees be damned, if he hadn't heard the distinctive sound of glass on metal. Laughter. Toby.

Luke skidded to a stop. Toby's back was to him, but there was a woman—older than them—facing him. She laughed, passing a bottle of something to Toby. She saw Luke standing in the shadows, which admittedly would have terrified anybody, and nearly choked on the wine. Toby spun around and froze.

"Luke?"

Luke hadn't meant to seem as if he'd been watching them. But now, as he stepped closer to the plane, he couldn't think of any other way it would look.

"Yeah. I was running."

It's all he could manage. Because there was Toby, sitting in the plane with a woman he couldn't have known for more than twenty-four hours, drinking from a bottle of wine.

Luke couldn't pull his eyes from the bottle. Sure, plenty of people drank. Parties, after football games. He could find a way to drink every night if he really wanted to. But there had always been an unspoken agreement that they wouldn't. They wouldn't let something they could control pull them off the rails.

"We were just, you know . . ." Toby dropped the bottle, trying to be casual. "This is Lily. She's my . . . friend?"

Toby and Lily laughed. They sounded drunk. Luke tried to keep his words even.

"Can I talk to you?" he said. Toby looked at Lily, then back to Luke, and nodded. When he stepped out of the plane, he almost fell down. More giggling. They acted as if they'd been friends forever, as if this visit wasn't the first, but the latest in a string of regular trysts. Toby's nighttime plane friend. When he was steady, he followed Luke to the edge of the tree line.

Luke didn't wait for Toby to talk.

"What the fuck are you doing?"

Toby ruffled like a bird. "What's it to you?"

Luke grabbed him, pushed him into the closest tree a little too hard. Toby gasped, but Luke didn't stop himself. How could Toby be so damn stupid? How could he suddenly start acting like Doreen and Jimmy and nearly every other damn adult they'd ever had in their life?

"You run away from Annie. You don't show up at school today. And now this. Drunk with some woman you don't know. What the *fuck*, man?"

Toby pushed against his arm in protest, and Luke let him go, suddenly aware that he had his friend pinned against a tree. That he had likely added two or three more bruises. He took a step back as Toby rubbed his shoulder.

"First? I'm not drunk. So go fuck yourself." Toby looked at his feet and then up at Luke. "And like it matters who we bring out here. I know that now."

"Oh, bullshit. How many girls have you tried to bring out to this plane? Five? A hundred? C'mon."

Toby stood completely still and looked Luke right in the eye. "It's not the plane. You let her see me. You let her see me like *that*, goddammit."

Luke felt like he'd been hit in the stomach again, doubled over and out of breath. But Toby wasn't done.

"And you know what? I didn't want to stay at her apartment, letting her treat me like some kind of broken fucking puppy, okay? So I left. I went home and I got in my car and I—"

Toby stopped abruptly, and it got Luke's attention.

"What?"

Toby kicked a pinecone across the clearing, looking like he was about to confess to a murder.

"Jimmy made me drive him to the Deuce, and while I was there I . . . shit. I got sick, okay? That's why I wasn't at school. Threw up everywhere."

Luke had no idea why Toby was sitting in the plane with Lily. Why he smelled like cheap wine. But compared with going to the Deuce with Jimmy, those were minor offenses. Something Luke could get over easily enough. But going to the Deuce with Jimmy was another story.

"What the hell are you doing, T?"

The fire went out of Toby, just a bit. He bit his lip and scratched his neck, looking as if he was trying to figure out the perfect way to answer Luke. Finally he shrugged and said, "Listen, I know I fucked up. What else is new?"

Luke took a chance. He motioned to the ridiculous shirt, the too-small corduroy pants. "You've started dressing like a ten-year-old, for starters."

"Yeah. Well. I puked all over my other clothes." Before Luke could ask, he said, "Lily gave these to me."

"Lily," Luke said, glancing over Toby's shoulder. The woman was drinking from the wine bottle, staring at Luke. Even in the darkness of the woods, the intensity of her gaze was piercing.

"How did, you know, that happen?"

"I'm basically irresistible." When Luke didn't respond, Toby sighed. "Lily brought me back to her house last night. Took care of me."

The entire story troubled Luke. A strange woman from a bar filled with petty and not-so-petty criminals brought a drunk, underage teenager back to her house, where he spent the night. And then let him skip school. Luke tried to tell himself that he should be happy Toby was safe. So he changed the subject.

"Mom and Ricky are missing," Luke said. "I came home from practice and the boys were on the landing, scared to death."

"Shit," Toby said. Concern tugged at his face. "Are they okay?"

Luke picked at a scab on his hand. He nodded.

"I think so. Annie is watching them right now."

They stood there, not looking at each other. A car passed on the highway, somebody whooping out the window. Behind them, Lily sat down in the hull of the plane.

"I'm sorry about bringing her yesterday," Luke said. At first, Toby looked surprised. But then he nodded. Flicked his eyes to Luke. "I should've figured something else out. But I was worried."

There were times, even as kids, when they didn't have to speak to each other. When wounds or arguments—anything, really—would vanish. Disappear without a scar. Two seconds later, and they'd be giving each other shit. Until this moment, Luke would've never said it was special.

Toby smiled.

"Well, no need to worry. Jimmy can't scratch all this." Toby moved his body, stringing together a few lewd gestures.

"So you feel fine."

Toby stopped rotating his hips and nodded.

"Yeah, dude. I'm good. I promise."

Toby clapped once and started gyrating again almost immediately. This time Lily called out from behind them.

"Do I need to be worried?"

Toby turned and gave Lily a thumbs-up, which made her laugh. Luke looked past Toby one last time and tried to see into Lily. To see if she was—what? Good? He didn't know, but he looked at her long enough that Toby cleared his throat and said his name low, so Lily wouldn't hear. Luke didn't care if he embarrassed Toby, at least not in front of this woman.

"Why don't you come back with me? We could hang out. The boys would love it if you were there in the morning. I'll ask Annie to leave, if you want."

"Leave? You need to be going back there and getting you some," Toby said loudly.

Behind him, Lily yelled out, "I'm still not changing my mind!"

Toby leaned close to Luke. "I'm going to try and see what's going on here. You know?"

It might've been the first time Toby had ever not taken an invitation from Luke to come home. And while Luke understood why, he still stood there dumbly for a few seconds, nodding.

"Yeah, I get it. Just be careful," Luke said. "Okay?"

Toby glanced at the plane, just long enough that Luke thought he might be reconsidering. When he looked back, Luke knew he hadn't.

"I'll pick you up for school tomorrow," Toby said. "If I don't show up, call the National Guard."

Luke didn't want to joke, didn't want to leave Toby in the woods alone with some woman he didn't know, would never trust no matter what Toby said, but he still walked away. The last thing he heard was Toby laughing, and the clink of that goddamn bottle hitting the side of the plane.

16

TOBY and Lily didn't have sex in the plane. But they talked all night. When he dropped her off, he realized it was the best day and night he'd had, maybe ever. Now, as he lay on the couch in his trailer, sun in his eyes, he was dead tired but still floating on air. All he could think about was Lily. The way she laughed. How she lifted the wine bottle to her lips, passing it so he could do the same. The subtle curves underneath her shirt.

Toby got up, walked quietly to the bathroom. As he was getting undressed, he caught a look at himself in the mirror. The new bruises were still bright, offsetting the old scars that mapped his body. What would Lily think? Would she cuss Jimmy again? As if on cue, the front door of the trailer banged open, and Jimmy yelled his name.

"In the bathroom," Toby said, hurrying to put on his shirt. When he was younger, he thought his father might see the havoc of his body and ease up. Be convicted by the damage. It had the opposite effect. Seeing the way he bruised only solidified Toby's weakness in Jimmy's mind. So Toby kept covered up, no matter how hot it got in the trailer.

"Where you at, boy?"

Toby opened the door. Jimmy and Bo were standing in the kitchen, bleary-eyed but pulsing with energy. Bo drank from a carton of orange juice, only stopping to pop a mini chocolate doughnut into his mouth every few seconds. When he saw Toby, he offered the bag. Toby shook his head.

"How you feeling?"

"Fine. I'm getting ready to go to school."

"Where were you all day yesterday?"

Toby grabbed his toothbrush and got to work, shrugging. He spit out the front door, and thought, Fuck it.

"I went to the mountains with Lily."

If it surprised Jimmy, he didn't let it show. Bo put down the carton of juice and wiped his mouth.

"That right?" he said.

Toby started walking back to the bathroom and Bo stopped him. "So you guys went up to the mountains. To do what?"

How could he explain sitting there in the rain? Drinking wine and watching Lily eat her guac to go? Any way he tried

to frame it would sound childish. But maybe more importantly, he wanted to keep it for himself.

"Why do you care?"

Bo looked at Jimmy like, "Can you believe this kid?" But
Jimmy was sitting on the couch with his arm over his eyes,
barely listening.

"Maybe I'll want to take sweet Miss Lily up to the mountains one of these days. What do you think about that?"

"I think she wouldn't even look at you twice," Toby said,
stepping around Bo to put his toothbrush away. He grabbed
his keys and his backpack and started for the door.

"You're pretty confident."

"And you're an ex-con," Toby said. "It isn't confidence."

Jimmy snorted. Bo's mouth dropped.

"*Ex*-con? Who said I'm retired?"

Jimmy gave the man a pointed look, but Bo ignored him.
He followed Toby outside, leaning against the doorframe as
Toby walked to his car.

"You don't know anything about that girl, do you?"

"I know enough," Toby said, opening the door.

As he was pulling away, Bo was still in the doorway, the
orange juice in his hands again. Swallowing right from the
carton in long, rhythmic gulps.

* * *

Luke was sitting on the steps of the apartment, Annie right behind him with her arms draped over his shoulders. They were laughing about something. When Luke noticed Toby, he acted surprised. It kind of pissed Toby off. He'd said he'd be there. Luke gave Annie a kiss and then loped to the passenger door. By the time he had his seat belt on, Toby forced himself not to bring it up.

"So?"

"So, what?"

"Did you hit that?"

Luke gave him a dopey smile. "I'm laying a foundation."

Toby laughed. "God help her."

As they drove to school, a familiar lightness started to seep into him. He turned on the radio—Elvis, again, loudly—and began to sing along.

"What about you?" Luke said over the music.

"I'm also laying a foundation," Toby said. "Hey, did your mom show up?"

Luke didn't answer at first, but then he shook his head. "We don't have practice tonight. So I'll be home for the twins if she doesn't come back today. Plus, it's not like I haven't watched the boys all weekend before."

Toby didn't say anything; he didn't need to. He turned the radio up a tick and let the music be the only sound in the car until they pulled into the school parking lot. Neither of them made for the door. The bell wouldn't ring for fifteen minutes, so Toby leaned back in his seat and thought about Lily.

When Luke spoke, Toby nearly jumped with surprise.

"So what were you doing at the Deuce?" he said.

Toby held completely still in the seat. He didn't want to get into this again, to be forced to appease Luke while still validating the fact that he went to the Deuce. If he hadn't gone, he wouldn't have met Lily. Was it a mistake? Yes. No. But Luke rarely saw things other than black and white.

Toby played it off like it was nothing.

"I told you. I drove Jimmy."

Luke barely moved, only his head fell back against the seat as he sighed.

Toby couldn't take it anymore. "What?"

"First the Deuce. And missing school," Luke said. "And then . . ."

Luke stopped himself, but Toby didn't want anything left unsaid.

"And then what?"

"That woman at the plane," Luke said. "Drinking?"

This time, Toby looked out the window. Of course Luke was right about the wine, the beers he hadn't copped to yet.

But at the same time, if Luke wanted to live his life like a monk—that was his choice. Toby had made a mistake. And it wasn't one he wasn't going to repeat.

"Lily isn't a problem," Toby said.

Luke shrugged, and it was so dismissive, so arrogant. Toby reached out and gripped the steering wheel, already exhausted by the conversation.

"I don't know her . . . and neither do you."

"So just because we don't know somebody, that makes them bad? C'mon . . ."

Luke shrugged again. This time, it was the smug, know-it-all smile on his lips. The way he raised his eyebrows. So Toby used the only ammo he had—Annie.

"You know what, fuck you. You don't have shit to say to me about choices. Not lately."

Luke finally quit the cool act, turning to Toby, surprised.

"How many times do I need to apologize to you?"

Luke leaned toward Toby, their faces only inches apart. It was enough to make Toby shut up. They sat there in silence, the last stragglers in the parking lot beginning to make their way to the doors.

"I'm sorry," Luke said. "But I can't help it that Annie and I, you know . . ."

Toby knew he was fighting dirty, but he didn't understand

why Luke held him to a different standard. Why Annie was okay, but Lily was dangerous. Even thinking about it made Toby want to punch Luke.

"It's fine. I just . . ." Toby hit the steering wheel with his palm. "Lily's good for me. I promise you. She's just like us."

Luke stared at him for a long time. They didn't let people in very often. Because who else would understand? Their friendship had always been thicker than blood. Thicker than anything you could put up against it.

"I was going to bring her to see your match against Herrera," Toby said. "I want you to meet her."

Luke thought for a second and then said, "Sure."

The bell rang and they both looked toward the school, already late.

Toby had just finished a quiz on a short story called "Bullet in the Brain" when the speaker in the classroom came alive and asked him to come to the office. Mr. Geiger, the bearded, hippie teacher cracked a joke about the principal, and a few people laughed. Toby grabbed his bag and shuffled out of the room.

The last time he'd been called to the office, Jimmy had been arrested for a robbery charge he ultimately beat. The cops had come to see him under the auspices of child welfare, making sure that Toby would have a place to stay for the night. However, once they got Toby alone, it was evident to him that they were fishing—looking for any checkmark against Jimmy. For a moment, Toby thought about saying whatever they needed him to say. But the truth was, he didn't know a thing about Jimmy or his alleged involvement in a pawn-shop robbery. That night, they had a huge party at the trailer, the highlight being everybody racing around on these mini dirt bikes that had mysteriously appeared.

So when Toby got to the office, he took a deep breath and pushed through the heavy metal door. The room had the same otherworldly quality it usually did, as if the regular rules of space and time that applied in the hallways were suspended here. But that wasn't what threw Toby. It was Lily, dressed like one of his teachers and standing at the desk.

"There you are," she said, smiling.

"Now, Toby. I didn't know you had such a fabulous family member." Mr. Townsend, the principal, was practically drooling as he spoke. Toby caught his eyes flick up and down Lily.

He shrugged like, "I can't believe she's my . . . ?"

"Your cousin was just telling me how she's in from Seattle."

Cousin.

"Oh yeah. Her band broke up and she's trying out the domestic thing," Toby said. He turned to Lily, stone-faced.

"What was the name of your band? The Boone's Army?"

Lily nearly broke character, coughing out a laugh. Mr. Townsend's smile faded a degree, trying to read Toby's tone. Giving Lily a second look. He shook it off when she said, "I really appreciate you being cool about this, Bob."

Bob. Jesus, she was good.

"Well, it's good to know that Toby is, uh, on the mend. I think another day of rest is exactly what he needs"

He winked at Lily, who turned and smiled at Toby, like she had just pulled the biggest con ever. He wasn't sure what to do, except stand there and keep nodding. Neither Mr. Townsend nor Lily said anything for a long moment, and then Lily reached out and tapped Bob's hand lightly again.

"You're a lifesaver, Bob."

"Well," Mr. Townsend said, clearing his throat and reaching for the sign-out clipboard.

Lily signed the paper and put a hand on Toby's shoulder, leading him to the door. As they were going into the hallway, Toby started to ask a question and Lily shot him a death glare.

So he shut his mouth and walked out the doors of the school, into the bright, crisp day.

Lily was still tight-lipped and smiling. Toby kept looking

over, waiting for her to spill the secret. He'd just walked out of school with a woman he barely knew—that part, Luke *had* been right about. It was exhilarating. Like jumping into a pool of cold water. And he was still in shock.

When they got to Lily's car—a beat-up Ford Ranger— Toby couldn't wait any longer.

"Uh, you just broke me out of school."

"I was bored," she said, smiling at him. "And I thought maybe you'd want to be bored with me. Plus, it's Friday. They never teach you anything on Friday."

"Okay . . . but how did you get me out?"

Lily laughed once to herself. "Listen, I could've told Bob I was taking you back to my house to have wild sex, and he wouldn't have said a thing."

"Uh. You said you were my cousin. It might've raised a red flag or, like, five thousand."

She waved the concern away.

"I would've changed that part. Don't be ridiculous," Lily said. "The point is, people like Bob will do anything a woman tells him to do. I knew that as soon as I saw him. So no need to go with plan B."

"Oh my god," Toby said. "Do I want to know plan B?"

Lily smirked. "I was going to tell him I was your youth pastor and I needed you for an emergency prayer warrior meeting. And yes, I'm going to hell. But at least now you'll be there with me."

Toby laughed. "I didn't do anything!"

"You're complicit. You should go right back into that school. That's the only way your eternal salvation will stay secure. I'm sorry to tell you this."

Lily hopped into the truck and cranked the engine. Toby gave a perfunctory glance back to the school. Luke would have something to say about this. But it was a matter of opinion. This was either wrong, or it was a moment—something Toby would look back on for the rest of his life.

"You coming?" Lily asked, patting the seat with a devilish smile.

Toby pulled himself up into the truck and didn't look back as Lily sped across the parking lot and out onto the country highway that crossed in front of the school. The last thing Toby heard was the faint sound of the bell ringing. Telling everybody it was time to move.

January 23

T—

It's hard to explain what it feels like to live with an ax above your neck. It's like trying to describe love, or maybe even hate. They're both nothing but feelings, right? But they're real, more real than we probably know. And how are you going to describe love to somebody? That's what it's like in here: you may laugh sometimes. You might even get a few hours of sleep that aren't haunted each night. But then something happens, and it all comes flying right back at you like thousands of daggers. All of them pointed at you from the very start.

Man, I don't want to wake up one day and realize all of this has become normal.

And I worry that's what's happening to me, T.

Sister says that I can't hold on to all of this hopelessness. That I shouldn't wake up every day and think about how my life is basically over. Because there's more good than evil in the world and we're surrounded by what she calls "opportunities for joy." That joy is something that lives outside of circumstance.

I seriously don't even know what that means, T.

Sometimes I can't even remember good days, let alone a moment of joy. But of course, Sister pushed me. Usually, I'd just say something like "pizza" or "the sun"—anything to calm her down. Once she was gone, I'd forget all about it too. But for some reason, when I was alone, I got more and more desperate to find something. Anything.

It hit me in the middle of the night.

When we first found the plane.

Dude, I don't think I've ever seen you that happy. You were straight up dancing around that thing, remember? Maybe that day. That day it felt like we won something.

But other than that, every single day felt like shit stacked on top of more shit. So don't tell me that there's good out there. Don't tell me that we have to search it out or that some god is trying to make things right in this world. Because I don't buy it. Not for one second.

That doesn't stop Sister, of course. Even though she knows I'm not interested in any of that voodoo, she can't help herself. It's a part of her, buried deep. She could find out the world was ending and she'd probably still show up here, talking all that hope.

Here's the thing Sister doesn't get: hope isn't any help to me. Hope doesn't get me out of bed. If anything, hope will knife me when I'm not looking. Because as soon as you start hoping something's going to happen, you get irrational. You stop seeing the world for what it really is.

And I know you don't need any proof that we live in a bullshit world, but maybe this will be the first lesson for Sister.

Because they gave Eddie a date.

In two weeks, he'll be gone. They'll kill him. Forget he ever existed.

How are any of us ever supposed to have *hope*?

Luke

17

LUKE was standing at his locker when Annie came up behind him and grabbed him. He jumped like a little kid. When he turned around, she fell into him. Her body, her lips—everything.

"Hey."

She was still so close.

"Hey," Luke managed.

"So, tonight . . ."

Luke wanted to kiss her again, wanted to grab her hand and run out of the school. He didn't care about the fight with Toby. All he wanted was to be close to Annie. To let himself slowly become comfortable with her. To make this normal.

"Yeah?"

"I could come over to your apartment," Annie said.

"Yeah."

Luke hadn't intended it to be funny, but Annie laughed. Suddenly she looked at him shyly, as if this conversation was making her nervous.

"Do you know any other words?"

"Um, yes? That would be amazing."

The shyness dropped away, and she grinned big.

"*Amazing*. I like that," she said. "Say more things like that."

All Luke could say was, "Okay."

She leaned forward and gave him a kiss, way longer than a peck. And then she was gone.

Luke needed to find Toby. To get his read on the situation with Annie. This meant sex, he was pretty sure. But then, he could be totally wrong, and he didn't want Annie to walk into his apartment planning another trip to Wilco. Not that he wouldn't walk anywhere with her.

But he was kind of freaking out, and he needed Toby's advice.

He walked into a hallway he only set foot in when he was lost. Behind the doors of the classrooms, the kids seemed smarter. Better looking, even, as they studied for AP tests and talked about GPAs and class rank. A world Luke didn't know anything about. Toby told him that when he graduated, he could've had almost a year's worth of college credit if Jimmy would've sprung for the test fees.

Luke was pretty sure Toby had physics this period, so he peeked into the classroom as the room began to fill up. The teacher was at his desk, oblivious. Luke stood outside, nodding when people recognized him and said hello. One of his teammates slapped him on the shoulder. When the bell rang, Luke looked into the room one last time, as if he could've missed Toby. There was one empty desk, all the way in the back.

Of course there were reasons Toby wouldn't be in class. But just to be sure, he feigned an excuse for the school police officer, who used to wrestle years ago and, as a result, liked Luke. Luke didn't need to go more than a few feet into the parking lot to see the El Camino sitting just where they'd left it that morning.

Luke relaxed as he walked back inside. On his way back to class, he stopped at the office to get a pass. As soon as he walked inside, the principal smiled.

"Hey there, Luke," he said. "Next week's the big match, right?"

"Yes, sir."

"Are you ready?"

He nodded. "Coach O thinks so."

"I wrestled my freshman year," Mr. Townsend said. "But then I hurt my shoulder and decided to become a hall monitor instead."

Luke didn't realize it was a joke until the principal smiled. Luke gave him a gracious chuckle.

"I was looking for Toby, and I need a pass," he said. "If that's okay."

"Toby?" Mr. Townsend said. "Oh, he left for the weekend."

Luke's mouth dropped open. "He . . . left. With who?"

Mr. Townsend smiled big, leaning against the big desk that dominated the room. "With his cousin, Lily. I suppose you know her."

Luke went cold. He should say something, but nothing came out. Every instinct told him to run out of school, hotwire the El Camino, and chase them across the entire state of North Carolina if he had to.

But what would that do?

He'd apologized to Toby. He'd pushed him up against a tree and gotten in his face. Short of chaining him to his side, Luke had done everything he could to keep Toby from making the mistake he seemed intent on making. And even though it killed him, Luke couldn't do it anymore. If Toby wanted to chase Lily around, getting drunk and skipping school, that was on him.

He took the pass from Mr. Townsend and said, "I don't know her. At all."

When he saw Annie at lunch, he was still surprisingly calm. He didn't even tell her about Toby until she looked around and said, "Are we going to be graced with his presence today?"

"He left," was all Luke said.

Annie stopped picking at what was left of her pizza and stared at him. "Like, he ditched school? Again?"

Luke nodded and took a bite of the apple he'd gotten from Coach O earlier.

"Are we going to find him?" Annie asked.

"No," Luke said.

This wasn't about Jimmy anymore. Right now Toby's biggest threat was himself. Annie still looked worried, like she thought Luke was going to run out of the school in a craze.

"He met this girl," Luke said. "Or woman, actually. She's like twenty-something, I'm sure. *Lily*." He spit out her name like a piece of spoiled meat.

"Whoa. I never thought the little guy had it in him," Annie said, giving up on the pizza.

Normally that would've cracked Luke up. Because it was true: for all the shit he talked, neither of them would've ever dreamed he could pick up an older woman at a bar. Of course Toby would've told you all about his plans, his *destiny*—because that's a word he'd use—but it would be bullshit. Something Luke would eventually laugh away.

"Are you sure you don't want to go look for him?"

Luke thought about this for a long time, or at least it seemed like a long time. He'd never understand why Toby left. But like every other fascination Toby cultivated, Lily was ultimately temporary. Something that would be gone from their lives in weeks, if not days.

He shook his head and stood up.

"No. This is on him."

18

THEY drove through the afternoon until the sun dipped into the Blue Ridge Mountains. Toby watched Lily the whole time. As she turned up the radio. Fought with her hair, pulling it into a ponytail and letting it go countless times. They were somewhere near Conover when she turned up the music and sang loudly, then looked to see if Toby was laughing, a dash of embarrassment in her eyes.

It was only when they stopped moving—at a lonely stoplight close to the county line—that the adrenaline of leaving school with Lily released its grip on Toby's brain. Enough to question what he was doing. Luke would be pissed when he figured it out. That much was certain. And it's not like Toby didn't know skipping school with a woman he barely knew could bring unintended consequences. But he liked it. He *liked* finally feeling like he was risking something that didn't end with a possible fist to the face.

He reached over and turned up the radio a little louder, matching Lily's volume. She raised her eyebrows, impressed, and they raced away once the light changed to green. Lily pulled off the road and guided the truck into an abandoned parking lot. An empty building, crumbling and covered in kudzu, sagged in front of them. Toby laughed. She pushed her sunglasses down on her nose, as if she'd been expecting this response for hours.

"You're going to like this," she said.

He wanted to tell her it didn't matter where they were going, what they were doing. He wanted to turn up the music so loud that Luke could hear it back at school. Instead, he nodded at the building.

"If I had to pick a place somebody was going to kill me . . ."

"Stop. I want to show you something."

She drove around to the back of the building. When they got out of the car, a few birds rose up, disappearing into the bright sky. Other than that, everything was still. They were in the sticks, completely isolated from everything. Toby looked around.

"You sure you didn't come out here to take advantage of me?"

"Well, maybe *that*." She nodded toward one of the doors. "C'mon."

Lily wiped years of dust and dirt from the window. The graphic underneath was at least twenty, maybe thirty years old. A cartoon sun sat underneath a palm tree, holding a coconut drink. The dialogue bubble above its head read TANNED, TONED, AND *READY!*

"What . . ."

"Trust me," Lily said, looking around before forcing the door open.

The inside was dusty, maybe simply dirty at this point. Every step they took kicked up more. Posters hung on the walls everywhere, yellowed by the sun. BERMUDA! JAMAICA! EVER THOUGHT ABOUT AFRICA? BOOK TODAY! Each one was more ridiculous than the next. Toby turned around, confused.

"This is like the time my mom told me having an imaginary friend was as good as a real friend," he said. "But really, thank you for bringing me to see all . . . this."

"This isn't it. I mean, it is. But just the beginning."

She reached out and squeezed his arm before leading him across the room to another door Toby hadn't seen. Lily opened it, kicking away empty bottles and crumpled newspaper. When Toby walked through, he couldn't help himself—he laughed. There was a huge, ancient-looking tanning bed.

"I trust you. I really do," Toby said. This time, Lily hit him.

"Still not it. Jesus."

Yet another room was filled with what looked like boxes of uninflated Mylar balloons. When they came to the final door, Toby had no idea what to expect—a video store filled with VHS tapes? A miniature zoo? But this door was different from the others. There was a new knob, a new deadbolt. Lily pulled a set of keys from her pocket, turned the lock, and pushed the door open. Inside, the room was bigger and lighter than the previous two. On the wall read IREDELL COUNTY TRAVEL MUSEUM. There were boxes and glass cases everywhere.

"What the hell is this place?"

"I found it once when I was . . ." Lily trailed off, running a finger across a dusty display case filled with old steamer tickets, diner car menus, and various advertisements for trips around the world. "I thought it was the coolest place ever. The kind of place that could lead you anywhere, you know? I used to come up here, always telling myself I was going to leave. And then one day I did."

Toby looked around. He wanted to tap into whatever nostalgia was taking over Lily's entire body, but it was just a room full of old shit.

"You're not impressed," she said.

He nodded half-heartedly. "I mean, it's interesting. I have no idea why it's out here."

Lily drew a heart in the dust, an arrow through the heart. When she looked up at Toby, she smiled.

"It's my plane," she said.

They sat on the tailgate of the truck, the air already beginning to cross over from chilly to cold. Lily wrapped her arms around her body and pushed herself closer to Toby, who was freezing too. She shivered once and stood up, walking up the bed of the truck and reaching through the cab window to pull out two blankets. The first one she placed flat on the bed. The other one she wrapped around her shoulders as she sat next to Toby.

"I wanted to go to Ford," she said absently. "I went to Tabernacle instead. You know, the Christian school? Anyway, Dad didn't want me having any bad influences."

"Purity," Toby said.

Lily chuckled. "Making sure kids didn't listen to rock-and-roll music since Moses."

"When did you graduate?"

Lily shook her head. "You'll think I'm old."

"I already think you're old," Toby said, smiling up to the sky. There were stars. "C'mon. Like I care. What are you . . . twenty-seven?"

She laughed. "Well, I didn't think I looked *that* old!"

Toby's body went hot, and he tried to explain. Lily shook her head, graciously stopping him from doing any more damage.

"Twenty-two," she said. "At least for a little longer."

Toby shifted sideways, so he could see her better. He stared at the side of her face, thinking.

"We could've been in school together. If you'd gone to Ford, that is. We might've known each other."

"Like I would've ever given your skinny ass the time of day," she said, trying not to smile. When she failed, she rolled her eyes and leaned back into the bed. Toby froze as she playfully tapped the side of her foot against his hip, tapping it again and again like she was keeping time. He took a deep breath and slowly lowered himself down next to her, one hundred percent sure she was going to yell, or worse—laugh. Instead she scooted closer to him, their ears almost touching.

He could feel her breathing next to him, could see the puffs of steam rising from her mouth before disappearing into the cold sky. Suddenly Toby was very warm. And he decided to push it.

"You could probably still go to jail for all this," Toby said.

"Wouldn't be the first time," Lily said.

Toby turned onto his side, his mouth open. "What—
how? Are you saying I'm not the first guy you've brought
here?"

Lily smiled, her face lit by the stars. "Yeah, because
I totally go around picking up high-school dudes on the
reg."

"I don't know your life," he said, laughing.

She turned and hit Toby, which he took gracefully.
Anything to connect. Anything to feel her against his
body.

Lily was staring at him, the same smile playing on her
lips. "Jesus. You're cute as hell."

Toby coughed. Tried to say something smooth. Nothing
came out.

"Have I finally got you speechless?"

And he was. The way she was looking at him right
then—nobody had ever looked at him like that, like she
was going to keep him forever. Like she could devour him.
Instead, she leaned forward and kissed Toby lightly on the
lips.

It was the single most erotic thing Toby had ever
experienced.

"Oh shit. You look freaked out," Lily said. "I thought you
wanted me to do that."

Toby kissed her back, pushing himself closer to her body, which was so warm. The entire kiss was messy, but glorious. Lily pulled back slightly, their noses still touching.

"Are you okay with this?"

"Oh my god, yes."

The words were barely out of his mouth when she dove on top of him.

January 25

T—

Marilyn came in today, armed with her usual stack of papers and folders, like a hurricane of white and yellow. She was picking through some file and making small talk while I sat there thinking about Eddie.

Dudes in here have a way of isolating you, a sort of passive violence. Like they're already erasing you from their minds, from the world. Once people found out about Eddie's date, they immediately started treating him like he was infected. As if those judges and prosecutors would catch a whiff of them too. Start handing out dates like they were candy.

Anyway, I was off in some other world when I realized Marilyn was staring at me. Waiting for me to answer a question I hadn't heard. Before she could ask the question again, I was like, "What's going to happen to Eddie?"

She looked down at one of her folders, picking at the corner. When she looked up, she smiled politely and told me it wasn't the best use of our time to talk about other people's cases.

She opened her folder, but I was like, "How long is it going to take? You know, how long does he have?"

This time when she smiled, it wasn't polite. It was the way the woman at the gas station would smile at us, knowing we were stealing. Maybe knowing that we needed it. It wasn't pity; more like a patient empathy. She closed the folder and cleared her throat.

"Well, when an execution warrant is signed . . ."

She paused, like she wasn't sure I could take hearing it. But man, she has to know—I've been hearing this stuff my whole life. Maybe not these words, but second, third cousins to them.

"When that happens, they'll typically move the client . . . um, Eddie, to a death-watch area."

I nodded. She hesitated but kept talking.

"That could happen immediately, but it might also take a few days, because this is the first execution in North Carolina in, well, in a while."

A few days, man. It hit me hard. Eddie would be here, and then he wouldn't. There would be a hole in the world, and there wasn't any reason for it. It's not like he's sick or had an accident. And if that weren't fucked up enough, people would be *happy* he was gone. This is a dude who hasn't done shit to anybody in fifteen years. And they're going to kill him.

It doesn't make any sense, T.

My entire body felt overloaded. I couldn't get enough air, and every time I opened my mouth, I felt like I was going to choke. Like somebody had put a giant block of ice in the middle of my throat. Marilyn stopped talking and cleared her throat one more time, picking up my file like she was ready to get started. But what she said next, man, that's what really killed me.

"I'm sorry, Luke. I really am."

Luke

19

ANNIE and Luke were already in the kitchen cooking spaghetti when the boys' bus dropped them off and they came rampaging up the stairs. If being left alone yesterday had affected them, it didn't dampen their excitement for the coming meal. They jumped around, asking if there was garlic bread. Telling Annie that she was the best cook they'd ever met. They didn't seem to notice that Doreen and Ricky still weren't back. When Luke tried to help, Annie pushed him into the living room and told him to find a movie.

She brought the plates out to them, and the steaming pasta was met with *oohs* from the twins. Annie handed Luke his plate last. It had a single noodle on it.

"We can't take any chances," she said, knocking his knee with hers. He stood up and went to get a small helping. He skipped the garlic bread, though. When he came back into the living room, Annie put a hand to her heart.

"Are you sure? What if your tights don't fit for the match Monday?"

"It's called a singlet," Luke said. "And it will be fine."

She leaned close to Luke and whispered, "Maybe you can put it on for me later."

Luke's entire body went flush and he stammered, "It's at school. In my locker."

"Too bad for you," she said, leaning back on the couch and taking a bite of her garlic bread.

Once dinner was finished, the boys sat between Annie and Luke, talking nonstop about the movie Luke had put in. Had she seen it? Did she have a DVD player, because they'd gotten this VHS player at a thrift store for only five dollars—*Five dollars!* The movie was something Luke hadn't seen yet, animated and fifty cents from the same store. Instead, he watched Annie, doing it as subtly as he could. Still, she'd catch him every so often, smiling as she played with Petey's hair. Nodding her head as she listened to Jack-Jack explain how he thought girls should have been allowed to be soldiers back in ancient China.

They fell asleep well before the movie ended, but Luke let them lie on the couch until the credits rolled. He picked up Jack-Jack and took him to the bedroom. It smelled like sweat and cigarettes. He put his brother on the mattress in the corner and turned on the fan. As he was leaving, Annie appeared in the doorway, holding Petey.

"Where should I put him?" she whispered.

Luke looked around the room, as if he didn't know where to put Petey. But it wasn't that. He was looking at the ashtray. The piles of clothes. The half-broken mini blind that would surely invalidate their deposit if they ever moved out. He didn't want Annie to see this, even if it wasn't his fault. He didn't want her to see how they only had one bedroom, how the boys had to share a twin mattress in the corner.

Annie saw Jack-Jack and pushed past Luke. When she had both boys covered, she walked back to Luke, smiling. She must have seen the embarrassment on his face, because she came close and whispered in his ear.

"I don't care. I'll never care."

Luke couldn't pull up from the nosedive he was on, so she forced him to look away from the bedroom, only into her eyes, until he finally got the message. He moved slowly toward her, not closing his eyes until their lips touched. He didn't know where the electricity came from, how it was powered. But once again his body was completely on.

"We should go to the living room," she whispered, so close to his face that when he nodded, he almost hit her. They both laughed. Both looked to the mattress. Neither of the boys had moved.

They sat on the couch, trying to stay connected. Touching in simple, almost accidental ways. Luke wanted to kiss her again, but whatever bravery he'd mustered had been left behind in the shadows of his mom's room.

Annie was quiet for a few seconds. When she spoke, the bravado was gone. "So, do you want to, you know . . . go get those things?"

"What?"

She rolled her eyes. "The condoms. You know."

Luke wanted to sprint to the bedroom, because he did know. He *knew*. He tried to play it cool, though. Sat there and nodded like it wasn't a big deal. Just another Friday night.

"If you want to," he said.

"I think I do."

So Luke stood up, trying to cross his legs as he did—hoping that situation would calm down a bit before he got back to the couch. He power walked through the kitchen and tiptoed into the room, trying not to be weirded out that his mom not only had condoms, but actually thought it was helpful to tell Annie where to find them. Not that he was complaining. Because if he was being completely honest, he wasn't sure this would be happening if his mom hadn't told Annie.

They were hidden under an empty pack of cigarettes, a long string of squares that looked more like candy than he thought they should. How many did they need? He took them all.

Annie was still sitting on the couch. She had the remote in her hand and was rewinding the movie. Luke shoved the condoms in his pocket before he went back into the living room, momentarily worried she'd been joking. But when he sat down next to her, she moved closer. Put a hand on his thigh and rubbed it, slowly. He was almost too scared to move, to do anything. But he forced himself to reach over and kiss her, missing her lips and only getting a mouthful of hair.

She laughed and turned toward him. "So . . ."

He pulled the condoms out of his pocket. "I have no idea what to do with these."

"You're not giving me much confidence," Annie teased.

"It's just—I've never, you know . . ." Luke didn't want to finish the sentence. It wasn't like he didn't know what to do—Toby alone had given him enough information to last a lifetime. He just wasn't sure if he was supposed to tell Annie about his lack of experience. He wasn't sure if that would make it better or worse.

"It's fine," Annie said, turning off the light.

And in the darkness—the movie, paused, making it seem like this moment could last forever—they kissed, undressing each other with fumbling hands. Laughing the whole time.

20

TOBY covered himself with his T-shirt as they lay in the back of Lily's truck, staring at the sky and talking about anything other than what had just happened. Not that Toby didn't want to relive every single moment of it. But Lily was talking about Seattle, a place Toby could barely picture, let alone care about the weather.

"It doesn't really rain there. Not like it does here," she said. "I mean, it rains all the time. But it's light. A constant drizzle. Like this."

She ran her fingers lightly up Toby's arm, making him shiver.

"It sounds cool."

"And everything is always green. You've never seen green like that."

Toby didn't know what else to say. He'd never been a "Southern by the grace of God" type, but he also couldn't imagine anything outside of North Carolina. Even when he and Luke talked about going to Iowa, he always came up against a brick wall. A road that only went so far in his imagination.

Lily turned on her side, still naked. Toby tried not to look at her, a weird politeness considering their new familiarity. He looked into her eyes instead, to the point that it might've been creepy.

"We should go," Toby said. "This summer."

She laughed, thinking Toby was joking. It hurt his feelings at first, and then she said, "I thought you were moving to Iowa. With your friend."

Lily sat up and shimmied into her shirt. Then she pulled on her pants. Toby was suddenly bashful of his nakedness. When they'd started, it had been wild. She'd shucked him like a piece of corn, throwing his clothes in all directions. He was naked and she was on top of him before he even had a chance to process what was happening. Or to be more accurate, what had happened. It was over not long after that, both of them in the back of truck and her breathing so hard it sounded like she might be crying. Him, too scared to move.

"It's not like we have a plan," Toby said, reaching for his shirt. He held it in front of him as Lily jumped down from the bed.

"You don't need a plan to go somewhere." She threw his pants to him. "Trust me, I know from experience. You just decide and go."

Toby had been avoiding bigger questions about his and Luke's "plan" for months, mostly because Luke told him not to worry. They'd figure it out. Still, they lurked. For years, the questions hadn't mattered because leaving was so far away. But the closer they got to graduation, the more Toby wondered how he fit in.

"Well, what if I just decided I wanted to go to Seattle?" Toby said.

Lily kind of smiled as she pulled on her boots, but she didn't respond immediately. When she was completely dressed, she leaned against the bed of the truck and stared at Toby.

"Listen, I have a life in Seattle. Do you realize how hard it is to just move somewhere?"

"But you just said . . ." Toby stopped himself. "When are you going back?"

"As soon as I can buy a ticket," she said. "Train. Bus. I don't even care."

"Why not drive?" Toby asked. The truck was a beater, but it could surely make the trip. He had a sudden vision of them driving down sun-soaked highways. Ending each day in the bed of the pickup, sleeping under the stars.

Lily patted the truck one time and shook her head. "Some things need to stay here."

Toby scooted to the end of the truck, and Lily handed him his boots. "Okay, so how much does a train or bus ticket cost?"

"A lot," Lily said, running her hands through her hair. She smiled quickly, like she'd just said something impolite. Toby had seen this before.

He'd been blown off plenty of times before, most notably by a girl named Becky who'd given him her phone number at the mall. At first they talked every night. Jimmy would sometimes come in and make him get off, but fifteen, thirty minutes later, they were back on. Talking until his mouth was dry. And then one day she started making excuses. Suddenly she wasn't racing her mom to the phone. When he finally did get her, he could hear her friends laughing somewhere in the background as she explained that she was really busy. That she didn't have time for a boyfriend.

"Hey . . . is everything okay?" Toby felt stupid asking, considering they had been grinding into each other just moments before. Lily's eyes went wide, like something from a cartoon.

"What? Why?" She laughed and gave him a hug, which

felt just as fraudulent. "Are you getting weird on me, buddy?"

Buddy. Toby tried to ignore all of this, to let himself be cool with whatever might happen. He didn't want to assign too much meaning to the sex, and neither, it seemed, did Lily.

He could do this.

"No, sorry. I'm just trying to wrap my head around what happened," he said. "You might be surprised, but I don't get a lot of requests for sex in the back of pickup trucks. Or anywhere, really."

"And I didn't really request it, did I?" Lily said, biting her lip. She came over and sat next to Toby on the tailgate. "Listen, I don't want you to get the wrong idea. I like hanging out with you. And that was fun. I'd like to do it again, maybe. But when it comes to Seattle, I'm . . ."

She blew air between her lips.

"I have to make sure I don't get stuck here. And I'm really, really close to making it happen. You know?"

Toby didn't know why these were separate things, but he nodded and, for maybe the first time in his life, didn't say every word that was coming shooting into his brain. She patted him on the thigh.

"Want to see something else even cooler?"

"Cooler than all this?" Toby deadpanned, trying to rally

himself. "I really hope it's an abandoned hosiery mill. Oh! Or maybe a raccoon-infested bus station!"

Lily's eyes narrowed. "You're making me rethink my decision to get you naked."

Toby jumped off the tailgate and stood at attention. He zipped his lips and saluted, which made Lily laugh.

"Okay, okay. Calm down."

She led Toby to the side of the building and stopped in front of two restroom doors—both padlocked.

"Even if you told me to take my wildest guess, I never would've picked *bathroom*," Toby said, laughing. Lily rolled her eyes, but Toby didn't stop. "Let me guess. This is where you hide the World's Largest Bag of Grits. Or maybe—"

She reached out and put a finger on his lips. When he stopped talking, she produced a single key and unlocked the bathroom. Before she opened the door, she turned to Toby.

"When I came back, I thought I was going to be able to sell my dad's house and leave immediately," she said. "But I guess he left the house to the church, which . . . whatever. They're letting me stay there until I figure things out."

Lily wrapped both her arms around her body like she was trying to keep herself from flying away. She looked up to the sky, and her face went from distant to angry in a flash. Just as quickly, it all drained out of her.

"Anyway, now things are figured out."

She pushed the door open, and the bathroom was crammed with hundreds of boxes. There was an opening big enough for the door and one person, but the rest of the room was nothing but cardboard. Toby stepped inside and pried one of the boxes open. It was full of cigarette cartons.

"Where did you get these?"

"They're not mine. Not *really*. I'm just holding them for a day or so."

Toby looked around at the boxes, stacked deep into the surprisingly large bathroom. He did some quick math. "There's a couple hundred thousand dollars of cigarettes in here."

"Maybe more," Lily said.

Toby closed the box and paused, trying to figure out what to say. "You realize you can go to prison for this."

"Hopefully not."

He turned around and stared at Lily. She looked like she wanted to say more but was forcing herself to stay quiet. When he walked back outside, she immediately padlocked the door and—looking around the empty lot—started walking back to her truck. Toby followed, watching every movement Lily made.

* * *

Toby didn't say much as they drove back to the school to pick up his car. He was trying to put together the pieces. The way Lily had casually shown him the cigarettes, as if trafficking stolen cigarettes—and they had to be stolen; he couldn't see it any other way—was as normal as a trip to the store. If anyone had taken those cigarettes across state lines at any point, it was a felony. They'd do real time. Toby wasn't sure if him seeing them could be trouble, but he wasn't going to take any chances. As far as he was concerned, he would never acknowledge that bathroom ever again. Still, something troubled Toby.

He looked over at Lily. The headlights from passing cars highlighted her face every few seconds.

"What are you going to do with those?"

Lily seemed to be far away. She shook her head, as if she was trying to wake herself up.

"Sell them."

"Where did you get them?"

"I didn't. Somebody asked me if I wanted in and . . . well, I don't have a hot-shit wrestler for a friend. So this is my escape plan."

Toby didn't return her smile. He looked out his window, thinking. They were pulling into the school parking lot when Toby turned to her.

"How much does a train ticket to Seattle cost?"

Lily thought about it for a second. "Five hundred, maybe a thousand dollars?"

Relief shot through Toby. She didn't have to do this. She didn't have to worry about cigarettes or anything illegal. They could make this work.

"You could get a job—hell, *I* could get a job. I'd be happy to help you. It wouldn't take a month, maybe two to make that much money."

Lily stared out the window as she answered. "Do you know how expensive Seattle is?"

Toby wanted her to look him in the eye. He wanted her to accept his help, which he would give blindly. Completely. But more importantly, he wanted her to see that she didn't even have to go to Seattle. What was in Seattle? They could go to Charlotte or Greensboro together. Or maybe even back up to Asheville. Camping in the woods and living off vending machines. It sounded like heaven to Toby.

"You don't have to go to Seattle," he said.

Lily sighed and then turned to look at him, smiling. "I know you want to get out of here. I do too. And this is the way I'm going to do that. Okay?"

For a second, Lily closed her eyes. When she opened them and stared at Toby, he realized she'd been working up the resolve to say something he wouldn't like.

"Listen, I think I made a mistake. . . ."

Toby dropped his head. He had no idea what was happening, or why she was suddenly pushing him away. He laughed to himself.

"Usually girls tell me that before I get the chance to have sex with them," Toby said.

Lily's face softened, and she took Toby's hands. "It's not that. I just . . . You have to understand that I can't stay here. I can't get stuck. And I'm afraid if we do this too much, that's exactly what's going to happen."

"But . . ."

Lily smiled, and it made him forget all his objections.

"Give me the weekend, let me figure this stuff out. And then we can talk. Okay?"

Toby didn't get a chance to answer. Lily leaned over and kissed him like he was going to war. Afterward, she wiped her lips as Toby got out of the truck with barely a word. He stood there for a moment, waiting for her to say something—anything.

"I like you," she said.

"Thank you."

She chuckled once, and for a moment, Toby thought she might get out of the truck. But she gave him one last smile before slowly pulling out of the empty parking lot. Toby didn't move, watching until her taillights disappeared.

Bo and Jimmy were sitting at the kitchenette table, a case of beer open between them. They were laughing, tipping cans back. As soon as Toby walked into the trailer, Jimmy folded up a notebook they'd been writing in and nodded at Bo.

"Look at this kid," he said.

"I'm looking," Bo said.

Toby tried to read the look on Jimmy's face. The smirk, which really didn't tell him anything. His tone was light, the words playful. Toby reached for a beer—because, fuck it—opened it, and took a long drink. It still made him gag.

"Shiiiitt," Bo said, hitting the table as he laughed. "This kid is just like you, Jimmy. I swear to God. Doesn't give a *fuck*."

Normally, Toby would bristle at being compared to Jimmy. But right now, he just wanted to go back to Lily's house and sweep her away. To make her believe they could both be happy, could forget everything about this bastard town.

Jimmy stood up and took a few steps toward Toby. He put his hand on his chin, like he was investigating a crime.

"This is a dude who just got his dick wet," Jimmy said, finally laughing.

Toby brought the beer to his lips, trying to deflect the question. "I don't know what you're talking about."

"Boy, don't even try to lie to me. Look at his neck, Bo."

Bo leaned over and laughed—was it a bite? Some errant lipstick? Toby didn't know.

"I hope you wore a rubber," Jimmy said, opening another beer.

Toby laughed nervously and tried to walk away. If he could end it here, there wouldn't be any problem. Just get back in the El Camino and drive away. His dad stopped him.

"C'mon, I want to hear about this."

His hand was hard against Toby's abdomen, and Toby wasn't sure if he could push through it. When he relaxed, Jimmy lowered his arm.

"There's nothing to say," Toby said.

Jimmy laughed, looked over at Bo, who didn't say anything as he smiled and swallowed beer at the same time. "So who was it? Hazel?"

Hazel was easily fifty, if not older, and a more regular part of the Deuce than the cheap beer and watered-down metal bands that toured through. Toby shook his head, horrified. Bo about died right there.

"He'd need some WD-40 to dust that thing off," Bo said.

His dad kept naming names—Jenny? Twyla? Who was

that one girl who dated the state trooper?—and Toby shook his head to each of them, trying to think up a name that wouldn't have consequences. Wouldn't have a connection.

"Hell, it wasn't Doreen, was it? That would be really fucked up."

Toby took a drink of beer, hoping the answer would come like a prophetic vision. A prayer with every ounce he swallowed. Jimmy called for another beer and Bo tossed it to him. He opened it and smiled.

"I'm messing with you," he finally said, draining his beer. He burped loudly and then turned to Bo. "You got everything we need?"

Bo nodded, but he was still smiling at Toby. His smile was different from Jimmy's, which was a kind of mean-spirited playfulness. This was harder, like he not only knew Toby was lying, but knew the truth. Bo fingered the top of his beer and watched Toby until Jimmy yelled his name from outside. Without a word, Bo stood up, grabbed the beer, and walked out the door.

Toby lay down on the couch, trying to go to sleep. But every time he closed his eyes, he saw Lily. He felt her against his body. Fifteen minutes later he was up and in the El Camino, driving to her house.

As he drove, Toby encountered a brief moment of panic.

Was he being weird? Probably. But he wanted to think it was more sweet than pathetic. He imagined her opening the door, a wry smile on her face. At first, she'd play at being angry—"I told you we were taking the weekend." Something. And Toby would nod, biting his lip because he was going against the plan. What he'd say next would have to seal the deal. It would have to be perfect.

But when he pulled into her driveway, the house was completely dark. Even the porch light was off. He still knocked, thinking maybe she was asleep. After two more attempts, both louder than the last, he went back to the car to wait.

January 26

T—

I was still thinking about Eddie went I went to bed tonight. He's always been upfront about what he's done. About who he used to be. And man, I want to believe that I'm like that too. But every time Eddie gets done talking, he's smiling. I don't even know who I used to be, let alone who I am right now, T.

After I confessed, they sent me straight to get sentenced. And that went quick because I wouldn't help the lawyer at all. Sister says I was still in shock about what I'd done. I guess that's the technical term for it, *shock*. But when I hear that word, I think it should mean something that sets you off. Something that's alive, right? But there wasn't anything alive about me then. I was walking around in a cloud, one of those thick ones that don't come around North Carolina that much.

You remember when we hiked up to camp on Bakers Mountain and the fog rolled in? That's what I called it—fog. Of course you knew how far up we were, we had to go that high to make sure the sheriff's deputies didn't see us. And you were like, "This ain't fog, dude. This is a damn cloud!" You were adamant about that shit too. I'm cracking up thinking about how your face looked. Like you were ready to fight me.

That night, after you fell asleep, I got out of my sleeping bag and walked around. I can't remember why I couldn't sleep. Maybe Doreen had done something. Or your dad. But how did I not fall off the side of that mountain? I couldn't see a damn thing. I think we were what—fourteen?

Anyway, that's what it felt like sitting in that courtroom. Like I was stuck in some kind of fog and I couldn't escape. I was so pissed off. At myself. At you. At the whole world, T. Sister was right about that much. My lawyer asked me to give him a name of somebody who would come to speak for me. You know Coach would've come. Annie. Somebody. But I kept my mouth shut the whole time. I let the newspapers and everybody else tell the world who I was.

A killer. A monster. A tragic story all around.

As I'm sitting here in my cell, middle of the night, trying to write so nobody can see or hear me, I don't know how to think about all that.

We'll Fly Away

Am I supposed to say I'm sorry? Can I even do that now? And who am I supposed to apologize to anyway? You, maybe. If I'm being completely truthful, there are moments when I see your face and it's everything I can do to stop myself from bashing my head against the wall.

Luke

21

THEY'D spent the night content to do nothing but explore each other's bodies. Sleeping had never been something Luke enjoyed so much, their arms and legs intertwined. When the first light of morning peeked through the blinds of the apartment, Luke leaned over and kissed Annie gently on the ear. She giggled.

"I could get used to this," she said.

"Well, what do you think about Iowa?"

It came out confident, but now that the words were floating between them, Luke worried she'd dismiss the idea of coming with him in a hundred different ways. She tried to turn and face him, but instead fell off the couch, laughing as she lay there. Luke slid off and joined her on the floor.

"I'm going to get dressed before your brothers wake up."

Luke reached for her playfully and she laughed again, jumping out of his reach. She looked over her shoulder just before she turned the corner and disappeared into the bath-room. Luke stood up and got himself dressed. He probably needed a shower, but he could do that after the twins were awake. Other than that, he tried to make the living room look like he and Annie hadn't been having sex all night.

Somebody knocked on the door.

When the second knock came before he could even take a step, Luke knew it was Toby. Normally he'd push his way into the apartment, already halfway into a sentence and forcing Luke to play catch-up. But when Luke opened the door, he was standing on the landing, looking small in the weak parking-lot light.

"Hey," Luke said. He stepped onto the landing, closing the door behind him. Toby kicked his heel into the concrete. It didn't escape Luke that he wouldn't look him in the eye. Could barely keep himself still.

"You okay?" Luke finally asked.

"Spectacular," he said.

"You look like shit," Luke said.

"Well . . ."

Toby looked so run-down, and it shook Luke. This was the bottom of the ocean for both of them, the farthest away they could go from the plans they'd made. Luke had to decide he didn't care about being right anymore. Because they were out of their depth. But if he was going to do it, he needed Toby to come up for breath with him.

"Do we have a plan?" Toby asked.

"A plan? For what?"

Toby's eyes shot up, searching Luke's face. "About next year. Iowa."

Luke leaned back against the wall in relief. He had no idea what had precipitated this, but it was at least a question he could answer.

"Of course, T. We're going. As soon as we can." The answer hadn't changed since he signed that paper. "Unless you changed your mind?"

Toby stopped kicking his heel and sighed. "Where are we going to live? Or more importantly, where am I going to live? What happens to me when we get to Iowa and there's no place for me? What if they make you live in a dorm, which I'm pretty sure they're going to do?"

He paced like a caged animal, and Luke had no idea why. They had months to figure this out. And they would do just that—figure it out.

"I don't understand. We can . . ."

"Of course you don't understand. Of course."

Luke threw up his hands. "Just tell me! Don't come here acting all mysterious. I've been through everything with you, man. *Everything.* And now because you meet some girl, you think I'm going to change my mind?"

"This isn't about her," Toby said.

"Yeah? Well, I bet if she showed up right now, you wouldn't take a second look in my direction. That is, until you need me to help you fix it. Then you'll come running back just like you always do."

"Fuck you," Toby said, pointing a finger in Luke's face.

"Get your hand out of my face."

"Or what? You're going to hit me?"

Luke faltered, and he stood there wordless and wondering what he could say to get through to Toby. Behind them, the door opened. Annie was holding Jack-Jack, who was rubbing the sleep out of his eyes.

"You guys woke him up," Annie said, glaring at Luke. When Jack-Jack saw Toby, he bolted awake.

"Did you spend the night too?" he asked Toby, looking around at all of them. When no one answered, he said, "Annie will make you Mickey Mouse pancakes if you want."

Toby shook his head. "I only eat regular, round—American—pancakes."

Jack-Jack turned to Annie, his face worried. She leaned her forehead against his and said, "I got this. Go get your brother up for me, okay?"

He ran screaming into the apartment. When he was out of earshot, Annie turned to Toby and Luke and gave them a clipped smile.

"You two should come inside."

They both paused, waiting for the other to say something. To apologize. But Toby waited for Luke and Luke waited for Toby and when the wind blew, it shook Luke violently. He nodded to the door.

"It's freezing out here. Do you want to come in or not?"

Luke could hear Annie gathering the boys in the kitchen. The twins laughed, almost immediately followed by one telling the other to stop. Toby walked past Luke, into the living room.

Annie was singing in the kitchen, the boys helping her mix the batter. Before Luke could even sit down, Toby sighed and said, "Well, it's obvious you two fucked."

Luke nearly fell down. His eyes shot to the kitchen, making sure the boys—Annie—hadn't heard him. When he turned back, Toby was stretching out on the couch.

"What the hell, man?" Luke said.

"Dude, she's in there making *breakfast*. You guys are practically married."

Luke looked into the kitchen. Annie was smiling down at the boys and, for a moment, he wondered: is this good enough? Sure, Iowa was great. The type of opportunity only a few thousand people have ever gotten. But there was more than one way to escape. More than one way to be happy.

"This is my fault—I never told you," Toby said. "You don't have to marry the first person who touches you."

"Please shut up," Luke said, checking the kitchen again. Annie had two plates in her hands, pointed for the living room. The anger he had felt earlier was replaced by a rapid embarrassment. But when Annie walked into the room, Luke and Toby were both smiling.

"What?" she asked.

"Nothing," Luke said. "I promise neither of us is ever going to speak about it again."

They spent the morning watching television, cartoons that kept the boys entertained. Toby sat on the floor, at the far end of the couch, not saying much after the initial outburst. Every so often, Luke looked over at him and tried to figure out what he was thinking. Toby laughed at the cartoons and joked with the boys, just like every other time he'd been at the apartment. But as the day wore on, Luke could feel the tension building between them again.

Annie looked up from the pillow she had put on Luke's lap and tapped him on the knee. She crossed her eyes, and even though it was simple and a little stupid, he laughed. Toby looked over at them and smiled politely, immediately going back to the television.

At dinnertime, Luke got up and put the cold spaghetti into the microwave. As he waited for it to warm up, he looked in to the living room and imagined it as a painting. One of those ones they saw on a field trip to the small art museum downtown. They had pictures of the oddest things there. A bench. An apple. Stuff that Luke had trouble calling art until his teacher told him to think about it as a slice of life. A way we are able to see what another person saw at a very specific moment.

And maybe that's all this was with Toby—a moment. Something they would knuckle through and remember, although likely not fondly.

Annie bolted upright on the couch and told everyone to be quiet.

"Do you hear that?" she asked. But before anybody could answer, she ran to the window and looked through the blinds. "Oh *shit*. Shit, shit, shit. I have to go."

Luke tried to slow her down, but she ran through the apartment grabbing clothes and shoes. She was trying to put her jacket and shoes on at the same time when Petey, oblivious, said her name.

"Is there any more garlic bread?"

Annie shook her head, speaking as she fixed her hair and checked her face in the glass of the window. "We ate it all, honey. I promise I'll make you more."

She almost ran out the door without a word to Luke, who was still trying to figure out what was happening. When she saw his confusion, she stopped, but Luke could tell she didn't want to.

"It's David. My stepdad. He just pulled up in his truck and . . ." Luke followed Annie's gaze out the window. In the parking lot, a semitruck cab was parked in the far corner. A short, slightly overweight man was lowering himself down. "I'm not in trouble. Everything is fine. I just really need to be down there when he gets inside. Okay?"

Luke still must have looked worried, because Annie paused long enough to take both of his hands in hers. "Really. I'm fine. David's started going to these truck-stop churches. So he's gotten kind of annoyingly religious lately. Him leaving me alone is a big deal. It's just . . . I'll explain later. Okay?"

She gave Luke a kiss and ran out the door. When she was gone, Toby pulled the blinds down and looked at David.

"Shit. Look at the size of that cup."

Luke looked over Toby's shoulder. David was fumbling with a hundred-ounce insulated mug emblazoned with the

Mountain Dew logo. Luke shot a glance toward Annie's apartment. The door was just closing as David started across the parking lot.

"That's commitment to keeping a lot of liquid cold," Toby said. "And oh damn! I think he's wearing a headset!"

Toby went off on an extended riff about the benefits of having a CB radio in the El Camino, what his call sign would be—"This is HoneyBear signing off, good buddy!"—until he fell on the couch, tickled with himself. Luke watched Annie's apartment for fifteen minutes after the door closed, making excuses to go to the window. Ready to jump off the balcony and bust down her door if anything seemed wrong.

The last time he stood up, Toby said, "She's fine. It's just parent stuff. Speaking of that, is Doreen *ever* coming back?"

The twins both perked up at the mention of their mom. Luke went over and turned up the television. It was enough to redirect their attention while he motioned Toby outside onto the porch. Luke leaned against the railing and looked around the parking lot.

"I could call Ricky's cell again," he said. "But hell, what does it even matter at this point?"

"Do you think they're okay?"

Luke did a few push-ups on the railing. "Probably? I feel bad for saying it, but if they got into a car accident I'd be relieved. At least that's a reason to ditch your kids for two days."

Toby grunted. "I can watch the kids if you want to go run or something. I know you've got Herrera Monday."

Luke stopped with the push-ups. When was the last time he and Toby had spent more than a few days apart? When was the last time they hadn't shared every single moment that happened, nearly in real time? And now they were standing out here with too much to talk about. Luke had no idea where to even begin.

"Actually, I made weight," he said.

Toby threw his hands up in the air. "It's a damn miracle!" Toby said. "Maybe next time we go out to eat you can order something like a normal human being."

Luke smiled to himself, knocking out a few more awkward push-ups. When he stood up, glancing at Annie's apartment, unease fluttered in his stomach for what he was about to say.

"I told Annie she could come to Iowa," Luke said.

At first Toby didn't react. When he did, it started in his eyes. A flicker of annoyance. A sharpness that finally manifested itself in a simple, stilted shrug.

"Hey, I'm just along for the ride."

Luke had no idea if this would've annoyed him before, but now it did. It was the sort of response Toby excelled at when he felt slighted. One or two words that came out like a razor.

"That's it?"

Toby held his palms up. "What do you want me to say? I'm glad you're happy, but . . ." He laughed.

Luke already knew what he was going to say. "It's totally different. You barely know that woman."

"*Lily.* Jesus. Her name is Lily. And I've known her—what? Two days less than you've known Annie? You're right, I should be careful."

Luke didn't want to start a fight, but if they stacked up the evidence side by side, he was pretty sure the case for Lily would crumble. Met her at a bar, check! Got an underage kid drunk, bingo! And let's not forgot the two days of ditching school—a rotten cherry on top.

Oh yeah, she and Annie were exactly alike.

"You know what?" Toby said, watching Luke. "I'm going to go hang out with the boys. If you want Annie to come to Iowa, great. But please don't pretend like anything you're doing is better than what I'm doing."

And then he walked inside.

22

IN the middle of the night, Toby snuck into the kitchen and pulled out the phone book. There wasn't a listing for Lily Griffin, but there was a Reverend Arlo Griffin, and Toby dialed it. It rang and rang with no answer, probably fifty times, before Toby hung up. He spent the rest of the night on the kitchen floor, dialing and waiting.

The next morning, Toby barely said a word to Luke. Part of it was the new, knee-jerk anger, but mostly he was thinking of Lily. He couldn't figure out if she was simply ignoring his calls, or wasn't at home. And neither made him feel any better.

At lunch, Luke made another pot of spaghetti while Toby sat in the living room with the twins. As the smell of the sauce reached the living room, Petey and Jack-Jack perked up.

"Did Annie make more garlic bread?" Petey asked Toby.

"No," Toby said.

"I love garlic bread," Jack-Jack said.

"I know," Toby said.

Petey paused and then said, "Because she said she was going to make more garlic bread."

"Have you seen Annie here?" Toby snapped.

Luke leaned his head out from the kitchen and shot Toby a dirty look. Toby stood up and walked into the kitchen, starting to get plates down from the cupboard. He stopped at four and looked at Luke.

"Should I get one down for Annie?" he asked.

"I don't know if she's coming back or not," Luke said.

Toby reached and took down another plate, putting it with the others as Luke began spooning noodles onto the boys' plates. All Toby wanted was for everything to fit together. He wanted Luke and Lily to fit into the same equation. He closed his eyes, trying to force the exhaustion out of his body.

"I should apologize to the boys," he said, pushing himself away from the counter. "I was a dick."

"Hold up," Luke said. Toby readied himself, but Luke looked just as tired as he did. When he called for the twins, they snatched the plates, nearly throwing the noodles on the wall in the process.

"Slow down," Luke said.

Once Petey and Jack-Jack were in front of the television again, Luke said, "At least tell me you get how this looks on my side."

With great effort, Toby nodded. "Okay, fine. But when have I ever done anything wrong? When have I ever done anything I wasn't supposed to do? I just . . ."

He wanted to cut to the center. To wear Luke down until he finally—even begrudgingly—agreed that Lily wasn't bad news. Toby had known him long enough to believe that Luke wanted him to be happy.

So he looked Luke right in the eye and dropped all the bullshit, all the subtext.

"I like her. I like her a lot," Toby said. "And if you don't get that, I'm not sure what I'm supposed to do. Okay?"

Luke made a plate of spaghetti and handed it to Toby. For a second, he didn't think Luke was going to respond.

"It's probably too late to invite Lily over for spaghetti," Luke said.

Toby didn't immediately register what Luke was saying. And in fact, his body stiffened at hearing Luke actually say her name. But when he searched Luke's face, his entire body relaxed for a second, and he smiled.

"Well, I don't think she's happy with me right now."

He could tell Luke was trying hard to keep it light and

conversational. "So you've already pissed her off. That's probably a good sign."

Toby chuckled and took a bite of spaghetti. "She told me to leave her alone this weekend. I want to say it's because she needs time to recuperate. But, shit, I tried calling her like ten times last night, and she's either ignoring me or wasn't home."

Luke was obviously swallowing back so many things he wanted to say. He looked like he was trying to keep a live fish in his mouth. But to his credit, he nodded and smiled as Toby talked.

"Did you ask her to come to my match tomorrow?" Luke asked, the words quick and practiced. He'd probably been building up to this for fifteen minutes.

When Toby mentioned it before, it had kind of slipped out. A way to extend the night in another way. But in all honesty, a wrestling match was the perfect opportunity for Luke to meet Lily. It required the very barest amount of commitment or expectation. Luke would jog over sometime before the match and be as pleasant as possible. And then he would lose himself to the routine, the way he always did. That would leave Toby and Lily in the bleachers, watching. Their legs touching. Whispering in each other's ears.

Jack-Jack and Petey ran to the kitchen, dumping their

empty plates into the sink with a loud clatter. Luke yelled at them to scrape the noodles off, but they were already wrestling on the floor of the living room.

"I need to get them out of the apartment," Luke said, grabbing the plates.

Toby watched them roll around on the floor, laughing together. Jack-Jack was just a hair bigger than Petey, but he didn't use it to his advantage. If anything, he'd let Petey take control just long enough to feel good about himself.

Toby had an idea.

"Do you guys want to see something really cool?" he asked.

Both Jack-Jack and Petey stopped. They'd only recently learned that "cool" was a category they should pay attention to. And while they didn't quite understand what made something cool—Petey especially seemed to struggle with this, pulling a spoon out of the drawer and spending fifteen minutes fawning about how cool it was—they found the entire idea irresistible.

Luke's face was just as confused as the kids.

"Get your jackets," Toby said.

The boys didn't see the plane at first and were ecstatic just to be in the woods. They had stick swords and pinecone grenades and ran as fast as they could through the trees. Every so often, Luke would tell them to slow down. But eventually he gave up and let them run. Toby was content watching them fly around, the anticipation building in his own mind. Hoping it would conjure the same magic for them.

When the twins burst into the clearing that held the plane, they both froze.

"Holy *shit*," Petey said, immediately turning to Luke with an apologetic look on his face.

"It's fine," he said. "That's how we felt when we found it. Right?"

Toby nodded. "Go check it out."

The boys charged for the plane, jumping onto what was left of the nose and raising their sticks into the air like victorious knights. He and Luke hadn't been much older than Petey and Jack-Jack when they found it, not really. They were so damn scared that it wouldn't be there the next time they came to the woods. Or that some older kids would show up and claim it.

The boys screamed with laughter, trying to chase each other down as they popped through holes in the body of the plane. As he watched, Toby hoped Petey and Jack-Jack would come back to the plane on their own someday.

"Maybe they can fix it up," Toby said to Luke, shaking his head. "Jesus, how stupid were we?"

"It wasn't stupid," Luke said.

Suddenly Toby felt bad for saying it. Because he still wished they could piece it together too. He imagined them in the air, the wind attacking their hair. The way the ground would get smaller and smaller until it disappeared completely.

"You know I want you to come to Iowa, right?" Luke said.

Toby watched the boys without answering. It didn't solve the problem, but Luke was trying. "Yeah, I know. Did you really ask Annie?"

They'd always been perfect as two. But once they left North Carolina, everything could change. They could expand. Remake their lives in whatever way they wanted. It was exciting and terrifying and it shot through Toby like lightning.

"Yeah," Luke said. "But I don't know if she's going to come."

"You realize there will be all kinds of fine-ass women on that campus," Toby said. "Right?"

Luke gave him a dirty look.

"I'm just saying—if she doesn't go, you will be okay."

Even as he said it, Toby's mind shot to Lily. He wanted to apply the same logic, the same trajectory, to his own future life in Iowa. But whenever he tried, the sound of the phone ringing endlessly played in his ears. The way she looked at him, as if she'd made a huge mistake, played across his eyes.

"You okay?" Luke asked.

Toby shook himself. "Yeah, man. Yeah."

The boys ran around the plane. Jack-Jack shouted some sort of command at Petey and they both shot into the woods to gather more sticks for whatever game they were playing.

"I've been an asshole about Lily," Luke said, surprising Toby.

All Toby could say was, "A huge asshole."

Luke nodded once, as if he wasn't expecting confirmation. "Anyway. I need you to promise me you won't go back to the Deuce."

The twins came roaring back into the clearing, laughing as they jumped into the body of the plane like there were incoming missiles. Jack-Jack peeked his head up before immediately dropping back down.

"What reason do I have to ever go back to the Deuce?" Toby said.

"Seriously, T. There's nothing good about that place."

Toby didn't particularly want to hang out in a bar with his dad or Bo. He didn't want to lose every night to neon beer signs and stories that were never as funny to the people who were hearing them. But he also didn't want to have to keep proving his integrity to Luke. At some point, Luke had to trust him.

Still, it was an easy promise to make.

"You'll never see me in there again," Toby said.

January 27

T—

Sister came by my cell today, wanting to know how I was doing.

I was like, "I'm good. You know."

"Marilyn said you had a lot of questions," she said.

I shrugged her off. I didn't want to talk about Eddie. Or about what was going to happen—not right then. Of course Sister never lets anybody get away with that shit.

She kept saying, "It's okay to be upset. Eddie is a great person."

And I'd immediately be all, "I'm not upset."

Because if you don't double down, you're a punk. If you don't keep yourself bulletproof, you'll get shot. Sometimes when I'm doing it, I know it isn't right. But I honestly don't know how else to be. It's like I've become this whole other person. Grown a new skin that I can't seem to shed.

Anyway, Sister has heard it all before. But this time, she didn't come at me hard the way she normally does. She looked down into her lap.

"Nobody thought I should be here. Chaplain Cortes didn't want me here. My parents. And the prison definitely didn't want me here. But this is where I'm called. Do you know the number one thing I've learned doing this?"

I wanted to make a joke. Something like, "How many places a dude can hide contraband?" Something like that. But she looked dead serious, man. And honestly, I don't want to joke about Eddie. Any of this.

So I said, "I'm sure you've learned a lot of cuss words they don't use up in the convent."

That made Sister laugh. "Well, this might surprise you, but I have been known to say a choice word from time to time. And I don't live in a convent."

T, I'm not going to lie. Thinking about Sister cussing some dude out got my mind turning.

For real, man. I thought I had her. She was smiling. Shaking her head. I thought she was going to bust out a story about her cussing out some priest. I didn't even know. And the more I thought about it, the more it started to work its way inside me.

Like when we were kids at school or wherever, and some adult told us to be quiet. Don't laugh! So of course every damn thing cracked us up.

I couldn't hold it. I started laughing my ass off. Pretty soon, Sister was laughing too, and I couldn't even tell you why. But it felt like something was leaving my body. When we got done, my stomach hurt. Sister must've felt the same way, because she looked happy in a way I hadn't seen in a while.

It took a second, but she eventually got back her Sister eyes. Staring right into me until I had to look away. When she started talking, it was all about how nobody is defined by any one thing they've done in their life. There are no best or worst moments. It's all a part of a long line that continues and continues and continues. She must've realized she was losing me, because she smiled and said, "That's what I learned when I came here. Every single person has worth. Every single person is capable of shocking transformation."

I like the idea that we're a part of a long line, T. I can't even really say why, except that it makes me feel connected to something. But everything else she was talking about? How there's always a second chance? I don't know that I believe that. There are certain things that you cannot come back from. You and I—more than anybody else in the entire world—know that. There are some things you can't take back. There are some things you should pay for.

We'll Fly Away

So I was like, "Sister, I don't believe that."

To her credit, she didn't try to convince me.

All she said was, "We will have to disagree for now."

Luke

23

LUKE carried both the boys back to the apartment, his arms burning by the time they climbed the steps, and he set them on the couch. The boys turned, trying to get comfortable, and finally settled. Luke put a blanket on top of them and walked into the kitchen. Toby was hanging up the phone.

There was an awkward moment when Luke had to rewire the connection between his brain and his mouth. To fight back—or maybe just redirect—his feelings about Lily. He still didn't trust her, but maybe that would come? How long that would take, he couldn't say.

Toby watched him like he was reading a transcript of everything going through his head.

"I won't call her again," Toby said.

"Dude, I don't care."

Toby opened his mouth but closed it quickly. It took barely a second for him to decide not to fight. "Any word from Annie?"

Luke looked toward the front door, as if she had only been waiting for an invitation to walk back into the apartment. "I thought about walking down there. I don't want to get her in trouble."

Toby scoffed. "C'mon, what is that guy going to do? Hit you with his travel mug? Go down there and tell her you're going through withdrawal."

Toby made a lewd gesture, and Luke turned away.

"I don't know. What do I even say?"

They were getting comfortable again, Luke could feel it. Especially when Toby sighed heavily and pulled a plate down from the cupboard and started spooning cold spaghetti onto it. He moved efficiently, a learned behavior that wasted no movement. That allowed him to accomplish his task as quickly as possible. Always leaving time to escape if the temperature in the room changed.

He covered the plate with foil and shoved it into Luke's hands.

"Take her this. Tell her you were worried she might waste away. She might jump you right there on the landing."

Luke was unsure. But when Toby pushed him toward the door, he couldn't deny the thrill of anticipation. And it had nothing to do with Toby's perverted idea of how the world works. It would be enough to see her, even for a moment.

Luke forced himself to walk down the stairs; the only thing that kept him from running was the plate in his hands.

He knocked, and at first, nobody answered. The next few seconds were endless and brought about an unexpected dilemma. If he knocked again, he might wake up David. If he didn't, he wouldn't get to see Annie. And he'd have risked getting her in trouble for nothing.

His fist still hovered over the door when he heard the deadbolt slowly unlatch.

The door cracked open, and Annie whispered, "Wait one second."

Inside, the glow from the television lit the walls as newscasters droned on, their voices interrupted by a subtle snoring every few seconds. A moment later, Annie was standing in front of him.

"Hey . . . what are you doing?" She looked nervous, perhaps amused. She wrapped her arms around her body and Luke wanted to pull her close—to make her warm. When she saw the plate of food, her face changed and she smiled at Luke.

"Did you make more spaghetti?"

Luke was so bad at this. The first thing he thought was, should he have made something different? Was it weird to bring her a plate of food? Even the foil on top made him feel sheepish.

"The boys were hungry. I probably should've asked before I cooked your stuff."

Annie gave him a look, shaking her head. "No, it's totally sweet. Thank you."

Luke leaned forward to give her a kiss and she stepped back, looking to the apartment. His face tightened, and he could already feel the warning sirens starting up inside his body. He'd messed up.

Annie put a hand on his forearm.

"Hey, it's not you," she said, squeezing. "I want to make sure I introduce you to David in the right way. And that's not just after he's gotten off the road. And it's definitely not him catching us making out on the landing. Okay?"

Luke still felt a little foolish, but he nodded. Annie looked back at the apartment one more time and—with an air of urgency—leaned forward and kissed Luke hard. It only lasted a second, maybe two, but Luke was spinning when she pulled away and wiped her lips.

"I'll see you tomorrow at school."

"Maybe we can see if the janitor's closet is open," Luke said.

Annie chirped out a laugh, covering her mouth and

looking back at the apartment. Before she turned around, she took the plate from him and winked.

The kiss powered the rest of the night. It was like a dream, but one that moved too slowly. He wanted the evening to burn away. The night to go twice as fast. He didn't even realize he'd fallen asleep until he heard his mom laughing and saw the early morning sun lighting the apartment.

The door flew open. Ricky carried Doreen across the threshold as they laughed and kissed sloppily.

Luke thought, oh hell no.

"Wake up!" Doreen said, laughing out a scream as Ricky dropped her onto her feet. "We've got news!"

Ricky looked as if he'd been up for a month straight. A rash of stubble was on his chin and his eyes were bloodshot. Doreen didn't look much better, but the exuberance of her entry was enough to overshadow any haggardness.

She held out her hand and showed a gaudy ring. Toby yawned, nodding. Luke didn't say a word.

"This was the surprise!" Doreen said. "Ricky and I went to Gatlinburg, and well, we got married!"

"The Get 'Er Done package," Ricky confirmed.

When the boys came running into the room, Doreen went through the whole production again. Luke could tell the boys weren't sure if they were supposed to be happy or not. Was Ricky their dad now? They looked at Luke and then back to Doreen and finally to Ricky, who was ready to drop.

"Nobody's going to school today," Doreen said. "You neither, Toby. We're celebrating. What do you guys think about . . . Chuck E. Cheese?"

The twins tackled each other with excitement.

"I can't skip school," Luke said.

Doreen was still smiling at the boys, so she didn't hear him at first. Luke tapped her on the shoulder. "I have Herrera tonight."

"Oh, well. Afterward, then. Maybe we can all go out for a fancy dinner?" Doreen said. "We can celebrate *two* things."

She reached out and hugged Luke. Normally, he'd jump back, but she came at him with such conviction, such force, that he couldn't get away in time. And once she had her arms around him, he did the same. Luke felt like a kid again. Like he should be on the floor with Jack-Jack and Petey, lost in the excitement.

He coughed and said, "I'm going to get ready for school."

As Luke was walking out of the room, Toby said, "If we go to Chuck E. Cheese, can we get game tokens?"

24

DOREEN and Ricky were in the bedroom, getting the boys ready for the day's adventure, and Luke was in the shower. Toby picked up the receiver and dialed Lily's number, which he had already committed to memory. This time it was busy. He hung up and dialed again—busy. He had started dialing her number one more time when he heard Luke open the door to the bathroom. He quietly put the phone back on the receiver and pretended to be looking for breakfast.

"Hey," Luke said.

"Hey."

Luke was pulling on a shirt, staring at Toby. "You look like you're going to be sick."

Toby tried to play it off. "I'm fine. Still trying to wrap my head around Doreen getting married. At least Ricky is a good guy. Oh, wait."

He knew Luke wasn't ready to laugh about this, but Toby

needed a distraction. And maybe Luke did too.

"What do you think his mom will say about this? Will there be room in his twin bed?"

It worked. Luke was trying not to laugh. For a second, Toby was transported back to the easy familiarity he didn't have anywhere else in his life. Even Luke didn't have the clenched asshole look he'd been carrying for the past week. Hell, the past three years.

"I'll go right after school and get Lily," he said, watching for any flicker of annoyance. But all Luke did was nod, still smiling about Ricky's bed.

And for a second—maybe for the first time—Toby got a glimpse of the future. It was him and Lily, Luke and Annie. Maybe they lived in the same apartment, but maybe they didn't. Maybe it was down the road, just a stone's throw away. For so long, they would've called it growing apart. But maybe it was just growing.

"And then we're going to watch you going to put a hurting on Herrera," Toby said. "I want to make sure that Lily sees peak Luke."

"I'll try my best," Luke said.

"Let me see your killer face," Toby said, turning to Luke.

Luke shook his head. "You're an idiot."

"C'mon, I want to see the face you're going to give Herrera

when he steps out on that mat." Toby opened his mouth into a snarl and gave Luke the crazy eyes. "Your killer face."

"First, that is not what I look like," Luke said, laughing. "And god, I don't need a *face*."

"Well . . ." Toby shrugged. "Don't say I didn't try to help you."

Luke glanced back to the bedroom. The boys were loud enough they could hear every word, breathless and excited for a day of adventures. Toby reached out and flicked Luke's arm, trying to distract him.

"You think I should stick around for the entire school day?"

"Not funny," Luke said.

Toby put three fingers against his temple.

"Scout's honor. I may not even go to lunch, because that might be too fun."

Luke sighed and said, "You can go to lunch."

"Oh, wow. Thanks. Can I really?"

Luke gave him a dirty look, and Toby laughed.

Toby walked to his first class and sat down at the desk. Tyler Simpson and his friends came in and immediately started laughing and pointing at Toby. He ignored them, ignored the stage-whispered "his dad" and "look at his face" comments that slowly disappeared once the room began to fill.

Eventually Mr. Geiger, the English teacher, came in and started talking. Toby blocked everything else out until the intercom crackled and the office assistant's voice broke into the classroom. Toby sat up in his seat, sure she was going to say his name. Instead, it was Tyler's mom, bringing him his lunch. It got some hoots and hollers, which Toby enjoyed, but once Tyler was gone and the class had settled back down, the disappointment snuck in.

Toby sat on the edge of his desk the rest of the class. Despite what he had said to Luke, he was waiting for Lily to come with a new story, maybe a disguise this time, that would spring him for a few periods. He'd be back before Luke ever knew he was gone.

But the intercom never came back to life, and as soon as the bell rang, Toby ran to the office.

"I need to call my . . . cousin," Toby said, wishing it was Mr. Townsend and not the suspicious office aide sitting at the desk. Since everybody else had a cell phone, the only people who went to the office were usually in some kind of dire situation. The aide eventually nodded and turned the phone around for Toby to use.

He dialed the number, and it immediately went busy. He

clicked the receiver and dialed again, smiling over at the aide.

"Sometimes she can't hear the phone over all her cats," Toby said, laughing even though it got no reaction.

Busy.

When he tried to dial a third time, the woman stopped him. "Shouldn't you be going to class?"

Toby could run out the doors right now, and nobody would likely say a damn thing. If it wasn't for Luke, he might've done it too. He looked at the office worker and forced a pleasant tone.

"I'll try again next period."

And he did. He came back after every class, dialing and cussing under his breath. How could a simple beep be so frustrating? By the time he walked into the cafeteria, Toby was wearing his disappointment on his face, his sleeve— anywhere it would fit. Luke and Annie were sitting face to face, as if they'd just been making out. Toby hoped they hadn't been making out.

"Get a room," he said as he sat down.

Luke recognized that he was upset immediately, but Annie fired right back.

"We might. But we need a cameraman. Interested?"

That might've been the only thing that could've drawn

Luke's attention away from Toby's moping. He looked horrified, which would normally be enough for Toby to ratchet it up another level—asking about lubrication or whether he needed to wear a smock for the filming—but he set his books down and went to get a tray of food instead.

When he got back, both Annie and Luke were staring at him.

"What's wrong with you?" Luke asked, not unkindly.

Toby waved his concerns away. "Nothing. I was just being a dick. Did you see this pizza they're serving?"

Annie pointed to Luke's plate, which was just a collection of carrots and apple slices. "Somebody is back to worrying about his figure. A little too much spaghetti this weekend?"

Luke laughed uncomfortably. "I already weighed myself three times. I'm fine."

Annie looked at Luke like he was crazy and then to Toby for support. "Yeah. That's totally normal."

The rest of lunch went much the same way. He could still see people looking at him, at the cuts and bruises on his face. Normally it would make him self-conscious, enough that he'd skip out of lunch and go sit in an empty hallway. Or maybe find a teacher to chat up. But the entire cafeteria, the conversation he was having with Luke and Annie, felt like they were happening to somebody else.

When the bell rang, Annie gave Luke a kiss and hustled out of the cafeteria. Toby was about to follow her when Luke called his name and jogged to catch up.

"You sure you're okay?" he asked.

People liked to ask this question, especially adults. Most of them didn't want the real answer, or at least they didn't want to deal with the complications. Luke usually was different. And while Toby knew he cared, he knew Luke didn't want to hear about the wildfire spreading inside of Toby right now. Telling him to kick through the front doors and drive his El Camino straight to Lily's house.

Luke didn't want to hear any of that, so Toby smiled. Waved his friend off. And then he walked away.

As soon as the final bell rang, Toby ran to the parking lot and jumped in his car. He nearly killed a group of sophomores who, as he sped by, cussed and raised their fingers into the air. He was on the road before a second car had even pulled out of its space, but he waited to really hit the gas until he passed the old sheriff's deputy who cherry-picked speeding tickets off kids who didn't know or momentarily forgot where he sat every afternoon. He gave the man a wave and, once he was out of sight, gunned the engine.

When he pulled into Lily's driveway, the house was dark.

On the front porch, there was a bag of trash. Toby shot out of the car and hammered on her door. He jumped from foot to foot as he waited, every drop of expectation he'd stored inside throughout the day coming out.

Lily opened the door, her hair wild and her eyes half closed.

"Toby? What—" she looked behind her and closed the door a little. "What are you doing here?"

"I've been trying to call you since yesterday. Can I come in?"

She looked into the house again and, with a sigh, nodded. "Yeah, yeah. Come on."

Toby pushed through the door and did a double take immediately. There were beer bottles everywhere. An ashtray of used butts was emptied on the coffee table. The room smelled like Luke after a match. Lily fixed the cushions on the couch, wiping away some chip crumbs, and told him to sit down. In the kitchen, the phone was off the hook.

"What the hell happened here?"

"I had a little party. Kind of." Her words were choppy, and she rubbed her temples as she spoke. "I'm sorry, I have a massive headache."

Toby looked around. It looked like the sort of post-bender scene that only lived in movies. He half expected somebody to come stumbling out of one of the closets, a nerd who had snuck in when nobody was looking. The quarterback, fresh off a make-out session with a band geek. In the far corner of the room, he saw stacks of cigarette boxes.

He didn't want the betrayal to grab him the way it did. He didn't want to feel like the only kid not invited. But he did.

"You should've called me," Toby said, keeping it so damn chipper it sounded like he was reading a greeting card. "I'm great at parties."

"Next time," Lily said quietly. "Anyway, what's up?"

Who came to this party? Why did she have it? He could probably piece together why she hadn't called. Why the phone was off the hook. But he didn't ask. Instead, he reached for her hands, which she reluctantly let him take.

"Listen, I have an idea," he said. He'd never been this nervous in his entire life. "You can come to Iowa with me and Luke. And Annie, I guess. But whatever—it's perfect. Cheap. Closer than Seattle. And then you don't have to worry about the cigarettes or anything."

Lily coughed and rubbed her eyes. When she looked at Toby, her eyes red and unfocused, she said, "This is going to require coffee. Can you give me a minute?"

Toby waited as Lily looked for coffee, then filters. He waited as the machine warmed up and slowly began dripping into the glass carafe. When she poured the first cup and stood across from him at the kitchen island, already looking more awake, Toby dove back in.

"So what do you think?"

She took a long drink. "I think you're making a mistake."

Toby deflated. She stared out the window, still talking.

"You don't want me to come to Iowa," she said. "This is your chance to break away. To start over. And you have to take it."

Toby still couldn't say anything. What did he care about breaking away? He'd seen the future clearly. And that was him and her in Iowa. Figuring it out and forgetting this place together.

"What if I said I didn't want to go without you?"

Toby assumed that would get a positive reaction, either tears or an emotionally charged smile. She'd walk around the kitchen island and pull him close as they kissed.

Instead she put the cup down hard. "Then I'd say you're an idiot."

"Why are you doing this?" Toby asked.

She opened her mouth and then dropped her head back as if she were searching for an answer somewhere on the ceiling. When she looked back at him, she smiled weakly.

"I'm sorry. I didn't—I've had a lot of fun with you. And

if we were in a different situation, maybe it would work. But . . ."

She shrugged, and it destroyed Toby.

"Oh my god. You must think I'm a total asshole," he said.

He wanted to walk away, to make a dramatic exit, but he couldn't move. He was frozen by embarrassment.

Lily walked around the island. "I don't think you're an asshole."

"Yes you do. How could you not? Like you were ever going to come with me. I'm a total *asshole*."

"Toby, please. I promise I—" She stopped and rubbed her temples. "I didn't know we were going to end up . . ."

He wanted her to say it, to put some kind of label on whatever it is they'd been doing the past week. Dating? Or were they just friends, friends who could get naked together in the back of a pickup? Because now all of his emotions were knotted together.

She took both of his hands. "I didn't know you were going to be totally awesome."

She was smiling, trying to charm him. But it shouldn't be so easy.

"I wish you'd never brought me here," he said quietly.

Lily let go of him, and they stood across from each other for a moment. Then she sighed and walked into the living room, falling onto the couch. She laughed bitterly as Toby sat down next to her.

"You're right," she said, her entire attitude changing. Suddenly looking just as wrecked as Toby. "But . . . I used to be you. I used to be in that fucking bar and nobody—*nobody*—watched out for me. You wouldn't believe some of the shit I did. Shit I'm still repeating. I guess I thought I could help you."

"You did help me," Toby said. "And that's why I'm here. You could break free too. Start over. In *Iowa*."

He threw his arms out, announcing a state neither of them had been to with the sort of flair reserved for the circus and late-night infomercials. Jazz hands and everything. Lily laughed, wiping her eyes.

"You're so different from your dad. You know that, right?"

It surprised Toby, not because he didn't know—he'd spent his entire life trying to be different. Instead, it was realizing that, maybe, after years and years of trying, he'd finally outrun DNA and come out on the other side.

He leaned forward and kissed her. In the two, three seconds it lasted, the world seemed different.

Lily looked down at her lap, still smiling, but it wasn't as bright. As if she was deciding something important. When she looked up, she kissed Toby back. And then she straddled him, taking off her shirt and directing his mouth to her neck. Her shoulders.

When they finished, Toby sat on the couch both shocked and ecstatic. Lily jumped up and hurried to the bathroom. She was gone long enough that Toby got dressed and thought about knocking to make sure she was okay.

A few minutes later, she came out and started buzzing around the house, picking up wrappers and bottles. Barely looking at Toby as she cleaned. He stood to help and, without a glance, she tried to hand him a garbage bag. He took her hand instead.

"Did I do something?"

"What, no? Of course not. I just need to clean the house."

The words were a staccato blur, and with every one of them, she tried to pull away. Toby tried to catch her eye, but she was intent on avoiding him.

"We didn't have to do that. That's not why I came over."

"Then why did you come over?" she said.

"I wanted you to come to Luke's match," Toby said. "And Iowa. As previously stated."

"I'm supposed to drop something off at the Deuce. And the house is a wreck. I can't leave it like this, in case somebody from the church comes over."

"Sin all over the place," Toby said, picking up a bottle and wagging it in her direction. He'd intended it to be funny, but she finally pulled away and began cleaning up like it would solve world hunger.

He watched her for a few seconds, hoping she'd stop. When she didn't, he picked up a garbage bag and helped. It took less than an hour to get the house back in order, and it couldn't come soon enough for Toby. He gathered the bags and carried them to the trash cans behind the house. When he came back inside, Lily was hanging up the phone.

"So what do you think?" Toby said. "Wanna go watch some guys in tight clothing?"

"I'm already late," she said. "Could I meet you afterward?"

Toby didn't want to let her out of his sight, even if it meant going back on his promise to Luke. He smiled.

"It's just the Deuce," Toby said. "I'll take you. You do whatever it is you need to do with the cigarettes, and then we'll go to the match."

When he said "cigarettes," she flinched. She started shaking her head, but Toby wasn't having it. They would be in and out, quicker than you could say his name.

"That way I don't lose you."

Lily hesitated for a moment before finally nodding.

January 28

T—

The next time I went outside, I didn't think I'd see Eddie—not to mention play ball. So I was surprised to see a bunch of dudes standing around him on the court. The first thing I thought was he was about to get jumped, so I ran over, ready to do whatever needed to be done. As soon as I hit the court, Eddie looked up and started clapping.

"I'll take Luke on my team—you guys are gonna need all the help you can get."

Every dude on the court laughed. Man, I couldn't even think of a comeback. So I stood there looking stupid. Eventually Eddie came over, smiling and still talking shit over his shoulder to this dude who was an absolute monster.

I was like, "What was that about?"

And he said, "I told him you were going to embarrass him out here."

You should've seen the way he smiled, T. Like he was on fire. When I looked back at that monster—he had to be at least seven inches taller than me—he was staring at me like I'd said something about his sister.

I must've looked crazy nervous, because Eddie laughed and slapped me on the shoulder. Started telling me how I shouldn't worry, because Sister got him totally rehabilitated. Then he started talking strategy!

I wasn't even listening to what Eddie was saying because that giant wouldn't stop looking at me. When the game started, he got right up on me too. Started pushing me all over the place. The first time we came up the court, Eddie passed the ball to me, and this dude didn't even pretend to play defense. Knocked me right on my ass.

Eddie picked up the ball and checked it. He pretended to pass it in my direction and then he took off, right to the basket. I swear it was one dribble and two steps and then he was up in the air, flying above everybody. Nobody bothered playing defense after that. We were all watching Eddie.

Every single thing he did had a specific purpose. None of it looked particularly important, but when he put it all together, it was beautiful. We won ten to zero.

Eddie was everywhere. Anytime they got close to the basket, he'd take the ball away. And even when he wasn't scoring, he was making everything happen on offense.

After it was over, we were all sitting on the grass—sweating, starting to get cold because of the wind. Eddie leaned back, resting on his elbows with his eyes closed and his nose in the air. When he started talking, I jumped.

"Back when I was a kid, when my mom didn't give a shit and I was basically living by myself on the streets, you know what I had?"

He palmed the ball and held it out to me.

"This. This right here. The only good thing I ever had in my life was hoops. When I was in high school, a reporter said I played like somebody was chasing me. Nobody stopped me on the court, Luke. *Nobody*."

I know that feeling. When I was on the mat, it was like somebody was trying to take something away from me every time I had a match. I never could've told you that until I got here, though. In here, they take everything. Every damn bit of every damn thing you got. Snap your fingers and it's all gone. But Eddie wasn't trying to hear anything like that right then, because he was like, "This might be the best day of my life."

And I was like, "C'mon . . ."

Because that's crazy. A half-assed pick-up game on a windy day on death row? Best day ever? Eddie opened his eyes and stared at me as if he was reading every thought that came through my head.

"Feel the leather on your hand. Talk a little trash. Put the ball through that hoop." Eddie closed his eyes and smiled again. "Nobody's taking that away from me. And that's enough. I don't need anything else."

I thought about that really hard, T.

I don't know if I have anything like that in my life. Even when I wrestled, I don't know if I loved it on that sort of bone-deep level. So as we sat there in the sun and the wind, I tried closing my eyes too. Wondering if maybe that could be a start to what Eddie was talking about. A start to trying to figure things out, you know?

Luke

25

LUKE was the last one to get to the locker room before the match. He got dressed and walked out into the gymnasium, where the mats were already rolled out and taped down with precision. He stepped on them, feeling the cushion, and closed his eyes.

"You beat me out here."

Luke turned around. Connor Herrera was standing just off the mat, his singlet down around his waist and his headgear strapped to the loop.

"I didn't realize it was a competition."

Connor rolled his neck and stepped onto the mat. He was right next to Luke when he said, "It's not. I just like to be the first one on the mat before a match."

"Well, I hope it totally ruins your night," Luke said.

Connor smiled. "I was kind of worried when you first dropped weight. And then the more I thought about it, I decided I was kind of pissed. I don't plan on losing."

"Well, you can always jump up and wrestle 181."

Herrera's coach came walking out of the locker room and yelled his name. Connor nodded, pulling his singlet up over his shoulders. When it was in place, he reached a hand out to Luke.

"Make it a good one," he said.

Luke shook his hand. "You too."

Luke was trying to warm up when he heard his mom's voice. She and Ricky were walking into the gym, followed by Annie, holding each of the boys' hands. Annie smiled and mouthed, "Good luck." His mom saw him and started yelling and waving, laughing as Ricky bear-hugged her from behind. Annie led the boys to the top of the bleachers, a destination they'd obviously chosen. Luke scanned the top row for Toby and Lily too, but they weren't there yet.

He started the pre-match routine he'd done hundreds of times, circling the mat and trying to get warm. Working everything but Connor Herrera out of his mind. He didn't feel tired or out of sync. Just ready. When Coach O came over and asked him how he was doing, Luke told him he felt great.

"I'm good to go," he said.

"I know you are," Coach said. "Six minutes of pain for that kid, you hear me?"

Luke nodded, but when a side door of the gym opened, Luke's head shot up, expecting Toby and Lily. Instead it was a few cheerleaders he barely knew, both of them waving at him too.

Annie caught his eye and nodded toward the girls, a single eyebrow raised the whole time. Then she laughed, loud enough that the entire gym stared up at her. He started jumping rope, and damn if he wasn't grinning like an idiot. Enough that Coach came back over and stared at him like he had a second head growing out of his body.

He kept catching Annie's eye—why wouldn't he?—and she would smile. He would smile. Once the matches started, he was still smiling.

And then he saw a kid who couldn't have been more than twelve, dancing in the stands. Pretty soon the twins joined him. Of course it wasn't Toby, didn't even look like him. But the way he moved, as if he didn't give a damn about anybody—the way kids always danced—hit Luke. He scanned the crowd, making sure Toby hadn't snuck in. When his eyes landed on Annie, her smile faded and she mouthed, "Are you okay?"

Luke nodded absently, trying to focus on what was happening on the mat.

103 won by decision.

113, a pin.

They were dominating, as expected. But they were making their way through the weight classes in record time. Across the room, Herrera shot across the practice mat, a graceful mix of power and speed. One of their assistant coaches saw Luke and bent down to whisper something in Herrera's ear. Connor looked over his shoulder at Luke and grinned.

Normally, Luke wouldn't move. Would give him the death stare from across the gym, even if it meant losing a little warm-up time. Half of his matches at this point were mental. He could beat an unconfident wrestler before he ever got on the mat. But instead he stood there aimlessly holding the jump rope, until Bryant at 165 was having his arm raised after an early first-round pin.

Coach O was yelling his name.

"Take his fancy ass to school!" Coach yelled as Luke walked onto the mat.

Herrera reached out his hand, and they shook.

When the ref's whistle blew, Luke shot forward and took Herrera down almost immediately. Two points, and he was already pushing him onto his back for more. For the pin. While he normally never heard the crowd, today it was impossible not to. The entire gym was shaking as Luke worked his body around. He went high and Herrera bridged, trying to save himself. Luke was a fraction out of position, and Herrera took advantage immediately. His coach was yelling, "Half! Half!" But Herrera had already slipped one under Luke, wrenching his neck. Turning him toward the mat.

Luke flipped to his stomach easy enough, but he couldn't get up. He could barely move as Connor looped a leg around his and rode him until the period ended. When he stood up, Coach clapped and pointed at the scoreboard.

"Two-two, son. Your house. Let's do this!"

Luke dropped to the mat, getting into the referee's position. But he couldn't escape the crowd. Annie gave him a little clap; his mom yelled. Even Ricky clapped once, nodding his head. Luke didn't see Toby.

When Connor got on top of him, Luke focused on his hands, his feet. Both of them solid on the mat. He visualized every point he would take, the road toward the pin. Explode up, one point. Attack the legs, two more. And when he brought Herrera to the mat a second time, he wouldn't make the same mistake again. He would hammer Connor Herrera into the mat so hard, the next time he heard Luke's name, he'd run the other way.

He could see every step he was going to take, every single movement of his body.

But then the whistle blew, and Luke's face went straight into the mat.

His coach was yelling.

The other coach was yelling louder.

Luke had been in tough matches before. Last year's opening match at the state tournament had everybody talking. The kid had it in for Luke, had made *that* match—win or lose—his state championship. It went three periods, and Luke won by a single point.

So he'd been here before. He slowly worked his way up, first to his knees. Then to his feet, peeling Herrera's hands from around his waist until they were both facing each other again.

One more point, three-two in Luke's favor.

The crowd was cheering, and Luke was starting to feel it. Finally starting to push Toby from his mind.

Luke circled Connor, who was smiling. Ready for the fight. The first thing you learned as a wrestler was, nobody could do anything for you on the mat. You were alone out here. And nothing you said was ever going to change that. You had to put action behind your words. Work. Even a marginal athlete could be a legendary wrestler if he worked hard enough.

Luke feigned a single leg, and when Herrera sprawled, Luke put him in a front headlock and hooked his arm. As he expected, Herrera posted with his leg and Luke spun around—two more points—and used his arm to drive Connor down. The entire gym exploded when Herrera's shoulders touched the mat.

And then it happened.

Connor slipped away from Luke's grip and was on top of him before he could move. When Luke tried to bridge, Herrera snuck an arm around his chest and locked Luke's head up with the other arm.

It was the first time Luke had been pinned in nearly four years.

Luke wasn't sure what to do, how to hold his body when he walked off the mat. It seemed quiet, the sort of shock he'd only heard in movies. After the other matches, as his teammates came to shower and get dressed, a few of them stopped by his locker. He hadn't moved. His headgear was still on his lap. Coach came by and put a hand on Luke's shoulder, not saying a word. Even if he had, Luke was somewhere else. Back on the mat. Trying to figure out what had happened.

When he looked up, the locker room was empty. A single shower was still on, spraying into the darkness. Luke took a quick shower and slowly dressed back into the jeans and hoodie he'd worn to school. Eventually there was no other reason to hide in the locker room, so he pushed through the doors to what he hoped was an empty gym.

He didn't know what he expected when he saw Annie, Doreen, and Ricky sitting on the bleachers. The twins were out on the mat, wrestling each other hard. At first none of them saw him. But the door closed behind him, and they all stopped and looked.

Jack-Jack came flying up, trailed by Petey. They jumped without asking and Luke caught both, one in each arm. They were talking a mile a minute about the match, detailing every move they remembered. Every point.

"And then you lost," Petey said matter-of-factly.

Both boys looked like they'd been told Santa wasn't real. Jack-Jack suddenly couldn't get any words out. Petey was equally stumped. Luke dropped down on one knee and stared at both of them.

"What do I always tell you?"

"Clean up your crap?" Petey offered.

Luke couldn't help but laugh. "If you're not losing, you're not wrestling. Remember? That's one of the first things I ever taught you two. Everybody loses."

"Yeah, but . . ." Jack-Jack looked at Luke, then over his shoulder to Ricky, dropping his voice to just a whisper. "*You* don't lose."

Ricky and Doreen walked up behind them, holding hands.

"I've seen some tough shit in my life," Ricky said, shaking his head. "And that was tough."

Doreen came up to Luke and put an awkward hand on his shoulder. "Are you going to be okay?"

Luke nodded. Behind Doreen, Annie was pretending to check her phone as she listened to every word they said. Luke smiled at his mom. He couldn't remember the last time he'd done that.

"I'll be fine. You should get the boys home."

Doreen stood there, obviously wanting to say more. When Ricky called her name, she decided against it. She told the boys to hug Luke, looking back at Annie. "I suspect he'll be home late," she said.

Annie walked onto the mat slowly, staring at Luke in a way that was either sad or embarrassed. He didn't know until she was right next to him, and saw her eyes. She wasn't crying, but they seemed to hang a little lower than normal.

"Hey, you."

"Hey."

"That was . . ." She looked around the gym. "Kind of exciting? And kind of the hottest thing I've ever seen?"

Luke couldn't muster much more than a nod.

"Like, really. You were so . . . dominant."

"Yeah, until I got my ass handed to me."

Annie tackled Luke, bringing him down to the mat and pretending to wrestle him until she was simply holding him in her arms. She didn't say anything, just held him, which was exactly what Luke wanted. As they sat there, he fought the urge to completely lose it. Over the match. His mom. And, of course, Toby.

He wasn't sure how long he was sitting there when Annie said, "So do you think we could have sex on this mat, or would that be completely disgusting?"

"Um, I don't think we should do that," Luke said.

"Yeah, of course," Annie said, laughing nervously. "I was *totally* kidding."

Luke sat with her for another two or three minutes before the janitor came in, earphones on, and nearly fell over when he saw them sitting on the mat. Annie tripped trying to get up, laughing even harder when Luke tried to explain why they were still in the gym. Stumbling even more on his words. When they were finally outside, Annie leaned against the building and pulled Luke close to her.

"I feel like he would've been less shocked if we'd been naked," she said.

Luke laughed. He leaned close and kissed her.

"Mmm," she said. "Is there any way we can make your mom disappear again for, well, ever?"

"Have you thought about Iowa?" Luke asked.

She looked up, as if pondering the question. "Maybe . . ."

"No parents up there."

Annie leaned her forehead against Luke's. "I like you. I like this. Now let me drive you somewhere so we can make out with integrity."

Nothing sounded better to Luke than that right now. But he was still trembling with energy. Energy that would slowly turn frantic as the night went on. He needed to run. Just to the apartment. Maybe a little farther. He'd stop right in her doorway, if she wanted.

"Can you wait an hour?"

Annie leaned back and considered Luke. "You never know what might happen in that hour. What if Toby actually shows up and I suddenly get interested in that skinny dork?"

As soon as she said it, Annie grimaced.

"Don't worry about it," Luke said. "And I'll take my chances."

"I'm sure he has a reason," Annie said cautiously.

Luke wasn't. Before, him not showing up would elicit a National Guard–sized response in Luke. But even though they'd spent the last couple of days together and things had slowly returned to a familiar shape and size, he realized he fundamentally couldn't trust Toby. Not as long as Lily was around.

"I'm just going to run and . . ." He bit his lip. "Whatever."

Annie leaned forward and kissed him gently. As he started jogging, she yelled out, "Don't get *too* tired!"

He didn't run fast.

Despite Annie waiting for him, despite his first loss in four years. Despite all the work of cutting weight to meet Herrera. And maybe most importantly, despite Toby's disappearing act—he finally didn't feel like he was trying to outrun a demon. Now, it would be enough to let his legs slowly seep the extra energy out of his body. To clear his head so he could go back to the apartment, take Annie in his arms, and fall with her into the couch, laughing as quietly as they could.

Toby could wait until tomorrow.

He took turns as they presented themselves, slowly putting a loop together in his mind. He passed now-closed mills, tall and haunting in the shadows. A small breakfast spot that catered to the lone furniture factory on the road and, just as he was about to link back to the road that would lead him to Annie and the apartment, the Deuce.

Luke skidded to a stop.

Toby's car stood out among the heaps, Harleys, and hulked-out trucks. Luke's stomach dropped. He wanted to believe Toby wouldn't keep making the same mistakes. That he wouldn't lie to his face. But standing there, staring at the El Camino, it was clear Toby had made a decision. For a half second, Luke thought about running back to the apartment and forgetting all of it. The next time Toby came by—be it a beating or because Lily had dropped him in the way Luke knew she would—he would meet him with indifference for the first time in their lives.

But he wanted Toby to know.

Luke wasn't even angry when he walked into the bar. Toby was in a booth at the back of the bar with Lily, Jimmy, and a tall guy Luke had never seen before. Toby was raising a beer to his lips. By the time Luke made it to them, Toby was staring at the table.

That's when he got angry.

Luke wanted Toby to live in the shame, the knowledge that he'd messed up. More than anything, he wanted the recall of this moment to be immediate the next time he saw Toby. The moment when Luke would tell him it was either Lily or him.

He glared at Toby for a few seconds before Lily finally

stood up and reached her hand out.

"We haven't met yet—I'm Lily."

Luke took her hand reluctantly, and as soon as he touched her, Jimmy's voice rang out over the music and talking in the bar.

"Better watch it, son. That there is what you call *competition*."

People laughed, and Lily dropped Luke's hand like it had caught fire, giving Jimmy a nasty look. Toby stepped out of the booth and got between Luke and Lily.

"What are you doing here?"

Luke looked around. Jimmy's collective of drunks and petty criminals was draped over one another, watching everything. The rest of the crowd seemed just as interested. Luke knew he'd never get Toby to be real in here. As he was standing there, the tall, rangy guy joined Toby and Lily, giving Luke the eye.

"You said you were coming to the match," Luke said. "What happened?"

"That was my fault," Lily said. "I . . . Toby helped me at my house, and then I was late getting here."

Luke didn't even look at Lily. He didn't care what she said or did. But he did meet the stare of the tall guy, smiling as he drank his beer. Eyes never leaving Luke.

"Do you have a problem?" Luke asked.

"Me?" the man said, considering his beer for a moment. "Nah. No problem here."

Lily pulled Luke and Toby away from the table as everybody laughed. When they were out of earshot, Lily turned to Luke.

"Please take Toby home," she said.

They both turned to stare at her.

"What?" Toby said.

Lily was still staring at Luke. "I shouldn't have brought him here. And . . . shit." She turned to Toby. "I'm sorry. But this place is bad news for you. Especially tonight. I . . ."

She looked back at the booth, where Jimmy and the other man were watching. She shook her head and said, "Just go. Please."

Luke looked at Toby, gauging his reaction to Lily's words. Toby didn't even glance in Luke's direction, though. Everything he had was on Lily, his body turning more pitiful by the second. Like he might break down in front of everyone. Luke wouldn't let that happen. He grabbed his wrist.

"Come outside with me for a minute," Luke said quietly.

Toby ripped his hand away from Luke, still looking only at Lily. When Luke tried to grab him again, Toby turned on him, wild like lightning.

"Don't fucking touch me," he snarled.

Lily dropped her head and tried to talk to Toby. "Just go with him. We can talk later."

"When? After you have another party?"

The words didn't make sense to Luke, but they stopped Lily cold. She only snapped out of it when the woman behind the bar said, "Lily, take that shit outside. Right now."

As Lily was nodding and pulling Toby toward the door, the tall man came walking up behind everybody. He put both his hands on Lily's shoulders.

"Did somebody say something about a party?" he said, smiling. "Am I invited?"

Lily shrugged him off, but he traced his finger down her back, letting it linger just above the waistband of her jeans.

Toby watched the whole thing.

"Could you please get fucked, Bo?" Lily said.

Bo ignored her, pointing at Luke and then Toby.

"You heard Val. Time to take this party on the road."

"I'm not leaving," Toby said.

Luke and Lily groaned.

"You sure it isn't past your bedtime?" Bo said, laughing at Toby.

Lily called Bo an asshole just as Luke pushed him. He went flying into the bar, knocking over a couple of glasses.

Toby was still staring at Bo as if he'd finally figured out the answer to a problem.

Bo had Luke by the shirt almost immediately, his hand raised. Before he could swing, Luke dropped down and hit Bo with an uppercut to the jaw. Two more times in the face, splitting his eye open. He was ready to hit the man again when Jimmy picked up a beer bottle and cracked Luke just above the eye.

The room blinked out for a second.

Then both of them were on him, a blur of ringed fingers and cowboy boots going to work. Luke kicked Bo off him as Jimmy landed a hard punch on Luke's temple. He delivered two or three more hits before Luke spun away.

Luke was fire and twisted metal. Hands up and ready for whoever came at him. Blind with it. But when Val yelled that somebody had called the cops, Jimmy froze and pushed Bo toward the back of the bar.

Luke grabbed Toby's arm and tried to pull him in the other direction, but Toby was dead weight. Still barely paying attention to anything but Lily.

"What are you doing?" Luke said. "Fuck her. We need to go."

That shook Toby from whatever dream world he was in. He stared at Luke hard.

"What did you say?"

The adrenaline was draining from Luke's body, replaced by a familiar cold fear. His words shook with it. "They called the police. We need to go."

"No, what did you say about Lily?"

Luke couldn't believe it. He leaned close to Toby and said, "Are you kidding me? Wake up. She doesn't want you here."

"I don't need your help."

Luke laughed. "Yeah, okay. When *haven't* you needed my help? I've been sticking up for you your entire life. Every single time your dad kicks your ass—"

Toby charged forward and hit Luke with everything he had. Luke barely moved, but it didn't stop Toby. He came again and again.

"Don't do it," Luke said right before the third time. And when Toby charged, Luke reacted. Popped him once on the jaw. As soon as he connected, Luke wasn't sure if he was going to throw another punch or throw up.

Toby looked more shocked than hurt. He didn't move or say a word. The only sound in the room was sirens getting closer and closer. Before Toby could say anything else, Luke ran out of the bar and down the road as fast he could.

26

THE two sheriff's deputies looked more annoyed they'd been called to the Deuce for another fight than concerned about what had actually happened. As soon as they arrived, the entire bar went into a sort of practiced precision. Val rubbed the bar top in never-ending circles, her eyes following every step the deputies took. The only time she stopped was when Jimmy and Bo appeared from the back. Bo's left eye was swollen shut, like a piece of fruit that had been left in the sun to spoil. His right one wasn't much better. Every few seconds, he flinched in pain and touched his face cautiously.

Jimmy barely had a scratch on him.

They told the same neatly coordinated story: It was nothing but a high-school fight, couldn't say what about. His son could probably shine a light. When he said that, Jimmy's eyes flicked to Toby briefly, as if daring him to tell it any other way.

Even if the deputies didn't believe their convenient account, even if Toby wouldn't say a word to implicate Luke, it didn't matter. Every person in the bar had something to say about Luke, half of them pulling out phones and bringing up the aggressive headshot every newspaper had used when he won the state title last year.

Luke threw the first punch, they all said.

Looked like he was going to kill them boys.

But as soon as the deputies asked if anyone wanted to press charges, the entire bar acted like they couldn't get away fast enough. It didn't surprise Toby. He knew his father was involved with the cigarettes, and hell, everybody else in this room could be too. They wanted the cops to go after Luke and then forget they'd ever stepped foot inside the Deuce.

When the deputies finally came to talk to Toby, he was holding a bag of ice to his swollen jaw and trying to stuff all the anger inside him into a pocket in the back of his brain. He'd pull it out later, if he ever saw Luke again. The words like acid. Like bullets. And he'd pump every last one of them into Luke.

"So, you know Luke Teague," the first deputy said, checking his notebook.

"You guys go to school together?" the other one asked, like he didn't already know the answer.

"Yes," Toby said.

"What were you fighting about?"

Toby readjusted the ice but didn't answer. If Jimmy had taught him anything, it was how to stand up to questioning. How to get it over fast without doing a bit of damage. Single words were preferred, and if you could get away with just nodding or shaking your head, even better.

Behind them, Bo was holding a new beer to his eye, while Lily whispered something to Val. His dad sat in a corner booth, watching every move Toby made. For a half second, Toby thought, What if I just blew it all up? Let slip the tiny scraps of information he knew.

Cigarettes. His dad. Lily and Bo.

He was suddenly very tired. So tired he could barely move or focus on the questions the deputy was asking him. At some point, he had to take control. He had to stop letting other people direct his life.

The deputy pointed to Toby's face.

"You should press charges," he said. "Bo over there won't because he's on probation. And your dad, well . . ."

The deputy laughed, like he knew all about Jimmy. And he probably did. Every cop in town did, or at least it seemed that way. They'd get pulled over, and it was dealer's choice as to whether the cop would lean in and bullshit with Jimmy before letting him off with a warning, or pull him out of the car so he could make good on any number of slights Jimmy had handed out over the years.

This guy was a bullshitter to his core. Toby shook his head.

"I'm not going to press charges," he said.

The deputy looked at him strangely, then shrugged.

"Well, that's on you," he said, closing his notebook and putting it into the pocket of his shirt. He motioned to Toby's face. "But somebody who does *that* to another person? It isn't an accident. It will happen again."

Before Toby could say anything, Jimmy put a hand on the deputy's shoulder and, beer in hand, smiled like he was about to sell the man a new car.

"Shouldn't you be out chasing meth heads and busting prostitutes, Darryl?"

The deputy chuckled. "Well, Jimmy, maybe if your boy here wasn't earning the family name, I could be."

They both laughed, and Jimmy slapped Toby on the shoulder, proud. Like he'd just hit the winning home run.

"He took a wallop, that's for sure. But you know what that's like, don't you?"

The two men laughed again, and Toby tried to slip away. When he did, Darryl stopped him.

"Hold up there, son." He looked at Jimmy and spoke low. "I'm not about to tell another man how to raise his kid, but . . . you'd be making my life easier if he got gone."

Jimmy mulled it over. "Who am I to argue with the law?"

He slapped Darryl on the arm, and the deputy gave Toby one last nod before he walked away, joining his partner, who was talking to Lily.

Once Darryl was out of earshot, Jimmy said, "Go wait in the car. Once they're gone, come back in. We need to talk."

There was no emotion in his voice, and when he walked to the bar without another word, a shot of cold went through Toby. He watched his dad laugh with the deputies, not moving until Jimmy finally turned around and acted surprised to see him.

"Shit, boy, you heard the deputy. Get out of here!"

Toby walked outside and sat in the El Camino. As he stared at the Deuce, he was tempted to crank the car and drive away. He didn't have any money, but he could probably ransack the trailer for enough pawn-worthy stuff to get him to Tennessee, at least. He lived in that brief fantasy until the deputies got into their squad cars and pulled out of the parking lot. Almost immediately, Lily pushed through the door and scanned the parking lot, stopping when she saw his car.

She walked straight for him, her mouth set in a hard line,

and stopped just to the side of the door, as if she expected Toby to pull away. When the car didn't move, she sighed.

"Your dad wants you."

Toby nodded. Lily stared at the sky and didn't move. She pulled out a cigarette and lit it, taking a drag and showing it to Toby. "I haven't smoked in three years. A couple of months back here, and voilà. Every bad habit I had, back on me like a tick."

She leaned against the hood of the El Camino, smoking her cigarette and blowing smoke into the dark night sky. Every so often she'd look at Toby, like she had more to say, but chose to inhale instead. When she finished, she dropped the cigarette to the ground and rubbed it out with her heel.

"If you left right now," Lily said, "he wouldn't have time to come find you."

"Because of the cigarettes," Toby said.

Toby wanted a reaction. Lily barely moved.

"I guess I'm not surprised you figured it out. But yeah, because of the cigarettes."

"Any other reason you want me to leave?" Toby asked, his voice even. She shook her head, like the question wasn't important. But this was all Toby wanted to know. He'd seen Bo's hands on her. He wasn't going to let her make him a fool too.

She came over and leaned into the door of the car.

"Luke fucked Bo's eye up." Lily laughed, amused. "So Jimmy's going to ask you to help. And he's going to offer you money."

She said his name so familiar. So cavalier. *Bo*. It was a sudden torrential rain, overfilling the river, and Toby couldn't stop the water from coming over the banks. He opened the door and she jumped back, surprised.

"What the hell?"

"Probably should get in there," he said, talking too loudly and moving like he couldn't get past her quickly enough. Lily ran to catch him, her fingers barely brushing his shirt. As if she could stop him with the lightest touch.

"Wait—*wait*." She finally grabbed him, but he didn't want to stop, didn't want to give her any sort of chance to explain what he'd been too stupid to see from the very beginning. Her and Bo. Shit, her and Jimmy. They were all doing something behind his back.

"Stop. It's not worth it," she said.

Toby was tired of people telling him what to do. Tired of everybody thinking they knew what was best for him. For once in his life, he was going to be the one who decided what was happening to him.

"I can take care of myself," Toby said, his words still flat.

If his dad wanted him to help, great. He might only get a hundred bucks, but that would be a start. That would get him a few miles away. And then he'd find a way to make another hundred, go another few miles. Until he was as far away as he could get.

Lily cussed under her breath. "What's your problem?"

"Who was at your house last night?" Toby asked.

She froze so quickly, Toby was surprised she didn't fall over like a tipped statue. She wouldn't look him in the eye as she pulled another cigarette from the pack.

"I have a feeling you already know the answer to that question too," she said quietly. Toby wouldn't look at her, and she ducked down to look him in the eye. "What do you want me to say?"

All of Toby's bluster was gone. A single raindrop fell, landing in between them. He refused to look at her when he said, "I want you to say it didn't happen."

Lily's silence leveled Toby. He started toward the bar, but this time she didn't stop him. The last thing he heard before he walked in was her cussing, and the click of her lighter.

January 29

T—

Today I woke up with Sister sitting there staring at me. I was about
to crack a joke about her being a closeted creeper when I saw
her face. Like she'd been told the world was about to end. It's
this never-ending space that feels like the floor's disappeared and
all you can do is fall and fall and fall. I shot to my feet, already
knowing what she was going to say.

They took Eddie back this morning.

Now, I know there wasn't anybody looking. I know there
weren't any dudes out there trying to catch me in this moment.
But still, when she said that? Man, I just nodded. Even though
everything inside me started flying, T.

I wanted to punch the damn wall. To scream and cry and fall

apart. Because goddamn, even though I knew it was coming, even though I know it's coming for every dude in this place, it hurt me in a way that I didn't think was possible anymore. In a way that I didn't even remember was there.

That's when I saw it: Sister was trying just as hard to keep herself right-side out. When she stood up, I didn't know what to do. It was almost time for breakfast, but how was I supposed to sit there and eat when Eddie was back there all alone? Isolated like some kind of rabid animal.

And make no mistake, T. That's why they do it.

That's why they put you in a room all alone, away from everybody except your lawyer and, if you're lucky, any family that still claims you. Put you in a room right next to the one where they'll strap you to that gurney, stick those needles in your arm, and let you die in front of a room full of strangers.

They do it that way because your life doesn't mean shit to them. No matter what they say, that's how they let you die. Like some kind of dog kicked to the side of the damn road.

Sister bowed her head to say a prayer, the way she always does, and I grabbed for her hands. For a second, when I first touched them, small and cold, I thought she might pull back. That I might see she was actually scared of me, repulsed at hands turned claws, just like everybody else.

But she took my hands in hers as if she'd been waiting for them all along, and whispered frantic words to the sky. When the guards finally saw us, she refused to let go. And when they promised isolation, promised Sister would never see me again, I still held on.

Long after she left, I felt her hands on mine.

When I was brushing my teeth.

When they finally let me outside.

When the night came and I buried my face in my pillow and let years and years of pain come out, making the whole pillow wet. But man, I couldn't sleep. Nobody can, I think, when there's an execution scheduled. I spent all night lying on my bed, eyes wide open like some kind of zombie, trying to wipe my mind of everything.

Eventually I woke up and I wrote this letter.

I was lying there with my eyes open, hearing every damn cough, every step the guards took in that long shiny hallway, and I remembered something Sister said to me once.

"We are not living in a world that stands still."

At the time I was like, "Shit, Sister. Even I passed sixth grade science."

You remember when you told me the world was constantly spinning and I just couldn't wrap my head around it? And you were like, "It's moving so fast we can't feel it." And of course, that didn't make sense to me either. Man, you spent all afternoon trying to explain that mess to me. And at the end you said, "It's constant! It's always happening! That's why we don't feel it!"

I took your word for it back then, T. But last night, as I was lying there, some missing piece floated into my head, and it all connected.

Man, you and I lived for so long in a spinning world. So long that we started to think that shit was normal. Every day, spin. Spin, spin, spin. We got used to it. Everything about our life was moving so fast we never get a chance to see any of it.

We are not living in a world that stands still, T.

So the next morning, I hammered on my bars—yelling for somebody to bring the Sister to me as soon as she got on the block. A few hours later, she came right to me. I heard the cowboy boots as soon as she came in the door.

"Are you okay?" she asked.

I didn't have time for that, though.

"What do you mean when you say the world isn't standing still?"

She looked confused at first, so I told her about staying up all night, how me and you never stood still once in our life. As I was talking, her face started relaxing. She smiled.

"Well, I think it means that none of us are ever finished."

I stopped myself from saying anything right away, because that sounded like some bullshit to me.

"Luke, you have to understand that we are not defined solely by our choices. Even by our actions, to some extent. None of us are."

Sister knew what she was doing, of course. Ever since I met her, I've told her that I wasn't going to apologize for what I did. I wasn't going to betray the only truth I'd ever known in my life. And she must've already seen my head getting pointed in that direction, because she reached through the bars and touched my arm.

"Every single person in the world—me, you, Eddie—is in the process of creating themselves. Every single person, every single day. But to do that, you have to be able to let yourself accept the fact that what you did or didn't do is not all of who you are."

She took her hands away and waited for me to say something, but what am I going to say to that, right? I stared at my lap for a long time. I swear I could feel the earth moving. My entire body felt like it was floating. God, I wanted to crack a joke. Get this planet spinning the right way once again.

But I couldn't say anything. I could barely look at her, because for the first time in I don't know how long, I wanted to believe that I could actually be a different person tomorrow. Not a lot. But little by little, I won't be this person I've become. And I know it's hard for you to understand what that means to me, especially now, but T . . . all I want is to wake up in the morning and not feel like the entire world is falling on top of me.

I don't know if it's possible, but I want to think it is, you know?

Luke

27

LUKE kept expecting spinning lights, unsure if the police would start searching for him immediately. If they'd show up at the apartment, or maybe pass his name to the news. Images of the boys at home, watching television too late, popped into his mind. All of a sudden his picture came up on the screen, followed by . . . what?

He pushed harder, trying to outrun his own imagination.

Around him, the North Carolina night looked just as quiet and peaceful as it always did. The scenery changed from bars, tire shops, and vague manufacturing buildings into smartly manicured lawns and houses. When he saw Coach O's house, Luke's panic spiked.

The first time he'd come here, the entire family had been invited over for dinner. Doreen was still working at the Waffle House and couldn't find a person to pick up her shift, so Luke brought the boys, nothing but toddlers back then.

He could still remember the way Coach's wife, Mrs. O, had looked at the three of them standing on her porch. Like she wanted them there. Until that moment, he'd never understood the pity in other people's eyes. The way they always viewed him and Doreen and the boys as in need. Since that first night, she and Coach had never turned him away.

The house was already dark and quiet. Even the simplest decisions seemed wrought with impossibly high stakes. Should he knock or ring the bell? Or maybe he could just sit on the porch, surprising whoever came out to pick up the paper that next morning. But then his brain started telling stories again, ones where the police drove their cars onto Coach's lawn, sirens blaring.

He knocked quickly.

A few seconds later, he knocked again.

This time, lights popped on in the back of the house. One in the hallway. A second in the front room. Finally the porch light came on, making Luke squint.

Coach opened the door in shorts, a T-shirt, and Luke almost broke into tears right there on the steps. He sniffed until there was nothing left. Until he could look Coach in the eye.

"Damn, son. Are you okay?" Coach asked.

Luke opened his mouth to answer, but the tears came charging back. This time he couldn't catch them fast enough. He wiped his eyes, ashamed. Coach put his hand on Luke's shoulder.

"It ripped my heart out to see you come that close," he said. "But we'll get his ass at state. Don't you worry about that."

Luke had barely thought about Herrera. And state felt galaxies away. He wiped his eyes, his nose. And then he pulled the hood down from his sweatshirt so Coach could see the cut on his head.

"I got into a fight."

Coach stepped close to check the damage, his eyes slowly betraying the confidence he normally showed, no matter the situation. Luke had lived in some sort of crisis for most of his life, but when was the last time he had let it burrow deep into soft places? When was the last time it had hurt him?

"At the Deuce, and they called the police," Luke blurted out. He didn't want to say the next part. "I punched Toby."

Luke avoided Coach's eyes. He'd never be able to shake the dead sound of his fist on Toby's face. Or how Toby flew back, as if he'd been thrown across the room. Coach put his hand onto Luke's shoulder, and it felt like a boulder.

"Let's go inside and get you cleaned up."

"Am I in trouble?" Luke asked.

Coach hesitated. "The first thing we need to do is get your hands—and your head—taken care of. Then we'll figure everything out. Okay?"

Coach looked tired, more tired than Luke had ever seen him before. When he was at school, Coach always seemed plugged in and ready to go. But the man in front of Luke looked small and, maybe, scared.

Luke followed him inside, sitting on the toilet as Coach brought out a small first-aid kit. He held Q-tips in his mouth as he worked small pieces of glass out of Luke's forehead. When he was finished, he stepped back and crossed his arms over his chest.

"You never were going to win any beauty contests, so this should do."

Luke nodded. All he could muster was a simple, "Probably so."

Coach sat on the side of the bathtub, nearly eye to eye with Luke.

"Can you tell me what happened?" he asked.

Luke's chest went tight. He tried to bring out the practiced breathing he used to make himself calm down during matches—in and out through his nose—until he could speak.

"I don't want to go to jail," Luke said, feeling like a kid again.

Coach nodded, held out his hands. "Nobody's going to jail. Okay? But I need to understand what happened."

Luke didn't know where to start. Was it just the last week? Or was it when he and Toby first met? When you had to survive every minute, you were always seconds away from making a decision that could ruin everything. And even Coach was blind to how that could build up

"We've just been arguing," he said.

"About?"

"He met a woman at the Deuce."

Coach relaxed a bit, rubbing his eyes.

"Shit, Luke. You know better than this. You've got so much riding on this year. You can't go around getting into fights—at a *bar*—just because your friend is with a girl you don't like."

Luke's mind went but, but, but . . .

"I think we need to drive down to the police station and talk to somebody," Coach said. "Figure this thing out."

"No," Luke said, starting to stand up. Coach stopped him.

"Luke . . ." Coach looked to the ceiling. Behind him, the tiles were light blue with tiny seashells set in the middle. Luke focused on them, trying to steel himself for what he knew Coach was going to say next. "There are moments in your life when you have to make decisions. And they seem like regular decisions, but they're bigger than that. Bigger than just right and wrong. They're the type of decisions that determine what kind of man you are. Do you run away from your problems? Or do you stand up and take responsibility?"

Coach waited, but Luke couldn't move, couldn't speak. He couldn't feel his head, his hands—anything.

"I know what kind of man you are," Coach said. "And even though you might be scared, we should go down to the police station and talk to them. Make this right."

Coach stood up, almost as if he was inviting Luke to choose: run or not. Choose what kind of person he would be in that moment, for the rest of his life. Instinct said run. Everything he wanted to believe about himself told him to stay.

Luke wanted to be a good man.

But as soon as Coach reached down to clean up the first-aid kit, he bolted out of the bathroom—past Coach's wife, sitting on the couch with a mug of something—and out the door. He barely heard them calling his name.

28

JIMMY was alone in the far booth, and Toby marched right to him. Before he said a word, Jimmy reached out and turned Toby's face side to side, inspecting the damage.

"You really did take that punch like a goddamn champ," he said, holding up two fingers to Val. "I mean it. Especially from a monster like Luke."

Toby didn't say anything as Val brought the beers and put one in front of Jimmy and the other in front of him. He didn't want to think about Luke. The savageness in his eyes when he threw the punch. The feeling of Luke's knuckles against his skin. They'd fought before, playground arguments that faded as soon as they got up off the ground. But this had been different. Luke had given him everything he had, and his jaw still throbbed.

"I'm in," Toby said, wanting to skip all the pretense. The proud father bullshit. "The cigarettes at the travel museum, right?"

A flash of annoyance crossed Jimmy's face.

"I guess I'm not surprised you know. Although Lily should learn to *keep her fucking mouth shut.*"

Jimmy yelled the last few words as Lily walked back into the bar and sat down. She stared at her phone without even a glance toward them. When Bo came up and sat next to her, she moved a barstool away and said something that made him laugh.

"But okay, yeah. Bo's out. That eye's so fucked up, he isn't driving anywhere. And then Darryl said something that got me thinking." Jimmy grabbed Toby by the shoulders and shook him enthusiastically. "Why risk having a damn felon drive the truck? It's brilliant, really. Because even if you get pulled over, they ain't sending you to jail. Hell, you'd only get juvie—and maybe not even that!"

The idea that Toby would "only get juvie" didn't seem as positive as his dad was making it out to be. He pulled his attention away from Lily and Bo.

"Wait a second," Toby said. "What do you want me to do?"

Jimmy gave him the proudest look Toby had ever seen from his old man. He rubbed his chin, like he was pondering an ancient proverb. After that, Jimmy finished his beer, taking his time with every swallow.

"Shit, son, you're driving the truck!"

Toby looked at the dirty Deuce floor, trying not to feel the weight of Jimmy's stare. His words. Toby wasn't sure what he'd expected, but driving a truck wasn't it.

"What kind of truck?" Toby asked.

"Nothing more than a moving van," Jimmy said. "You know the old hosiery mill on Main? Ridgeview?"

Toby nodded.

"You drive the truck there. Fifteen minutes down the interstate, and you're home free. Lily will go ahead and make sure everything at the mill is clear. You guys unload the cigarettes and . . ." Jimmy wiped his hands. "Well, that's the good news. . . ."

Toby glanced back at Lily and Bo. They were flat-out arguing now. When Lily stomped away, Bo opened the beer he'd been holding against his eye and took a drink.

Jimmy snapped in Toby's face. "Hey, there are fifty other guys in this place that would shit themselves to do this job. You got it?"

"Yeah, yeah. Ridgeview. Money. I got it."

"Not just *money*," Jimmy said. "More money than you've ever seen. The kind of money that could make a woman change her mind about anything."

When Toby looked at Lily this time, she was staring right

at him. She shook her head with barely a movement, enough that Toby did a double take to make sure he'd actually seen it. She mouthed one word: "No." All Toby could see was another person trying to bend him into a shape he didn't want.

Toby turned back to Jimmy and said, "When do we do this?"

Jimmy gave him one last look, like he was trying to catch Toby in a lie, before he set his beer down and fished the truck keys out of his pocket. He slid them across the table to Toby.

"You better be up for this," Jimmy said. "This ain't no minor-league shit."

Toby grabbed the keys without hesitation, and Jimmy smiled.

"All right, let's go get Lily's ass settled down."

Toby followed Jimmy over to the bar. Lily didn't turn around, refusing to acknowledge their presence. Jimmy said her name and she pulled out her phone, staring at it pointedly. Jimmy reached over and took it out of her hands.

"I'm not doing it," she said.

"Yes, you are," Jimmy said. "You'll drive him up to Statesville and then meet him back here in Newton. Just like it was Bo. Just like we planned."

Lily shook her head again, and Toby could see the muscles

in Jimmy's face tense. Lily spun around, talking to Toby as much as she was Jimmy.

"You're really going to send your son to drive that truck? Really?"

"Hell, this is the best thing I've ever done for him!" Jimmy said, elbowing Toby in the ribs. "And he's nearly a grown-ass man. He can make his own decisions."

Lily slid off the bar stool and stood in front of Toby. She was so close; he could touch her without moving his arm.

"Don't do this for me. Please."

Jimmy glared at the back of Lily's head. Toby imagined him going for her, the way he'd gone after Toby countless times before. He wasn't sure if it was panic or pride that brought the words to his mouth.

"I'm not," Toby said.

Jimmy put a hand on Lily's shoulder and whispered in her ear. "When it's all over, you'll thank me. This money is your ticket out of here."

Lily said something under her breath as she pushed past Toby, walking out the door and not stopping until she was in the passenger seat of the El Camino. When Toby got to the car, he expected her to yell—something. She didn't say a word.

Toby's hands were shaking so bad he could barely hold the

steering wheel as he drove toward the interstate. The silence between them was aggressive. Lily watched the passing cars on the interstate. Toby gunned the engine, faster and faster down the interstate until he whipped around a subtle curve and Lily grabbed the armrest with a quick, barely audible yelp.

The faster he could get out of the El Camino, the better. He'd drive the truck, get his money, and figure out what would happen next.

The same dusty parking lot greeted them at the travel museum. As Toby pulled around to the back, everything seemed less sharp. As if somebody had rubbed away all the detail. Even the moon looked duller as he put the car in park. Toby stared at the spot where, just three nights ago, Lily had been lying on top of him. Tickling his ear with kisses and whispers, both of which felt like lies now.

"You aren't proving anything by doing this," Lily finally said.

Toby wouldn't look at her.

"So you're going to ignore me?"

"I'm not ignoring you," he said. "All I want to do is get in the truck and drive it back."

Lily sat back in her seat, putting her feet on the dashboard. Back to the silence. After a few minutes she let out a monumental sigh.

"I thought you were different," Lily said. "But you're just like every other guy in this town."

Toby hit the steering wheel, vibrating the entire car. Lily jumped like the change in his cupholder, giving him a nasty look. Toby unloaded on her.

"You thought I was different? *Me?*" He was trying to breathe, trying to get the words out before he started hyperventilating. "Pardon me if I don't acknowledge your moral fucking high ground."

Toby threw himself back into his seat, an action that he knew made him look like a kid having a tantrum. Lily's righteousness faded. Toby didn't want to give her the satisfaction of tears, but they were close enough that he waited to ask the one question he had.

"Why?" Toby said, his voice breaking. But he didn't care. At some point, he wanted the good parts of the world to arc in his direction. He wanted to rise above all the shit, which seemed to be infinite.

Lily reached for a cigarette, but the pack was empty.

"Like I said, I was in the Deuce a lot," she said. "And I met Bo and he was older and, at the time, seemed impossibly cool. Especially when I was used to a bunch of literal choirboys."

The words coming from Lily's mouth were as flat as if she

were telling him directions to her house.

"And . . . well, I don't know," she said. "I was confused. And I was excited about the money. So when he came over, I . . . Sometimes I think this whole state is cursed."

Toby turned to face her, ready to yell. To call bullshit. When he was a kid, Jimmy would try to explain away the reasons why he beat on him. "You can't keep your mouth shut." "You need to learn some discipline." As if any of that ever made a bit of sense.

"So with me . . ." He swallowed a few times before he started talking again. "Was it all just a joke?"

Lily reached her hand toward Toby tentatively. "Of course not."

He wanted to believe her. He wanted to pretend that they'd had something real. Something that, given time and attention, would eventually work. Like a carefully rebuilt engine. But no matter how many ways he tried to believe it, what little faith he had in magic was gone. She wouldn't end up with Bo. She wouldn't end up with him. As soon as she got her money, she'd be on the first bus, train, or plane she could find. Back to Seattle, away from all this.

"God. This is what I always do. I swoop in and fuck up people's lives, my own included. I'm more aware of it than you can possibly imagine."

Outside, the rain started falling harder, streaking everything. He visualized the moment he handed the keys back to his dad. The moment he had the cash in his hand. Toby knew enough to expect a disappointment. But what if it really was more money than he'd ever seen? Ten grand. Hell, even five. That sort of money could get him out of the country, let alone the state.

"We should do this," he said.

Lily started crying softly. "I'm sorry. I really am."

Toby didn't know what else to do, so he reached for the door handle. Before he could open it, she pulled him close, clutching his body like he might disappear. And maybe that's exactly what they both were going to do—disappear. When he pulled away, her eyes were still wet.

"I'll see you at the mill, okay?"

"Okay."

Toby watched the taillights of the El Camino disappear around the building. He waited there, listening to the night, alive with sounds. Small animals scurried in the bushes. Birds, startled, rose from tree branches and disappeared into the dark sky. In the distance, the constant hum of the interstate reminded Toby that he had a purpose.

Toby walked around the side of the building and saw the

truck for the first time. The sheer size of the rig stopped him in his tracks. It was easily twice the size of the El Camino and probably weighed ten times as much. There might be moving trucks this big, but he'd never seen one. Where the hell had Jimmy gotten this monster?

He forced himself to walk to the door of the truck and unlock it. Inside smelled like cigarette smoke and stale potato chips. He wiped crumbs off the seat and sat down, trying to steady his hands. His entire body. The steering wheel was as big as a Hula-Hoop, and the shifter rose up from the floor like a baseball bat. Toby toed the different pedals, unsure if he was happy when he easily touched each one.

He pushed the clutch in and tried to start the truck. The engine coughed and sputtered at first, but then, in a sudden roar of effort, turned over. He let it rumble underneath him, watching the clock and waiting for Lily to get a far enough head start.

He reached over and turned on the radio. It was tuned to a country station, which Toby ignored until the jangly song ended and a man's gravelly voice announced that tickets were still available for the winter car and air show down in Charlotte. Thousands of cars. A couple of helicopters. And an old warplane that kids could investigate.

The ad ended with the sound of a plane roaring across the sky.

There were still five minutes before he should leave, but Toby couldn't sit here any longer. He touched the side of his face and then reached down and wrenched the twenty-four-footer into gear. The heavy truck hopped once, twice, before smoothing out. As he was rolling toward the road, Toby turned up the radio.

Thank god for the dark and empty country roads.

He swerved and nearly put the truck in a ditch two times before he stopped overcorrecting and got the hang of the subtle movements of the steering wheel. Soon the long white lines of the highway stretched out in front of him, broken up by the dark puddles between the streetlights. Toby turned the radio up louder, opened the windows. The cool air calmed what was left of his nerves, and he told himself, There's nothing abnormal about this. Thousands of trucks go up and down this interstate every single day.

He was one, two miles away from the exit when he realized, I'm going to make it.

Something flashed in the sky. At first he thought it was lightning. A shooting star, maybe. It disappeared into the clouds just as Toby realized he'd been staring a second too long. He was headed for the shoulder, fast.

He jerked the wheel, and the entire truck tilted like a bomb had gone off underneath it. He tried to correct, but the sudden spin of the wheel made the truck jump—Toby couldn't tell how long he was even in the air, but it felt like an entire lifetime—and then landed on the hard pavement.

The last thing he remembered was the horrifying crack of the glass. The way the entire truck seemed to collapse around him.

And then everything went quiet.

January 30

T—

Today, when Sister came to see me, she looked like she hadn't slept all night. I didn't have to ask. I knew she'd been up with Eddie. Holding hands the way she does. Whispering those prayers she's so sure work.

I wanted to scream at her.

What happens if all your praying doesn't work? What then?

But when she sat down, her face tired and her hands shaking, I calmed my ass down. I sat there, waiting for her to speak—trying to figure out what I could say to make her feel better. But every time I opened my mouth, nothing seemed right.

So we sat there for a solid hour, neither of us saying anything. That's when I realized there wasn't anything I could say. All she needed was for me to sit here with her. So I didn't say a word, T. Every few minutes I'd look at her, making sure she was okay. And then, right before lunch, Sister smiled at me.

"Eddie wants you to have a few of his things."

I had no idea what Eddie wanted to give me, what he even had. Probably not much. That's the thing in here, T. The weird way you try to leave a legacy. For some guys, that means telling jokes or giving away commissary. For others, it means getting up in your ear about God, the Bible. There's more than a few dudes in here who are like that. But Eddie—Eddie had never played any of those games. He'd always been different.

I nodded, but there was something else bothering me.

"Are you going to be with him?" I asked.

Sister closed her eyes and nodded, wiping away a tear.

"Until they force me out of that room."

Luke

29

LUKE didn't stop running until he reached the apartment complex, sprinting up the stairs and throwing the door open. The boys were asleep, one under each of Annie's arms. They jerked as Luke flew inside but stayed asleep.

"What are you doing?" Annie said.

His entire body was shaking as she took in the cuts, the blood, all of it.

She stood up and came to him. "Oh my god, what happened? Are you okay?"

"I have to go," he said, not sure where to start. What to take. His eyes stopped on the sleeping boys.

"You need to tell me what happened," Annie said, her voice rising.

"I will," Luke said. "If I left, would you come with me?"

She hesitated, looking at Luke's hands. The cut above his eye was bleeding through the bandage. Luke was already shaking his head.

"No, it's okay. I get it."

Annie reached out grabbed his arm. "Hey, that's not it. I just . . . I need to go downstairs and get a few things."

She slipped out the door, leaving him alone in the quiet apartment. He thought he should probably pack some things too. Clothes, at least. But as he stood in the apartment, he couldn't think of a single thing he wanted to bring.

As he stood there, Petey sat up, blinking.

"You hurt your eye," was the first thing he said. Luke knelt down.

"I'll be fine," he said. "Go back to sleep."

But Petey wasn't having it. He sat up, yawning and rubbing at his eyes. "Can I tell you something?"

A surge of emotions overtook Luke. He couldn't imagine not being around them, not seeing the daily changes in their personalities. They always surprised him in the simplest ways.

He choked his feelings back and said, "Of course, buddy."

"Okay, I'm going to tell you all the rumors I've heard about the new Pokémon game," he said.

Luke smiled and let him say every single word he wanted. By the time he was finished, Jack-Jack was awake and they were arguing about whether a certain Pokémon was legendary or, as Jack-Jack put it, "plain useless."

"Guys, I want to talk to you about something."

The phone rang in the kitchen and Luke ignored it.

"I'm going to leave," he said. "For just a little while, I hope. Annie's coming too."

The boys stopped talking and both stared up at him, as if they didn't understand. The phone rang again.

He heard the bedroom door open. Behind him, Doreen answered with a sleepy hello. For a second, she didn't say anything—only listened. Ricky walked past her, shirtless and annoyed, and looked from Luke to the boys, as if unsure where to start.

"What are they doing up?" he asked. Before Luke could answer, he pointed at the cut. "And what the hell happened to your head?"

Luke ignored him and turned back to the boys. "Lay down, guys."

Doreen came flying out of the kitchen, the cord of the phone snapping the receiver out of her hands. It clattered behind her.

"That's your coach," she said.

"It's not a big deal," Luke said, but his body was flush again. He couldn't swallow fast enough. "Everything's okay."

"He said he talked to the police, Luke. The *police*."

Luke didn't doubt for one second that Coach O had called the police. He may have used generalities, "What if a boy got in a fight . . ." to keep all the angles open until he'd investigated every single one. Luke imagined this is the way the tough bastard had wrestled too. Annoyingly patient. Slow until you messed up. And then you got the hammer.

The boys' eyes were wide with fear.

"The police? Is Luke in trouble?"

The twins started crying, and Luke bent down to calm them. But Doreen pushed him back and directed Jack-Jack and Petey behind her as she talked. "What about your scholarship? What about the state championship?"

In the kitchen, the phone was still on the floor. Ricky went to pick it up.

"Is this why you're leaving?" Petey asked, his lip trembling. Doreen looked down at him.

"What did you say, honey? Leaving?"

"Luke's leaving with Annie," Jack-Jack said.

Luke couldn't stop looking at the twins. He wanted to grab them from his mom and run to Annie's car. All of them disappearing, just like that. He didn't know how far they'd get before the police caught up with them—it could be the county line, it could be three states away—as long as it wasn't leaving them here.

Ricky came back into the room, eyeing Luke. "Your coach wants to come pick you up. I'm going to let you decide what you want to do . . . but you aren't staying here."

Luke looked over at his mom. She faltered only for a second before she nodded and stared at Luke with the same hard eyes. He bent down, and Petey ran over and wrapped his arms around Luke's neck.

"Guys, you'll need to really do a good job at listening to Mom," Luke said, calling Jack-Jack over too.

"I don't understand," Petey said. As soon as the words came out, Jack-Jack started crying.

"Can't we all go with you?" Jack-Jack asked.

Luke tried to move Petey's arm, but he clamped down so hard that Luke had to pull it off. He looked at the boys, both in tears now, and then up to his mom, wanting her to say something—anything to give him the peace of mind he needed to leave.

Instead, she grabbed Jack-Jack and Petey and hurried them to the bedroom. They both screamed and cried, pleading with Doreen to explain what was happening. The last thing Luke saw was Petey's arm, reaching out in one last panicked motion before they disappeared.

Luke stared at the bedroom, fighting a million different impulses, each of which pulled him in a different direction.

Run. Stay. Kick the bedroom door down and take the boys away. The result was a complete paralysis, only broken when Ricky said his name.

"Don't make me call the sheriff," he said.

Luke looked at the door one more time before he walked out of the apartment.

30

TOBY woke up to a woman yelling at him, the words coming more as sounds without any actual meaning. The first thing he felt was pain—glass everywhere—followed by a sudden hollowness that made him want to throw up.

"Are you okay?" the lady asked. When Toby unbuckled his seat belt, and tried to move, she yelped. "Don't! You could have a broken neck or . . ."

Toby didn't wait for her to finish. He pulled himself up and out of the truck, his vision blurry and every part of his body feeling like the broken glass that was spread across the highway.

He looked around, trying to blink the scene into focus. The truck was split open and cartons of cigarettes littered the wet road. Every few minutes, a car would pass slowly, gawking at the scene. Toby took a step and nearly fell to the ground.

"I saw the whole thing," the woman said. "What were you even doing driving that truck?"

In the distance, Toby heard the faint yell of a siren. It helped him rally enough strength to stumble from the truck's wreckage, pulling his arm from the woman's grip—promising he was okay. Even though every step hurt, he willed himself into a sprint toward the woods that lined the road. He ran through the overgrown grass with his hands out, hoping to avoid tree branches—anything hanging darkly in the night. He ran until his legs and lungs burned and the sirens stopped getting closer.

Of course, losing the cops was only the immediate problem.

Toby picked his way back to town by running through yards, dodging automatic floodlights that popped on, momentarily lighting up the world. The whole time, he was trying to figure out how to deal with his bigger problem. Jimmy would be livid. His first thought was that he should go to Lily, warn her. But he wasn't sure how she'd react. He'd ruined her escape plan too. And while he was sure she wouldn't turn him over to Jimmy, he wasn't so sure how she'd take the news that Seattle was off the table.

He stopped running, suddenly unable to breathe. As he stood there, bent over and sucking wind, he thought about Luke.

If Toby went to the apartment right now, a mea culpa

on his lips, Luke would forgive him. More than likely, Luke was already tearing himself apart because of the punch. He'd offer up a gruff apology and they'd do what they'd always done—adapt. Maybe he could convince Luke to leave with him, he didn't know. But as he stood there, panic still crippling his lungs, there was one problem.

Toby wasn't sure he could actually say those words.

He was tired of apologizing for other people's sins. Tired of letting other people move him around like a chess piece. And even if he went to Luke's, how long would it take for Jimmy to show? He might not even knock, just wait in the parking lot to snatch Toby as soon as they stepped outside. Or worse, come inside. Exposing Doreen, the boys—all of them.

He stood up and started running again, ignoring the pain. The panic. Running as hard as he could to the only place he'd ever been able to think. The place he and Luke had planned countless escapes.

The only place he'd ever really felt safe.

Toby reached out and ran a hand along the plane's rusted frame, almost testing if it were real. He lowered himself into the shell of the plane and pulled his legs up against his chest, trying to think.

BRYAN BLISS

He needed his car. And despite himself, he wanted to find Lily—to make sure she was okay. That she understood what had happened. But he couldn't risk going back to the Deuce tonight, or even the trailer. He would hole up in the plane and wait it out. Just like he had countless times before.

But he couldn't get comfortable. Part of it was his aching body, but something deeper nagged at him. There had been no precautions—no masks to hide his identity, no gloves to mask his fingerprints. No talk about how he should protect himself if something had gone wrong. He didn't even know where they'd gotten the truck in the first place. And maybe his denseness was the ultimate protection, the thing his father had been counting on all along.

Years ago, in the darkness of Luke's living room, Toby had cried after another beating from his father. Before that, Toby had never cried in front of Luke. However, once the lights went off—Toby unable to get comfortable on the couch because of the bruise his dad had tattooed on his ribs—he finally let go. The tears came and came and, finally, so did the cussing. Words that Toby had used countless times before but now were less rebellion and more an exorcism. He told Luke he would never let a beating scare him again, no matter what.

Luke didn't say much, not then or the next morning when Toby woke up and Luke had somehow cobbled together enough money for some frozen waffles. Or maybe they were in the freezer—this was before the twins. Before Luke was a wrestling star, before he had every college with a team sniffing around their shitty town. Before he'd raised a fist at Toby. Now, as Toby sat on the ground shivering, it felt like he was stuck in a nightmare and there was no chance of waking up.

And he was more scared than he'd ever been in his life.

Toby shrank into the metal of the plane, trying to find a place the cold air couldn't penetrate. Behind him, there was a rustle of leaves. Probably the wind or some squirrel. They always had a way of sounding bigger when they were hidden in the brush. But then it happened again. He turned around, expecting to see Luke.

Jimmy stepped out of the tree line.

His dad didn't say anything, just twirled a tire wrench back and forth on his thumb like a gunslinger.

"At first Lily said she didn't have any idea where you'd be," Jimmy said. "But once we got to talking, it didn't take long."

Toby went to stand up, but Jimmy held a hand in the air, lowering Toby back down to the ground with just the movement. Jimmy looked around and nodded.

"So this is it? This is where you've been running to all these years?"

Toby couldn't say a word. There had been moments when

Jimmy had chased him and Luke before, but they went miles in a different direction to keep him from finding the plane. Jimmy staring at the plane now was a kick to the stomach. An abomination.

"Not to a bus. Or a car," Jimmy said, swinging the tire iron. "No, you fuck up and you come . . . here. To some make-believe *bullshit.*"

When he said the last word, he slammed the tire iron down on what was left of the right wing. It shattered, splitting from the fuselage with a loud rip. Toby jumped. Jimmy had destroyed the plane with one swing.

"Every time you catch a whiff of a challenge, you go running. That's your whole life story, right there. You didn't learn a damn thing I taught you."

Jimmy swung the tire iron again, cleaving off the nose in one swipe.

"Taught me?"

Toby stepped toward Jimmy. He didn't care anymore. He was tired of hiding. He was tired of letting Luke stick up for him at every moment. He was just plain tired, and he wanted this shit to be over.

"That's what you call getting my ass kicked for not picking up my socks? For leaving a glass of milk on the table? *Teaching me?* Fuck you."

In one sudden movement, Jimmy slammed the tire iron down on the side of the plane with a metallic clunk. When it didn't go through completely, he hit it again and again and again until finally the tire iron struck dirt. Jimmy kicked the body of the plane apart, opening it like a can of beans. When he looked at Toby, he was breathing hard.

"You lost me a lot of money tonight. What do you have to say for yourself?"

Toby didn't answer. He was staring at the destroyed plane, his body numb. Jimmy grabbed Toby and threw him to the ground. As soon as he hit the dirt, Toby felt a surge of power go through him. He stood up and pushed Jimmy with every ounce of strength he had. Jimmy tripped, falling over the twisted plane's carcass.

How many times had Toby been here before? How many times had he stood toe-to-toe with Jimmy, only to go running away so sleep could dilute the anger, the booze—all of it. Toby was going to end it forever, right now. He picked up a piece of metal from the wing and walked to his father.

Jimmy snickered.

"You think—"

Toby swung as hard as he could, the metal connecting with a dull thud. Jimmy groaned, dropping the tire iron. Toby reworked his grip. Ready to hit Jimmy until he couldn't raise a beer or a hand or anything in his direction ever again.

He swung for the fences. Just before the metal crashed back into Jimmy's head, ending it, his father ducked. Toby spun, the piece of wing skittering across the clearing. Jimmy stood up, rubbing the side of his head.

"Shit, boy. That was close."

Jimmy took a step toward Toby, bending down to pick up the tire iron.

January 31

T—

It's almost midnight.

That's when they do it, which seems almost unreal, doesn't it? Duels at high noon and executions at the stroke of midnight. I don't think there's a dude in this entire place who's asleep right now. You can feel the vibrations, the way everybody can't seem to figure out what to do with themselves.

Part of it is just knowing Eddie, I think. Putting yourself in his place, trying to imagine what it will be like in that room. When they bring you Whoppers and steak and shrimp—too much food to eat. And shit, how fucked up is it that you get to have a special meal right before they kill you?

The other part of it is knowing that it doesn't take much

imagination putting yourself next to Eddie. It might take twenty years, but soon enough we'll all be on that gurney. We'll all be holding hands with Sister, begging for any last-chance miracle we can get.

I don't want to walk into that room like this.

I don't want to have anything left unsaid, which I guess is the why I started writing these letters in the first place. But damn, T. We could've skipped all the bullshit about basketball and lawyers. Because we both know I've been ignoring the only words that really matter. What I should've said to you first thing.

I'm sorry, T.

It's 12:07 right now.

I have no idea how long it takes for somebody to die.

Luke

31

LUKE was in front of Annie's door, dazed. He raised his hand and delivered three sharp knocks. There was a slight scuffle of feet behind the door, followed by Annie's clear voice saying, "I'm sorry! Please don't!"

The door flew open, and David was standing in front of him. He had a Bible in his hand, a giant cross formed from nails hanging around his neck. And those were the man's most memorable features. He was six inches shorter than Luke and at least seventy-five pounds heavier. One eye squinted as he spoke.

"You may want to join us in here," he said, using the Bible to punctuate the sentence. Luke looked into the apartment. Annie was sitting on the couch and had obviously been crying. Luke ignored David.

"Are you okay?" he asked.

Annie nodded quickly, just before David started talking again.

"She's not okay. Not at all. And my best guess is that you're the one to blame for all this?"

As he spoke, David walked into the apartment and pulled out a wad of cash. It was a few hundred dollars, easy. When he lifted it up, turning to speak to her, Annie dropped her head.

"I thought we were past the stealing? The running away?" He threw the money back down on the table and took a few breaths before turning back to Luke. A tight smile appeared on his lips. "Like I said, maybe you should join us in here."

Luke was trying to think, trying to determine if Annie was in any sort of danger. They didn't have to leave together, not even tonight. Luke could find a place to hide until everything calmed down. Until she could use school as an excuse and slip away. The future for both of them was wide like an empty highway.

It hit him the way realizations never did—quick, like a shot of lightning.

"I don't want to get you in trouble," Luke said to Annie. And then he looked at David. "I didn't ask her to do this. I'm sorry."

Annie sat up, her face going from distraught to seriously pissed in a matter of seconds. She was giving Luke a stare that even Toby couldn't have pulled from her in his worst moments. He didn't want to say good-bye—to see another thing end tonight—so he spoke slow, hoping she understood what he was saying.

"I have a plane to catch," he said, pausing for a second. Waiting to see a lightbulb, for that same lightning to strike twice. Annie's face softened only slightly, her words sharp as a blade.

"Well, I hope it gets delayed and you're there all night. Asshole."

David tsked at the cuss word, but when he turned around to face Luke one last time, Annie flashed him a smile so big, so alive with potential, that Luke knew it meant only one thing.

I'll see you soon.

Luke ran into the dark night, a strange sense of peace filling his body for the first time in years. The stars were now out, bright enough to make it seem as if the entire world was highlighted in silver. When he came to the path that led to the grove of trees, he stopped running and walked toward the plane.

This was it. Something he and Toby had dreamed about. Talked about and talked about until their voices were hoarse—always imagining what it would feel like the moment they knew were getting away. It might not be on a plane, or even in a way they ever expected. But they both knew they would feel *something*.

And now Luke knew. It felt like waking up in the morning after a good night's sleep. Like Christmas Day, or how his body would tense wonderfully when Annie appeared in front of him. Butterflies in the stomach. His hand being raised after a match.

It felt like hope.

A sudden pang of guilt stuck a knife between his ribs. This hope wasn't supposed to be for him and Annie. Sure, there was enough to go around. But what he was feeling had always been so closely tied to Toby, it was odd that his friend wasn't right behind him, talking about god knows what.

Luke flexed his hands, feeling the pain from the cuts. Toby's face still lingered on each of his knuckles like a shadow. It wasn't a feeling he expected to disappear, no matter how far he and Annie ran. As he started walking to the trees, he was already thinking of ways he could reach out to Toby once all the tempers had settled.

Luke stepped through the clearing with a smile on his face.

At first his mind couldn't process what he was seeing. The plane, broken apart like a child's toy. The wings had been hacked off and tossed aside in a heap. The nose was gone, the tail nothing but splinters. And the fuselage—the cockpit where he and Toby had spent countless afternoons, pretending to fly and then, when they got too old for make-believe, planning to leave—was curled in on itself. It looked like a tractor trailer had driven through the trees, leaving behind the twisted metal in its wake.

Luke's stomach dropped.

This, of course, had always been the fear—that some drunk, some group of high-school or college kids would be bored and use the plane as a temporary distraction. Even as Luke stepped carefully around the pieces of metal littering the ground, he was surprised by the ferocity of the job.

He picked up a piece of the broken nose and studied it for a second and then sat down, holding it on his lap. They never even had a propeller. Luke had never thought about this until just now, and it made him laugh, a little too loudly, seeing as he was officially on the lam. But damn. All the talk of flying away in that plane. All the belief—more belief than any person ever had in a god, Luke was sure—and they didn't have the one part *necessary* to get that plane up in the air.

Just then he saw what looked like the arm of a doll sticking out from under one of the wings. From a distance, it could've been anything. But the longer he looked at it, the more familiar it got. It had an unnatural, almost waxy appearance. Like a mannequin left out in the rain for too long.

He stood up, dropping the nose.

"No, no, no," Luke said, running to his friend.

Everything was slick from the rain. The ground. The wing that covered most of Toby's motionless body. Luke lifted the long sheet of metal and it slipped from his hands, crashing back down on top of Toby. He reached again and threw the rusted metal off his friend with every bit of strength he had. It crashed into a tree, the sound like a train driving through a house.

Toby lay with one arm outstretched like he was trying to fly. He was covered in blood, his body broken and bruised. Barely recognizable. Luke was frozen. He didn't pick Toby up or reach down to check for the pulse. He knew. The way he knew how to wrestle that first time on the mat. It was instinct, a prophecy almost.

They'd never spent a single moment imagining a situation where they wouldn't escape. It was preordained, a bulletproof future they'd tricked themselves into believing was guaranteed to them. But they'd been fooling themselves. They always had been.

Luke dropped to the ground, but he couldn't cry. He reached out and pulled Toby toward him. Toby was stiff from the cold, and heavy. Luke knew he should feel something, but his entire body, his mind, had finally gone empty.

He stood up and carried Toby to the place where the cockpit had sat, now an oval of exposed dirt circled by overgrown grass and leaves. Luke laid him in the middle of the space and then started putting the plane back together. First he moved the fuselage. The metal groaned as he bent the two ends until they were touching once again. He picked up the pieces of each wing, putting the jigsaw back together on either side of the plane. The tail on top of the bent body. The pieces of the nose in front.

He worked until the plane was right again. Or as right as it could be.

Luke would give anything to go back to pretending to fly missions, when they crash-landed behind enemy lines. Given orders only heroes could carry out. "We'll need our wits to survive this," Toby had said, making Luke laugh. But no matter how much he willed his brain to remember the plane the way it used to be, he could only see it the way it was now—broken and incomplete.

Luke climbed in and sat next to Toby's body. He needed to be close to Toby for as long as he could.

Around them, the world went quiet, matching the emptiness inside Luke. He wanted to feel anything but a cold, crawling sense of calm that was overtaking him. A sense of calculating purpose that snuffed out all the anger, dried up all his tears. Whenever he'd gotten on the mat, this was what he had always wanted. To have a singular purpose, a way of putting blinders on until nothing, not time, or the crowd, or even his own pain, would distract him from accomplishing his mission.

He had it now.

Every single step he'd take. Every movement. All of it collected into one perfect moment.

He was staring at Toby's hand—open, like he was about to catch a ball—when Annie came running into the clearing. Her face lit up when she saw Luke. He knew he should stand up, stop her from seeing Toby—he'd already made that mistake once before.

Before.

The word took on new meaning for Luke. Everything in his life would now be separated into before and after this moment. Everything would force him to ask one question for the rest of his life: What did you do to save your friend?

Luke still couldn't move when Annie got to the plane, when she started screaming.

"Luke! Oh my god!"

"I know where he's at," Luke said. For a moment, Annie paused, confused. "Jimmy. I know where he must be."

"We need to call an ambulance," Annie said, reaching for her phone. "The police. Are you okay?"

Luke stood up, and maybe Annie thought he was going to come to her, wrap her up in his arms the way he'd held Toby for the last hour, his arms cramping under the weight of his friend. She let the phone drop to her side as Luke walked by.

"Luke."

He stopped and turned to face her. "Take care of Toby. Please. I need to go do something."

And then he started walking to the trailer.

The door was locked, so he kicked it in. The cheap wood broke easily enough. Deep in the trailer park, a dog started barking. Luke stepped inside, barely taking notice of the beer cans littering the floor. The stacks and stacks of cigarettes Jimmy had in the kitchen. The only thing that made him pause were the rumpled clothes Toby had worn just a few days ago. He picked up the shirt and held it close to his face. It smelled like wine and sweat and, for a second that disappeared quicker than it came, Toby.

Luke walked to the bedroom. Straight to the closet. They

had been eleven, maybe a little older, when Toby snuck Luke into the trailer and showed him the revolver. Luke could still feel the weight of it in his hand when they went running back into the woods, his entire body shaking with either fear or excitement. That night he made Toby promise he'd never pick it up again, no matter what happened with Jimmy. To come running to Luke instead. Because he would always save him.

Luke picked up the gun. It still felt heavy in his hands.

Every time a car would pass, Luke hid the wrapped-up gun at his hip. It could've been a present, or even a bottle. He had no plan if the police stopped him.

Walking seemed to loosen the cold fist that had grabbed his heart when he first saw Toby. As it thawed, it was replaced with a hot rage, the sort that Luke had never felt before. With every step, it boiled in his bones a little deeper until his heart was leather.

It wasn't until he finally got to the Deuce's parking lot that he started running.

He pushed through the doors in a sprint, skidding into the nearly empty bar. For a moment, the entire room froze. Jimmy stood up, his eyes going wide with fear when he saw what was in Luke's hand.

One, two, three, four, five, six.

The revolver was still clicking when Bo tried to tackle him. He never got close. Luke swung the gun down onto the drunk man's head so hard, the crack shook the whole room. Blood everywhere. Behind him, Val swung a bottle at his head. It connected in a brilliant flash, and Luke swung the gun one time, right at her temple. She fell too.

Luke dropped to his knees, blood coming out of his ear. A new gash over the other eye now. From under the table, he heard a squeak of fear that slowly turned into a scream. Luke dropped the gun and stared right at Lily, finally feeling the weight and the pain of Toby falling on top of him.

All he could say was, "He's dead."

February 2

T—

When Sister came to see me today, she brought a box of Eddie's stuff—his basketball, a couple of books. Then she handed me a letter.

"Eddie wanted to say good-bye," she said.

Once Sister left, I stared at that letter like it might blow up. I don't get any mail here because Mom pretty much gave up, and Annie . . . well, I'm not going to hold anything against Annie. She tried, especially in the beginning. But they pressed her pretty hard. And she knew I was coming for Jimmy. So when they asked, she told them.

Three people, man.

I'm pretty sure nobody cared about Bo or Jimmy, but taking

out Val—that's what sunk me. They called her an innocent. And while I don't know if that's true, she didn't deserve what she got. What I did to her.

Anyway, I was sitting here staring at Eddie's letter, trying to figure out what it might say. Trying to figure out what I would write to somebody in the last few hours of my life. Who would I write to?

The twins. Mom. You.

The other day, when Sister asked if I was still writing these letters, I tried to play it off—I tried to be like, Sometimes. When I feel like it. You know.

All that hard-ass shit is getting so old, T.

The Sister didn't call me on it. Instead she was like, "Well, why did you keep writing?"

I sat there, searching for the answer—searching long after she left. But I think I've always known, even from that very first letter.

Man, I just want to be close to you again.

If I could have anything—anything in the world—it wouldn't be money. It wouldn't even be to get out of jail.

It would be more time.

Just you and me. Messing around in the woods, driving that crazy-ass car of yours down the back roads. Stopping at Wilco for some drinks. Snacks. Doing everything we could to find enough change to pay for it. Living long and getting old. Day after day until we were those dudes sitting around Hardee's for hours and hours solving all the world's problems over some shitty coffee.

Goddamn, T. Do you know what I would do to make that happen?

Later I walked into the yard for the first time since Eddie's execution. I brought his ball and was spinning it again and again in my palm—closing my eyes and lifting my head to smell the air. His letter, unopened in my pocket.

The sun is out, the sky is clear, and I've got my head pointed to the sky, letting that sun just shine on my face. I sat like that for ten minutes before I heard it. The plane was yellow, a fixed-wing somebody must've restored. The propeller was spinning invisibly in front of it, and then, like it was nothing, it made a lazy loop above us.

I looked around, but nobody was paying any attention.

The plane flipped.

It turned, diving to the ground, impossibly fast.

At the last second, it pulled up, shooting back up to the sky until it disappeared behind the only cloud in the sky.

Just like that, it was gone.

I sat there searching for that plane, trying to hear it. But it was like it never had even been there. The rest of the yard could care less too. Everybody was doing their own thing.

Lifting. Hooping. Talking.

We'll Fly Away

I stood there for a minute, feeling like maybe I'd seen a ghost. And then one of the dudes on the court started yelling, asking me if I was going to play or not.

I dribbled the ball once, twice. And without thinking about it, I threw up a jump shot. It arced against the sky—against that tall sun—and fell through the net without a sound. Like nothing you've ever seen in your life, T.

Everybody lost it as I walked onto the court.

Luke

AUTHOR'S NOTE

Fifteen years ago, I was a press witness to an execution. I saw a man put to death. Since then, I've searched for some way to express my shame and to understand the injustice of that experience. The pursuit took me to seminary. It pushed me to read every book I could find about capital punishment and mass incarceration. I attended vigils and protested at public forums. I taught classes at prisons and juvenile correctional facilities. And ultimately I befriended death-row inmates (that's the real work) and wrote letters until my hand cramped. All of it to make sense of/run away from/finally process what happened in that tiny, triangular room.

When I started *We'll Fly Away*, I always called it my "death-penalty book." It was shorthand, a way to talk about it before I had a working title. But the more I worked on Luke and Toby's story, the more I realized that "death-penalty book" no longer sufficiently covered the scope of it. Yes, it is a book about the death penalty. But it's also a book about friendship. It's about growing up hard, in a way that forces you to make choices you'd otherwise not make. It's a book about wanting to escape. It's about love and loyalty. It's about people who care, even when you don't. And maybe most importantly, it's a book that invites readers to ask the question: do I believe a person can ever be beyond redemption?

My hope is that, after reading *We'll Fly Away*, the only answer can be: "no."